DON'T FORGET TO LIVE

LIVE

A. C. Jack

Cover created by Alisson Valentim.

For Claire,

You are a beacon of light
when the world turns dark

1

The Final Decision

I lined up the pills in the same way I used to arrange toy soldiers as a child. Twenty-three of them. They did not fumble, fall, or even hesitate; they had a duty to fulfil. I pinched the first between my finger and thumb to study it. White as salt. Small as a penny. Powerful enough to shut down my organs.

It fizzed with bitterness in my mouth. I washed away the taste, then took the second and third pill before I gagged. If I were strong enough for the fight, I wouldn't have been in it in the first place.

I stuffed the remaining pills into my mouth and washed them down with the rest of my drink, but retched again. They had to stay down to work. I could feel their effects almost immediately. In movies, death by overdose is poetic, even pretty, but there was nothing romantic about my actions. People would want a reason for my behaviour, some external circumstance weighing on my mind for months before I finally cracked, but there wasn't one. There was no crippling debt, no childhood trauma, nor a whimsical tale of a broken heart. There was just me and the darkness.

I snatched the envelope from the desk and clutched it to my chest. My carefully crafted goodbye. When I stood, the white walls of my room danced around me, spinning in circles like a merry-go-round. Noises—music and laughter—bled through the walls, turned into piercing carnival shrieks which penetrated my skin. My room, both a prison and a sanctuary, was nothing but a matchbox, and yet I managed to stumble and fall between the built-in desk and the single bed. A stench rose from the carpet, filling my nostrils. The accumulation of years' worth of vomit and spilt drinks, common

1

remnants in student accommodation. I tried to stand, to bring myself to the bed, but my energy was spent. Instead, I cowered into a ball. The room melted around me, drooping like gooey honey, covering me until I couldn't breathe anymore. Each student who had lived there before had left their own mark. Death would be mine.

It wasn't enough to scrunch my eyes shut and wait to be taken out of this life. I had to lash out, scream, and cry, until my eyelids became so heavy they sank like the sun behind the horizon. I kissed the moon as I became a star in the night sky, floating high over the world I'd left behind.

You can only imagine my disappointment when I woke up.

I lay still, stiff as a corpse. There was a marching band pounding wild symphonies through my head, slamming off-beat quavers in rising crescendos against my skull. My brain throbbed. I thought it would inflate with pain until it could take no more and explode. Beside me, there was a small patch of crusty vomit spattered on the floor. Maybe if I didn't move death would still come. It was supposed to be irrefutable; yet there I was, awake and alive in the aftermath of a breakdown.

The flat's buzzer wailed, forcing me to peel myself from the floor. I walked into the hallway, pawing the walls to keep upright. My body ached, my bones dense and weary. The skin around my lips had dried and cracked. I had an intense desire to find a pin and prick the skin over my temples, let the blood and the pain and the marching band pour from me. Instead, I opened the front door. I didn't recognise the person on the other side.

'Rough night?' he asked, shuffling his weight from foot to foot. His hands, I noticed, were tucked into the sleeves of his jumper. When I didn't respond, he said: 'It's William, right?'

I nodded, unsure of myself.

'I was passing by and thought I'd see if you were home, see if you wanted to walk to class together, but you're obviously not ready,' he said. 'I'm Alex.' He shoved his arm out and in doing so, his jumper peeled back, unveiling a small, gentle hand which I limply shook.

'Alex . . .?' I said slowly, checking my mind for a picture of the person standing in front of me. There was nothing.

'You're in Professor Hall's class,' he said with confidence. When he spoke, he did so with the jolliness of a caricature from a children's cartoon — so alive and full of life. 'Professor Hall, Jurisprudence.'

'I'm sorry . . . I really don't know why you're here,' I said with expiring patience.

'You haven't checked the online portal, have you?'

'Guilty,' I said, with a shrug.

'We've been paired for the final assignment: you and me. I know your flatmate Amber, so I knew you lived here. I had an appointment this morning and was nearby, so I figured we should meet. We can talk about revision schedules and make a plan on the way to class,' he said. He was so full of energy I could almost feel his thoughts buzz in the air between us. I told him I wasn't intending on going to class, but as I pushed the door he deftly shot his foot against the wood, taking me by surprise.

'I've never been graded less than a seventy,' he said bluntly. 'I've never missed a single lecture or tutorial. You're not going to ruin that for me just because you're hungover. I'll wait in the kitchen while you get dressed.' His smile was soft and kind, but his unrelenting eye contact dared me to challenge him. I lacked the ability to produce a witty retort, so stood stupid and silent. It was no surprise he was a first-class student; he looked the type to be forever buried in a book. To reveal I hadn't planned on being around long enough to complete the assignment was out of the question. So with no other option, I steeled myself, pulled the door open and let Alex into my flat. Death would have to wait.

'Help yourself to tea or coffee,' I offered. 'I'll go shower.'

'There's no time,' he protested, glancing at his watch. 'Just get dressed.'

He made his way to the kitchen without having to be shown where it was and I disappeared into my bedroom. I frantically got dressed, wondering why I was obeying the demands of a stranger. Catching myself in the mirror, I saw there was no denying I'd had a rough night. I picked up a can of deodorant and sprayed myself from head to toe.

Alex was sitting at the breakfast bar with his chin resting in his palms when I entered the kitchen. He told me he'd been in my flat just a few weeks before, at a party. When I threw him a quizzical glance, he told me I'd locked myself in my room the entire night. But that didn't narrow it down; there had been a lot of parties. *A lot of parties avoided.*

Rain drizzled from the overcast skies as we walked to the lecture so I pulled my hood over my head which meant that Alex's voice was nothing but a distant, droning hum. He created conversations effortlessly but struggled to keep them alive with my lack of input. I didn't mean to be a killjoy; I just didn't have the words to give him. We were already late by the time we arrived, which I would normally have taken as a cue to turn around and head home, but Alex was adamant we attend the class. He pushed the wooden doors open and walked into the dry, cold lecture theatre. Every eye in the room fell on us, including those of the powerful and astute Professor Hall.

'How nice of you to join us,' said the Professor. More than half of the seats were empty, but his thick Scottish accent filled the voids in the room. *Nice of you to embarrass us.*

Alex muttered an apology and scuttled to the closest empty chair. I kept my head down and followed. Sitting, I threw a glance towards the professor. His disapproving stare burned into me.

'What's your name?' he asked. I pointed to myself in question. He nodded with a sarcastic grin in return.

I should have stayed in bed.

'William Walters,' I said.

'Well William Walters, it's nice to meet you. Is there a reason you're in this room today?' His glare was an impenetrable wall, daring me to defy him. Evidently, I was going to be his subject of torture for the hour. I explained that I was taking the module, and he asked why he hadn't seen me before. He also wanted an explanation for our tardiness, and then made a point to aim every single question directed towards the class at me, saying my name as though it were a cancer on his tongue. Not just an expert in jurisprudence, but also in exploiting emotional weakness in students. *Only written a book on one of those topics, though.* If I were female, he probably wouldn't have called me out like that, but such is the way of the world: it's run by rich, chauvinistic men. Perhaps I would have been one of those, if I hadn't been so broken inside.

'What did you think?' Alex asked when the lecture finished. We joined the flow of students pouring from the theatre.

'The guy's a—'

'—No, not of him. I know that. What did you think of the assignment?'

'It sounds interesting enough,' I said.

We left the building and I stepped onto the empty road.

'Interesting?' he repeated. 'It's an absolute minefield. If we don't get it just right, he'll make out we're incompetent, or worse. What are your plans for the rest of the day?'

I hesitated, tried to think of a worthy excuse, hated myself for not having one.

'Well,' Alex began. My time to answer had expired. 'You're not going to waste the day nursing a hangover when you're already out.' The force of nature that he was, he yanked my arm, sealing my fate. 'It's a big assignment. We need to get started straight away.'

In the short time I'd known him, I'd already learned Alex admired hard work and good grades above all else. I refrained from telling him I'd achieved at least a sixty-seven in every class I'd taken; that I wasn't the idiot he assumed me to be. We walked to the antiquated, geometric palace of concrete that is the Bodlian Law Library and joined the queue for the independent cafe because Alex wanted a coffee. He apologised for barging in that morning and for being so full on, then continued talking about the professor and the class assignment.

'I already complained that the grades shouldn't rely on multiple student's input,' he said. I lifted my chin, showing he had my full attention. 'But Professor Hall is adamant the experience will prepare us for working life,' he added with an exaggerated eye-roll. I needed to tell him he'd have to find another partner, but how could I do that without revealing my plan?

Without asking if I wanted anything, he bought me a tea. I thanked him, and made a mental note to either buy him one back before dying, or leave him the £1.95 on my deathbed. We entered the library, and climbed the stairs in hope of finding space to work on the second floor. With exams approaching, the building was busy, but not yet full. The hushed atmosphere around us was not entirely silent as restless students rustled through textbooks and papers in desperation to finish assignments and essays, or like us, get a head start on pending exams.

Alex dashed for an empty table and took a seat. The adjacent panelled window cast a shadow over him, making it look like he was in a jail cell. As I joined him, he pulled out his revision plan along with a colour-coded timetable and explained the rationale behind his polychromatic highlights and scribbles in great detail. I watched the tail end of people flurry, either to or from their classes, through the window. *We're all running from something: it's the cost of being alive.*

'Here,' Alex said in conclusion. He passed me a sheet of crisp paper. 'This is the recommended reading list. If I keep the table, can you go and find these books?'

I resisted rolling my eyes at his eagerness, reminded myself he was only trying to finish the race, just like everybody else. Plus, he had bought me tea which was nice. I walked through the aisles, running my index finger along the books as I passed. Between them, serenity was an almost tangible object, something you could reach out and grab, wrap around yourself if you wanted to. They comforted me. They had the power to transform the world, to protect from its harsh realities. I scanned the shelves and found one final copy of Professor Hall's book, sitting tatty and slanted. I was tempted to hide it behind the other textbooks so nobody would read it, or be able to quote him, but I picked it up instead.

'I would have died if I were you.'

I spun around to face the speaker. A nymph of a girl smiled at me through glistening eyes; the kind you could lose yourself in. Her blonde hair was pinned back with an Alice band, and her ears were decorated with studded, diamond earrings.

'Died?' I asked, conscious I was staring at her. My eyes searched for something else to focus on: the overhead lights, the shelving brackets, a piece of fluff on the carpet, *her dimples. . .*

'Yeah, the way Professor Hall embarrassed you in class. He's such a bully. I would have wanted the ground to swallow me whole, but you took it in your stride, smiled and everything. He thinks he rules the world just because he's written a book. Like, hello? There's more to life.' There was no sarcasm in her tone, but I was suspicious of her words. If she doubted my confidence, it didn't show at all. Funny, how some people can see you in a different light. She giggled in a way that made her whole body jitter, then grabbed my arm impulsively.

'I've got to go, I'll see you later,' she said as though she had remembered something. Her touch, though firm, was gentle. It was a lingering rain on a spring day which made the hairs on my arms stand on end. I had to shuffle them back down as she walked away. In a state of distraction, I found some more books from the reading list and took them back to Alex, hoping he'd be pleased with my selection.

'You took your time,' he said as I dropped the books onto the table. I wanted to ask if he knew of a girl with deep green eyes, but decided against it. She'd noticed me in class, and then recognised me in the library aisle. She had *seen* me, and that made my stomach churn gently, like the sea washing upon the shore. Speaking to her would be my little secret.

That night, I lined up even more pills along my desk, next to my final goodbye and a small pile of change adding up to £1.95. When I swallowed the first one, a pale and viscous bile violently erupted from my stomach. I ran to the bathroom, heaved again, and rested my head on the cool ceramic of the toilet bowl. I'd been failing at life, and I'd failed at death. With a burning throat, I carried myself back to the bedroom and stared at the mess I'd made. So mentally drained was I, that I couldn't bring myself to clean it up. I downed the contents in my glass; the chill of the drink soothed my scorched throat, and fell onto my bed. On the other side of the wall, my flat mates were having another party. I wondered if Alex would be in attendance; if his was the laugh mocking me from the kitchen. Student life, I thought, is comparable to living in a beehive: people buzzing about, coming and going, fulfilling the purpose of their lives. I wondered if when a bee dies, the other bees even notice, or if they were so busy working there was no time to mourn. Is it so normal for bees to die they don't even blink over it? *Can bees even blink?*

I wondered if anybody would mourn my death, or if I was just another bee in the hive.

Thoughts of bees transitioned into those of gardens in bloom and of pollen and plants, of shamrock-green leaves collecting water droplets from morning dew; individual blades of chartreuse fescue grass bowing to the wind and fat fern-coloured caterpillars who turn into butterflies. And thinking of that, made me think of the girl in the library. Her striking eyes were a perfect blend of all those greens and even more. They haunted me.

I got up, used tissues to scrape the pills and residue from the desk and watched them fall into the bin. They landed with pangs against the metal, the soundtrack of failure. I tossed the suicide note in too, so that the only thing remaining on my desk were the copious notes for the assignment I'd written with Alex, and the loose change. He needed a partner. Maybe I should live, I thought, for the time being, see the assignment through, at least.

With that in mind, I switched off the lights and crawled into bed.

I managed to get an emergency appointment with my GP the next day. I knew I'd need professional help to survive the upcoming weeks. Dr Guppa, a small Indian man with a brilliant mind, but a life so far removed from my own, sat adjacent to me. He listened intently as I half-heartedly explained how I'd been feeling and why I'd come to see him, censoring the more disturbing details. I'd decided before I even sat down that Dr Guppa would never understand my pain, and in my prejudice, I failed to give the doctor what he needed to help me. How was I supposed to trust a stranger with my deepest, darkest secrets?

'What makes you think you're depressed?' The doctor asked so casually he may have been asking for the time. He stared at me through brown eyes, magnified behind large, round glasses. I wished I had a definitive answer for him. I couldn't find the words to explain the way a darkness had taken residence in me, how it had shadowed my happiness for so long. I couldn't meet his sympathetic gaze, so I gave a shrug instead.

'Have you been sleeping?' he asked.

'Not well,' I said, incapable of elaboration. Answering his premeditated checklist was proving impossible.

'And eating?' he asked. I sighed internally.

'Sometimes I eat well,' I replied.

'It's exam season,' he said, like I wasn't painfully aware. 'You wouldn't believe the number of students who come to see me with depression during their exams. There's a tremendous amount of pressure on you these days. I understand. Take some time away from your phone, eat plenty fruit and vegetables—cut out the Pot Noodles and takeaways—exercise, and try to get a goodnights sleep.'

I nodded, as though those simple remedies were the cure to my deep-rooted problems. He told me if I still felt low in a months' time I should come back to see him again. I didn't tell him I may not be around that long.

I got up and nodded again, as though his advice was helpful. At least he had tried.

'Thanks,' I said, closing his door sharply on my way out.

If I was to find a way to survive until the assignment, I'd have to do it on my own.

2

Two Meals

As I was leaving the practice, I saw Alex walking up the path. He was so heavily engaged in conversation with another man that he didn't noticed me. To avoid small and forced conversation, I retracted my steps and cowered to the side of the lobby's lone vending machine, waiting until they'd passed before I made my getaway.

I saw him again, later that afternoon. His jaw visibly dropped when he watched me enter Professor Hall's lecture on time, and without his prompting. Both seats either side of him were already occupied, so I sat on my own near the front of the class. I scoured the lecture theatre in search of the mysterious girl from the library, but her dazzling eyes were absent. Professor Hall watched me suspiciously, but made no point to single me out. My lesson, it seemed, had been learnt.

After class, Alex ran after me, catching me on the pavement outside the building. He was wearing the same lime-green bomber jacket I'd seen him in that morning, but his cheeks were rosier and his hair a little more unkempt.

'Do you want to go to the library?' he asked.

I thought about it, but admittedly not for as long as I may previously have.

'Okay,' I said, a smile breaking over my face.

In the passing weeks, we struggled to find empty tables in the library, so we settled for working in the student-run coffee shop on the high street. With gloomy lighting and a constant babble of chatter, it lacked the quiet, safety and warmth the library possessed. On top of that, the drinks were more expensive and the barista was cold and rude, not like the university librarians. I paid Alex back for the tea I owed him and made a conscious effort to alternate who paid each time. In the past it had been rare for me to see someone so frequently, but I grew to enjoy—and even look forward to—our scheduled meetings. I hadn't forgotten about the green-eyed girl, but I began to suspect she had been a figment of my imagination—someone my mind had made up to comfort me during my lowest low. Too much time had passed for me to ask Alex about her, so I became resigned to the knowledge that I may never see her again. In those weeks, I gave myself a goal; not to die after Professor Hall's final assignment, but instead, after graduation — that way my life wouldn't have been for *nothing*: I'd at least have accomplished *something*.

As I was leaving Professor Hall's final class of the semester, the professor asked if he could have a word with me. Alex threw an alarmed glance which I dismissed with a feigned shrug of disinterest. I told him I'd see him after. The professor waited for the room to clear and the door to close before he spoke again.

'What are your plans after you graduate?' he asked.

'I don't really have any . . .' I mumbled. *A half-truth.*

'William.' For the first time the professor's face seemed to soften. 'I see through you,' he said. Dread slid down my throat as though it were a piece of glass, lodging here and there in my oesophagus, tearing and slicing me apart on its way down. It seemed the professor had been trying to form an opinion of me and had finally reached a conclusion. With tight lips and no response ready, I could only furrow my brow and wait to hear what he had to say.

'I've seen a real change in you lately. It's like someone's come along and flicked a switch on inside you. I checked out your transcript. You're a bright lad, lots of potential. Imagine what you could achieve if you applied yourself a little more. Anxious as a beaten puppy, but I bet you're riddled with confidence underneath it all. If you don't learn to play by the rules of the world, you're going to get left behind,' he said.

I only realised I was knotting my fingers together when his eyes fell on them. I stopped.

'Have you thought about London?' he asked.

'I have, actually,' I lied, deciding to feed him the enthusiasm he obviously wanted. There had been, deep down, an ambitious, career-driven side to me at one point in my life, but that had been drowned out by the darkness a long time ago.

'I have a friend, an old colleague, actually, meeting me for dinner on Thursday night. He's looking for graduates around the country and I think you'd be exactly who he's looking for.' The professor nodded in his own excitement, and after a second or two, I found that I was as well. 'He's Peter Truman,' he said, like I should have known who that was. The name sounded vaguely familiar, but I wouldn't have been able to pick the man out from a crowd. 'Join us.'

It wasn't a question. There was no way I could refuse. I hesitated, perhaps a little too long, before I agreed and thanked him, though my words were drowned by the throbbing of my heart. I was certain he wouldn't hear my voice over the pounding.

'Excellent,' he said rather pleased with himself. 'We're meeting in Hakusan at 8:30pm. You know it?'

'On the high street?' I asked, faking excitement in my voice, wondering how on earth I could get out of it.

'You can't get out of it,' Alex told me when Thursday came around. We sat in the library and I'd made the mistake of telling him that I wasn't planning on going to the dinner.

'Why not?' I closed my textbook, feeling depleted.

'Not showing up gives him a reason to fail you. Which gives him a reason to fail me. You signed up for this, so you're going. It's one dinner.'

Attending was the least I could do if Alex could get a good grade out of it. Plus, if I failed the class then I couldn't graduate, and then I'd have lived and died for nothing.

'I don't even know anything about Truman,' I whined, already exhausted by the prospect of playing the enthusiastic undergraduate. Alex twisted his lip as he eyed my laptop. With a friendly smirk, he took the machine and keyed Truman's name into the search bar. There was a plethora of information on the man. He'd started his own firm at the tender age of twenty-six and was considered both a shark and a god in the industry. The images of him showed a middle-aged man with glowing skin and an immaculate smile, winning award after award.

'What are you going to wear?' Alex asked. I looked down at the hoody and jeans I already had on.

'No,' he responded. 'Wear a suit.'

I looked at him blankly.

'You *do* have a suit?' he asked cautiously, checking his watch. I nodded, mentally rummaging through my wardrobe.

'It's at my gran's,' I said.

Alex held his breath after asking where she lived. He let it out in relief when I told him it was a twenty-minute walk away.

'I suggest you call her,' he said, 'because we're about to pay her a visit.'

Forgotten in time, Grandma Jo's cottage sat on the edge of the woodland surrounding the outskirts of the city. Thick black smoke plumed from the chimney, dissipating into the sky. I collected myself on the doorstep, letting the rush of the nearby river calm my nerves. Alex pushed the doorbell impatiently so I threw him a disgruntled look. He widened his eyes and shrugged. If he had wondered why I'd left my suit at my grandmothers, he showed exceptional restraint by not asking. Hearing Jo's footsteps on the other side of the door, I quickly warned him in a harsh whisper not to call her *Gran* or reference her age at all.

'William,' she gushed when she pulled the door open. Her grey hair was wild and knotty. I lost myself in it as she pulled me in for a hug. 'And you must be Alex,' she enthused, turning towards him.

'Come, come,' she ushered, sauntering away from us. Alex closed the door and we followed the scent of Jo's cooking to the kitchen.

'There's obviously an occasion because this one never visits.' She pointed at me with her thumb, 'let alone bring friends over.' She manoeuvred around the kitchen. I could never have brought myself to tell her I didn't have friends to bring in the first place. That information would have crushed her.

'Are you hungry? I made lasagne,' she said. Then threw me an accusatory look and removing the pleasantries from her voice, added, 'I would have made more, but I didn't have much warning.'

'Actually, we're—'

'—We'd love some,' Alex interrupted. He invited himself to take a seat at the old oak table with a confidence I could never have mustered in a stranger's home. Jo checked the oven and demanded I fetch my guest a drink. I poured us each a glass of water then dribbled some into the daffodils on the windowsill. Their natural colours were lost in the offensive hues of the walls. I took the seat across from Alex, my favourite spot, and absentmindedly thumbed the edge of the table where the letters of my father's name had been carved into the wood. From the stories I'd heard about him, I knew he was a rebellious child.

I often wondered if he saw the spark in life I never could.

'Alex dear, tell me how you are. Can I get you anything else? Wine perhaps?' Jo asked. She pranced from the oven to his side and lay a gentle hand on his shoulder. He politely declined; told her he'd have to keep a sober head for studying later. It was painful how attentive she was. Perhaps if I made effort to visit her more often, she wouldn't have been so flustered.

'This is a lovely home,' Alex said. 'It must have been nice to grow up by the woods,' he added, looking from the window to me. The back garden was a jungle of overgrown wildflowers, unkempt grass, and rogue bushes. Beyond the broken fence were the woodlands of my childhood.

'William used to love playing out there. It was his special place, his kingdom. He stopped going out—' she cut herself short, placed her fingers to her temples, then turned to me. 'It was the day we got the call. You never went back out there.' She picked up the dish towel and clutched it to her chest. Underneath, I imagined her heart beat with ache. To distract her from her thoughts, I rose, deliberately scraping my chair against the tiled floor. 'I'll go find my suit,' I announced, then asked Alex if he'd like to see my bedroom. I didn't particularly want to show him, but I didn't want to leave him alone with Jo either; there was no telling what embarrassing stories she'd divulge in my absence.

My bedroom hadn't changed since I was a child and was still littered with magazines and plastic dinosaurs. Alex picked up a tyrannosaurus rex and growled. I laughed, opened the wardrobe and picked out my suit. Slimline and grey. Unworn since I'd interviewed for a place on my course. I threw the jacket on. Still a perfect fit.

The noise of china clattering and smashing ripped through the cottage. I ran back to the kitchen with Alex at my tail. When I entered, my heart sank. Jo was leaning against the counter with a hand clutching at her ribs. Shattered fragments of china scattered the floor around her.

'What happened?' I asked, running to her aid.

'Oh, it's nothing, just some old lady problems,' she said. 'It comes and goes.' She exhaled deeply and stood upright. Any pain she felt, she hid with a convincing smile.

'See.' She held her hands up as if there were nothing wrong. 'It's gone.' I could see beneath her fake exterior and told her to have a seat and some water. Surprisingly, she obliged. I got the broom from the cupboard and cleaned the mess on the floor, embarrassed Alex had witnessed the event. I dished out the lasagne and garlic bread and carried the plates to the table where the salad had already been presented. Before I could push Jo to explain her episode, she asked Alex how we had become friends. As he helped himself to a generous helping of salad, he told Jo about the assignment and that we'd been partnered, carefully skipping the part where he showed up at my door and dragged me to class. She asked him what his plans were after we graduated, taking away my chance to steer the conversation.

'I've interviewed for the firm where I had a placement last year. It's only as a legal clerk, but it's a growing company and it's an excellent place to start.'

'That sounds like a wonderful opportunity,' Jo said, forking lasagne into her lipsticked mouth.

'It doesn't pay very well,' Alex admitted, as though to clarify an unmade point. He peeled stringy cheese from his chin. 'This is delicious.'

'It's meat free,' Jo said, throwing him a playful wink. Alex did a double take between his plate and the food on his fork. Jo was an expert at disguising plants within meals.

'I've never eaten meat in my life,' she said proudly, 'and I *don't* look seventy-two.' It was true, she didn't, but gone were the days where she could pass as my mother.

'You're vegetarian,' Alex said, 'but William—'

'—Is and always has been free to make his own choices,' she eyed me as she took a gulp of water and added under hear breath, 'one of these days I'm sure he'll make a good one.' She pulled a face, as cheeky as a child. Alex snorted but I missed the humour.

'I guess you enjoyed your placement if you want to go back,' she said, then asked what the firm specialised in.

'It's a small non-profit representing people who often struggle to find legal support,' he answered in an almost rehearsed manner. Then his lips became a padlock, keeping secrets inside. He obviously didn't want to give too much information away. I wished Jo wouldn't push, but there was so much unsaid and she couldn't help herself.

'People?' she asked, forming the single word into an entire question. Alex twisted his silver ring around his index finger. The unbearable silence Jo left was enough to crack the lock of his lips.

'People with disabilities . . . well, not disabilities. I didn't mean that . . . ' He trailed off, took a deep breath seemingly uncomfortable, as though he were sitting on a chair made of nails. I'd never seen him so reserved. I couldn't help but suspect it was because of Jo's age.

'Specifically, people who test HIV positive,' he disclosed. 'People disproportionally affected by socio-economic and mental health issues, that kind of thing,' he trailed off again. Jo leaned in, which fed him approval to continue. Perhaps some closed-minded people may not have wanted him to. 'Lawyers always get painted in dark colours, but we're not all evil and corporate. I have a voice and a privilege. If I do nothing with those, then that's the real evil.' He paused, appeared to read the room, and continued. 'There's such a stigma around HIV and AIDS that some people who test positive have their respect stripped from them. And they don't just lose their lives, their families or their self-esteem - they lose their humanity. It's . . . well, it's just not fair.'

It appeared he had said it so many times he was reciting the information rather than speaking off the cuff, but there was still passion in the way he carried himself. Jo looked lost for words, but gathered her thoughts quickly.

'Absolutely beautiful,' she said, reaching out. She put her hand over one of his, cupping him in a way I would never have felt comfortable with. 'Is there a girl on the scene?' she asked obtrusively.

'No,' he said with a polite smile.

'A boyfriend?' she asked.

'I wouldn't call him a *boyfriend*,' Alex blushed, 'but there *is* someone.'

'What?' I couldn't help but ask. They both shot me a look as though I'd interrupted. I had no idea Alex was gay. Thinking of it, I'd never seen him flirt with a girl, but then, I'd never seen him flirt with a guy either. For a fleeting second, I wondered if I was the someone he was thinking of. We *had* been spending a lot of time together. . .

'His name is Luke. We met during my interview,' Alex said.

I smiled to myself. Of course he didn't see me like that. I didn't even consider him a friend until Jo had said it. I saw him as more of an annoying acquaintance who made me study because he wanted a good grade.

'He's not the boss is he?' Jo asked playfully.

'No, no, it's nothing like that,' Alex laughed. Jo clasped her hands together, ready to hear more. Alex didn't dissatisfy. At first, he skimmed the surface, but the more he could see Jo loving it, the deeper he dived into the delicate details.

'Picture this,' he said. *An April morning. A light drizzle. He opens the door as he leaves his interview and bumps into a tall and handsome stranger.*

The stranger smiles and asks him for his name. It's Alex, he says. They dance around each other and as he's walking away, the stranger, Luke, grabs his arm. He spins, and they meet each other's eye. Their stares linger for a moment, or for an eternity, he doesn't know which. They walked the length of the canal before Luke pulled him in, held him tight, kissed him deep under the blooming cherry trees on the edge of town.

Jo brought her hands to her chest as though she were cradling her heart. 'Do we get to see a photo?' It was less of a question, more of a command. For a sliver of a second, Alex looked unsettled, but shrugged his discomfort away. He plucked his phone from his pocket and swiped the screen with an abundance of excitement I'd never seen in him before. He showed Jo the picture.

'Oh, he's gorgeous.' *There could have been a troll on the screen and she'd have said that.* Without permission, and with the ability of a teenager, she peeled the phone from his hand and pinched the screen, zooming in on the features of the person who had given Alex his flushed smile. Showing me, she asked, 'Isn't he just dashing, William?'

I studied the photograph. The boy inside stared back at me with intense blue eyes. His chiselled jaw stuck out from the picture the way a model's would, and his hair had been styled into a perfect quiff. I could see why she'd gotten so excited: he was conventionally handsome.

Alex's eyes shone, falling on the picture as Jo handed the phone back to him. It was obvious that he was completely infatuated, which is a dangerous thing to be. Infatuation, I have found, is an unusual concept. Stronger than love and arriving in full force with no warning or hesitance, it burns red: passionate and furious. A fire with enough fuel to burn down a whole village. Not like love at all. Love is a flickering flame on a cold winter's night, gentle and tranquil. It's rose petals on bed sheets and affectionate kisses on cheeks. That's why we hurt the ones we love, because love is soft and forgiving. We can take advantage of that. We never hurt those we're infatuated with because during the short life span of obsession we are completely and uncontrollably drunk on another person.

This could only end in unbearable heartache for Alex, I thought.

'I wonder when William will find someone,' Jo said dreamily. She exchanged glances with Alex, a look of guilt drawn over her time-weathered face. She knew the topic was out-of-bounds.

'Don't make me regret bringing someone over, *Grandma,*' I said playfully.

She winced, shivered.

'Of course, he'd have to speak to people for that to happen,' she said. 'He thinks too much.'

Retaliation for calling her Grandma.

'No, I don't,' I protested, whiney as a child.

'This one lives in his head. He's been this way since he was a boy, wastes all his time worrying. Worries about being on time, about what people think of him, if he's cool enough, liked enough, handsome enough,' she used her fingers as though ticking items from a list. 'Enough. Enough. *Enough.* Can you ever be enough if you're not enough?'

Alex looked like he wanted to save me, but I dismissed the notion with a small headshake. Needless to say, when Jo got carried away, there was no stopping her. I had no idea it was so obvious I was so self-conscious. Wondering if that impacted her at all, I sat still and expressionless, while my heart broke at the mere thought of burdening her.

'Remember boys, you—your soul—has an invitation to be here, on this earth, in this wrinkle of time exactly as you are.' She was growing preachy. If we didn't leave, we'd never escape.

'I think,' I cut in, 'it's about time Alex and I head off, Jo. It's getting late.' I pretended to check the time on my phone. I'd heard more than enough, and I remembered why I didn't visit more often. I filled the dishwasher and grabbed my suit, noticing a sadness in her eyes as we left. I couldn't help but forgive her abrasiveness and promised myself I would visit sooner than I otherwise would have.

Later, as I walked to Hakusan, I developed the theory that mental health and walking speed are correlated. The more my mental health deteriorated, the faster I walked, and I wondered if other speed-walkers were the same. Casual strolls weren't something I was capable of. Instead, I power walked across the park, deliberately taking perverse routes just so I didn't show up too early, and when I reached Magdalen bridge there was still too much time to spare, so I stopped walking and focused on my surroundings.

Ahead of me, the sky stretched vast and blue, littered with wispy clouds. Beneath the bridge, water levels were low and the banks dehydrated. Already, students had begun to fill the tables in the beer garden opposite. Leaning over the brick wall, I saw chicks waddling behind their mother and I spotted a small hedgehog, an early riser, grazing by a bush.

The world can be beautiful, if only you remember to look.

Even with my small rest, I still arrived with time to spare. I'd passed Hakusan a million times, but never been inside before. I didn't know anyone who had.

Sat on the brick wall where Longwall street meets High Street, I took in the restaurant, appreciating the grand mahogany doors and stone dragons carved onto the wall, features I'd never noticed before. At first, the opulence seemed rather unwelcoming, and I imagined myself simply getting up and walking away.

To steady my nerves, I picked up a broken twig, fallen from a nearby tree in Magdalen College's garden and ran my thumbnail down the length of it repeatedly. Chestnut-brown curls of bark fell lazily to the ground. When a taxi pulled up, the tugging sensation in my intestines told me Professor Hall and Peter Truman were inside. The back door opened and a man with peppered grey hair climbed out. He carried himself with the elegance of a man who had money. Real money. *Peter Truman.* Ungraciously Professor Hall followed, and they walked into the restaurant together.

The taxi pulled away and I crossed the street while practicing my "hello" aloud, to let myself grow comfortable with the shape and feel of the word. Suddenly, I was absolutely parched. I reached the door and froze. It wasn't too late. I could still turn around, pretend I hadn't arrived at all. But what would Alex say? What would Jo say? I let out a deep breath and—

'Are you going inside?'

I turned to face the speaker behind me, mentally wishing people would stop sneaking up on me and starting conversations. I knew him.

I just didn't know how I knew him.

He was my age, maybe a year or two older, and taller. A lot taller. He didn't carry himself as a student - he was much too sophisticated, with a Rolex watch around his wrist and a woollen Prussian-blue turtle-neck sweater.

'Sorry,' I said, even though I wasn't really sorry at all. 'After you.'

I held the door open and followed him inside, trying to place where I recognised him from. We stood inside a rectangular candle-lit space. Draped curtains hid the view of the restaurant, which added to the flare of my rising anxiety. Professor Hall and Peter Truman had already been seated.

'Table for two?'

'Yes,' the stranger said. 'But, no,' stealing a glance at me, he realised the hostess thought we'd arrived together. 'My friend's already here. The booking's under Caitlyn Donoghue.'

The hostess nodded, and without taking her eyes off the stranger told me she'd be back in a moment.

'Do you have a booking?' she asked on her return.

'It's under Hall,' I said boldly, then added, 'though it might be Truman. I'm not sure.'

She scanned her booking sheet then looked me up and down. 'Right this way.'

Behind the curtain was a world I'd never set foot in before. Beyond the steel frames of the open kitchen, flames burst towards the ceiling warning me to turn around and never come back. From behind the dimly lit bar, mixologists juggled cocktail shakers and performed elaborate tricks with liquor bottles. Every move was perfect, as practiced as a show. If I could make it through dinner, that would be the biggest act of all. The hostess led me through the restaurant to a secluded table tucked away in the corner. As I neared, I rubbed the sweat from my palms on the cotton of my trousers. Both Professor Hall and Peter Truman stood when they saw me arrive.

'Walters,' Professor Hall said. He shook my hand and then Truman did too. I recognised him instantly from his pictures online. His face was gaunt, filled with a prominent nose below two, small, round intelligent eyes. A tall and slender man, he carried himself with the swagger of a football player. A man's man, no doubt. He flashed an impeccable smile, unlike Professor Hall who bore nicotine-stained gravestones. My heart turned into a beating drum, reminding me I was alive. *What do they have up their suede sleeves tonight?*

Without checking if I had preference, Professor Hall ordered an assortment of food for the table along with a bottle of wine. Opportunities like dinner at Hakusan happened to other people, not me, so at least I would be able to take away a good meal from the night, if nothing else.

I had braced myself for interview-styled babble, but Truman barely asked me anything. Instead, he rattled on about himself, filling his voice with absolute authority. He sprinkled the conversation with highlights from his career, emphasising the names of people he had hand-picked to work for him. I already knew from my research he had a bank of the best lawyers in the country working at the firm he'd set up entirely on his own. And that was when he was just five years older than I was at the time, which begged me to evaluate my questionable life choices so far. I gave small sounds of encouragement in appropriate places, recognising some of the names, but less than a quarter. I nodded as though they were famous politicians or celebrities, because to him, they were. The evening wasn't an interview, I realised. It was a card game, and my opponents were other graduates. There was an expectation of me to play my hand.

In uninterrupted flow, Truman waved a hand through the air in front of the waiter who had poured a fraction of wine in his glass as though he were swatting a fly.

'I know what it's like, I've had it before,' he said, continuing his story as though the waiter no longer existed. Aware I had said very little, I tried to squeeze an opinion out when Truman paused and took a sip of his wine, only for Professor Hall to overshadow me.

'I taught him. What a good lad,' he toasted, after Truman name-dropped Christopher Michaels. I took a sip of wine to disguise that I'd opened my mouth to speak. An immense volume of flavours blanketed my mouth: an explosion of ripe pear combined with dashes of citric-lemon and hints of grapefruit. Slick tones of cream and exotic nuts cloyed to my tongue, adding a weight which had previously not been present. I'd never experienced anything like that before; I enjoyed the numbness of the feeling. Truman talked until the food arrived and Professor Hall dealt it out between us. Any anxieties I had slowly dissipated with each dish.

'How have you found Oxford?' Truman asked. Both he and the professor looked at me expectantly. The tables had finally turned: the attention was solely on me.

'Brilliant' I said, rather flatly as though I wasn't born and bred on the outskirts of the city. *Brilliant* except for the monthly mental breakdowns, the mountainous pressures which rained from the skies, the impending clock of doom which ticked louder each day and the never-ending worry of paying bills, saving money and drowning in debt.

'What's next?' Truman demanded.

I told him I'd applied for a few jobs but was weighing my options – a fairly benign answer. One he'd probably heard from a handful of graduates with better credentials than me.

'How are you finding rising tuition fees?' Truman asked after a second's silence.

'It's a struggle,' I laughed, hoping humour would win him over, wondering why I was even bothering. 'I stack shelves at weekends for some extra money. It keeps me humble.'

Only when disinterest plastered their faces did I realise how much I wanted to impress those implacable men.

'Do you consider yourself to be well off?'

A loaded question, surely a trap. I was a fox in a snare. In searching for an answer, realisation struck. I knew where I'd seen the stranger before—the man I'd come into the restaurant with—he was in a photograph I'd seen. He was the boy Alex was dating; Luke. I shifted in my seat and caught sight of him a few tables away. At the same moment, the girl dining with him also looked across the restaurant. Green eyes—the same ones which had haunted me since the first time I saw them—pierced the room and met my own. She'd made the booking - Caitlyn Donoghue, he'd called her.

I tore my eyes away, bringing myself back to the conversation with a boost of morale. I could have told them the unvarnished truth, left them with some alluring lies or given a blemish of both. Truman had just handed me an ace, and he didn't even know it. I didn't necessarily want the prize, but I was driven to win the competition regardless.

'I'm not well-off,' I revealed slowly. 'My grandmother took me in when my parents died. It's because of her I've come so far.'

'Your parents died?' Professor Hall asked. Pieces of rice had stuck to his lip. I nodded, proud of myself for taking control of the situation. Too often before I'd been hampered by self-doubt. It was low of me to use their deaths as an aid, but the evening was no longer about qualifications. It was about sticking out from the crowd.

'I'm so sorry,' Truman said. He clamped a solid hand on my arm. Professor Hall, who seemed to have no experience confronting death, shuffled awkwardly in his chair. I tightened my lips, nodded solemnly. Truman's years in the courtroom shone through as he held an impenetrable stare, trying to read beyond my poker face. I bit the inside of my cheek to contain emotion.

'I'm impressed by your attitude,' he finally said. From the twitch in his eyebrow, I thought he'd say more, but he picked up his wine glass and took a sip instead. Professor Hall looked at him expectantly. As Truman placed his glass back on the table, he met the professor's eye and sneered. Slowly, he turned his attention back to me.

'You'll apply for a place on my graduate programme,' he announced. With his tongue poking from the corner of his lips. Truman fished inside his jacket pocket and pulled out a business card along with a designer pen. Professor Hall beamed as Truman circled his phone number in the corner. He passed me the card along with a wink.

'My receptionist, Grace, will sort you out,' he said.

I couldn't help but stare at the card resting in my palm. It was a coarse material and Truman's name was printed in the centre, demanding my eyes fall onto it. It was proposition; an invitation into his world.

3

Freedom

Truman's proposition sat heavy in my heart over the passing days. Joining the rat race was of no interest to me. The thought alone was a puncture in my lungs. Happiness, I thought sourly, was a myth. And I could not afford to buy the dream that Truman sold. But still, I at least wanted to graduate. If not for myself, then for Jo and for Alex.

I stood outside the doctor's practice, bracing myself for what was to come. Dressed to reflect my mood, I wore dark faded jeans and an oversized muggy-brown t-shirt. When the doctor asked me how I was feeling, I planned to be melodramatic and reveal what I'd failed to before: that my depression wasn't situational, that I wasn't merely crying out for help. As I gathered my thoughts, the front door burst open and Alex walked out, followed by a man I recognised as Luke. Inwardly I cursed, outwardly I smiled.

'William,' Alex said, 'what are you doing here?' He greeted me with yet another hug.

'I was just out for a walk,' I lied, swinging my body as though I hadn't planned on going inside. 'What about you?'

'We had an appointment,' he waved a limp hand carelessly through air. Catching my wandering eye, Luke stuffed a prescription package into his tote bag. I nodded, and for a second we stood in shared silence, somewhat suspicious of each other. Alex introduced me to Luke, calling me his friend. The word hit hard. I'd been called many things in life, but never that. I wanted to wear the title as a badge.

'Are you busy?' Alex asked and before I had a chance to answer said, 'we're going for coffee. Do you want to join us?'

I paused. A pretence. Then politely declined. He reminded me we were due to study later that day. As I twisted away, Luke checked his phone.

'Caitlyn's just getting ready,' he told Alex. I turned as they began to walk away.

'On second thought,' I called, 'I'd die for a cup of tea.'

I stole a glance back at the doctors' practice as we walked away. Why, I wondered, could I never make the right choices?

The independant café Luke insisted on visiting was nestled between the city's tenacious medieval buildings in the heart of town. With the exception of a lone student typing ferociously on their laptop, it was empty. Luke announced he'd pay for the tea, so once again I found myself making a mental note of how much it cost in order to later pay him back.

I stirred sugar into my drink as Luke checked his phone. He slammed it to the table with an exaggerated sigh.

'Caitlyn's cancelled,' he said.

Flooded with disappointment, I tilted my mug, letting the contents sway in a feeble attempt to pretend I was unfazed.

'She's had a fight with Rose,' Luke said. 'Her mum,' he added to me, for clarification.

'Again?' Alex asked. Luke pulled a face which confirmed, yes, again. I tried to form a picture of Caitlyn arguing, wondered if her head would jolt minutely as she debated her case; mused if her eyebrows would rise or fall, and was curious to know if she'd win ruthlessly or sulk in loss. I struggled to conjure an image of her in any of those states, though, and was puzzled as to why she had wanted to study law in the first place.

'Have you called Truman yet?' asked Alex, pulling me from my wandering thoughts.

I shook my head.

'Why not?'

I'll be dead by summer.

I clicked my tongue. How could I explain that I couldn't face being the pauper in a room full of princes?

'I don't belong in a graduate programme filled with inherited credentials,' I said, picking up my mug for something to do. Both Luke and Alex wore stunned expressions, so I added, 'I wouldn't exactly fit in,' before taking a sip of tea.

After a moment, Luke put his mug on the table and leaned into me.

'That,' he said, 'is exactly *why* you belong there.' His stare fixed onto me like a target. 'You need to prove the underdog can win.'

In welcoming his support, I gave a fraction of a nod, contemplating the thought.

'Are you ready for your exams?' he asked. The weight of them was like walking around with a loaded gun pointed at my head.

'I think so,' I said. 'I know we'll do well with Professor Hall's assignment, at least.' Alex, who treated exam predictions as a bad omen, cringed.

'I wanted to ask Caitlyn how prepared she is for it,' Alex said. 'Do you know?' His face directed at Luke.

'So you're close?' I blurted, before I could stop myself.

'We're cousins,' he said. 'You know her?'

I hated myself more than ever.

'No,' I admitted carefully, 'I know *of* her. Since we're in the same class.' Somehow, they accepted my answer without further question, and I relaxed a little, but hoped for a change in conversation. A web of connections became clear in my mind: Luke and Caitlyn were related, which is why they'd had dinner together at Hakusan. Caitlyn and Alex were in the same class, and Alex and Luke were dating. Then there was me, on the outer rungs looking in, but if I wanted to get to know Caitlyn, I had been given a perfect opportunity to do so.

My final exams turned out to be no more or less daunting than any exams ever were. I coasted along, answering each question with undeserved confidence, writing until my fingers ached and cramped. On the morning of our final assignment, I met Alex outside the Bodlian Law Library and as we walked to the allocated room, I listened as he rattled on about how nervous he was. I played it cool, knowing he would be awarded the high grade he'd been determined to achieve from the offset. Ultimately, it didn't matter what I would receive; my destiny to graduate with a second-class degree had already been cast. We ascended the stairs and turned a corner, bumping into the students who had been assessed before us. One of them wore a tear-stricken face, but the other looked rather bored by the whole affair.

'Caitlyn,' Alex asked, 'what's the matter?' He wrapped his arm around her trembling shoulder sending an indistinguishable jab across my chest. The other girl snapped a bubble.

'It's nothing,' Caitlyn choked. In a failed effort to hide her pain, she shook her head and rolled her eyes, but her mascara-stained cheeks betrayed her.

'We tanked,' her partner said. From context, I translated that to mean they hadn't performed very well.

'We're about to go in, but maybe afterwards we can grab a drink and talk it over,' Alex suggested. I held my breath.

'I *need* a drink,' Caitlyn nodded. As comforting as Alex had been, he checked his watch and told her he'd text her afterwards. I followed him, stealing a glance back at Caitlyn who tried to compose herself. Later, I planned, I would offer her my shoulder to cry on.

Timidly, Alex knocked on the door, then poked his head inside the room. He entered truly believing in himself while I walked in with a fake air of confidence. The room was a small space, designed for an intimate presentation and was filled with only a dozen chairs, a podium and a projector which hummed quietly in the background.

Professor Hall sat in the front row accompanied by two other professors. He whispered to them as Alex and I danced around each other, preparing the space for our presentation.

In the beginning, the three academics took copious notes, but as Alex and I ebbed and flowed in perfect synchronisation they slowed with their written critiques. Where Alex had been detailed, I was succinct, making us a perfect team. At one point, I was certain I saw a flicker of a smile on Professor Hall's face, given away by the fine lines around his eyes. Though when he caught me looking, he frowned.

We finished on high notes, successfully answering their questions with persuasive examples. Thanking them, we left the room. Outside, we let out a small laugh and high-fived each other. The door opened and Professor Hall came plodding out.

'Walters, a word.' His tone was sharp. Alex took the hint and told me he'd see me later, then walked away. I faced the professor in earnest.

'You haven't called Truman,' he said. 'Do you think opportunities like this come along every day?'

Fear struck like lightning. I couldn't find the words to explain myself.

'No, sir. I haven't yet.' *Because what else could I say?*

'You gave an excellent performance today,' he snapped. 'It would be a shame to have to penalise you both.' Without so much as a second glance, he turned around and went back into the room. I stood on the spot with a racing heart. He couldn't punish me for not wanting a job, could he? Then again, he'd recommended me to Truman and I'd passed on the opportunity as though it were nothing. Of course the consequence wasn't going to be light.

I left the building by the main doors, expecting Alex to be waiting on the concrete stairs, or by the road, but he wasn't. Only my shadow filled the desolate street. Deciding he'd gone to the toilet, I went back into the building and stood near the librarian's reception, but grew bored waiting, so made my way to the men's room in search for him. Each of the cubical doors were askew and there was no one by the urinals. I left the building again, expecting him to be outside, inexplicably having somehow passed me in transit. I tried to remember where he said he'd meet me and remembered he hadn't. With a sinking feeling in my stomach I went back inside to look for him. He wasn't in the communal areas or waiting on any of the staircases. The group study rooms were empty with the exception of a group of students I recognised from Professor Hall's class, and the computers were only occupied by eager second years.

As I made my way back to the street, I replayed the conversation with Caitlyn over again. He'd said we'd go for a drink afterwards. Realisation stung like an injection.

We'd go for a drink.

That didn't include me.

With blurry eyes, I dashed back inside the library and burst into the toilets on the ground floor. Tears were falling, so I stowed away in a cubicle. It was pathetic to be upset, but I couldn't help but feel betrayed. The assignment was over, and apparently, so was our friendship. Alex was somewhere with Luke and Caitlyn. I imagined them laughing. Their happiness reverberated from the grubby, off-white bathroom tiles around me, bouncing from wall to wall piercing me with painful stabbing juts.

When I was able to, I collected myself and left the building for the last time. The thought of going back to my own place, where my flatmates were sure to be celebrating the end of exams with yet another party that wouldn't include me, was a knife in my chest. So I walked along Mansfield Road, navigating my way home, to Jo's.

The cottage lay idyllic as ever. I deduced that Jo wasn't home because the lights were off and the windows were shut. I didn't want her to see me upset anyway. The spare key was still under the rock by the steps even though I'd told her to move it a hundred times before. I let myself in. The hallway smelled of her baking, lingering even in her absence. I made my way to my old bedroom, heaved onto the bed and sunk into my sadness. The more I tried *not* to think of Caitlyn, the more vivid she appeared in my mind. I burrowed my face into my pillow to muffle my cries, mourning a relationship which had never even existed.

I replayed the morning over and over, each time finding, then approaching Alex and Caitlyn in different ways. If I'd just called Alex to find out where he'd gone; if I'd called Truman in the first place, I'd have never been held back. Perhaps then I could have changed the course of the day and still felt like I had a friend.

Without warning, an overwhelming sensation of suffocation arrived in my chest. I pictured Alex's face twist in hate as he learned he'd failed the assignment because of me. I longed for the shrill ping of a text to come through but the room remained silent. I picked up my phone and launched it in frustration. The screen crunched as it collided with the wardrobe handle. Defining depression as an imbalance of chemicals in the brain doesn't stop it from being devastatingly disabling. If the chemical store in my brain was a bathtub, then my pipes were broken and my taps leaky, because when I was all out of happy, there was no filling me back up. *Self-aware enough to diagnose yet too self-destructive to medicate.*

I didn't sleep, but I had a dream. *I stood in a glass box in the centre of the city. There were no doors and I couldn't escape. I banged on the walls until the skin over my hands tore and my knuckles bled. I shrieked and cried, but nobody could see me, and nobody could hear me. Water poured from the top of the box, filling fast around me. There were no obvious pipes or contraptions, no weak spot for me to hit. The water cascaded in from nowhere, flooding the box. Reaching first my mouth, then nose, and soon my lungs were filling with water instead of air. Nobody could save me, and everything turned dark.*

The darkness was a void, a bottomless pit of self-pity and torture. Riddled with anxiety, *Professor Hall had said. How did he know?* Lives in his head, Jo had cried. Lives in his head. *Their words spilled from above, growing into physical objects which deluged my room. Big, black, and ink-like, their words spiralled around me. Growing louder and throbbing, leaving nasty tar-like smudges and stains on the carpet, window and ceiling as they crashed around me. They hit my shelves and where they smacked the dry wall, flakes of plaster tippled down.*

With clasped hands over my ears, I wailed until the only sounds in the room were the aching sobs tearing from my lungs. Pain permeated my pounding heart. Was it all in my head, or were the shooting aches in my left arm the signs of a heart attack? *I tried to scrape myself up, twist into a position to alleviate the torment, but the words exploded and gummy liquid rained over me. I choked. Coughed and spurted. The viscous liquid became verbal vines, wrapping themselves around me like a python squeezing the life from me. My heart slowed to a stop and the world disappeared.*

'A second-class degree,' Jo gushed, almost two weeks later. She clamped her hands on my shoulders. Pride seethed from her skin, transforming to guilt as it transferred to me. Alex always scored grades in the 90s, but for Professor Hall's jurisprudence class, we'd each been awarded an 70. He'd hate me, I decided; being partnered with me had dragged him down.

The two weeks prior had passed as a blur. The moments are gone from my memory, like I hadn't existed in them, as though my head and heart had been switched off. *Living, but not living at all.*

It was the morning of graduation, and Jo was restless. She peeled her hands away and carried herself to the fridge and pulled out a bottle of champagne.

'Jo, we can't—'

'Nonsense,' she said. 'It's not every day my grandson earns a degree. She placed the bottle on the table, then collected flutes from the cupboard. Arguing would have been pointless, so I uncorked the bottle, thinking her nimble fingers wouldn't be adequate for the job, and poured. Bubbles burst into fragments of gold as the champagne tumbled into the glasses. As gentle as mice placing uncertain paws on unexplored territories, we clinked the tulip-shaped glassware and I took a sip of the liquid. If the bubbles were an orchestra, they rose to a sharp apex and fell into harmony on my tongue. I took another sip feeling that I was, for the first time in a long time, awake.

The city gleamed with pride as we sauntered to the ceremony. I couldn't quite bring myself to believe that I'd made it: both, in surviving so long, and that I'd earned a degree, but the swooshing of my robes around my feet reminded me with every step. I imagined the events ahead, created a whole future where I'd stroll confidently onto the stage, shake hands with somebody I'd never seen before and smile at a crowd who would applaud my accomplishments.

I led Jo to her seat then made my way through the buzz of students to find my own. The excitement in the room was suffocating and intoxicating but contagious and thrilling at the same time. My cheeks burned, but I couldn't help but smile. I kept my hands busy as student after student was called. When I heard Caitlyn Donoghue's name, my stomach crimped and cramped. The kaleidoscope of butterflies she'd given me had returned, their wings a force to be reckoned with. As beautiful and elegant as ever, she strode across the stage. She was only there for a few meagre seconds but her imprint lined my brain. Then my own name was eventually called, and the butterflies fell, turning into little balls on their way to the pit of my stomach. Ten thousand eyes fell on me, watching my every move. Don't fall, I thought, don't fall, don't fall. Then the ceremony ended, and I was free.

Like a bird of prey, Professor Hall spotted me from across the room. He made a beeline towards me and Jo. There was no escape.

'Walters,' he said, announcing himself with a prominently forced smile. He introduced himself to Jo and congratulated me. 'Truman's graduate programme is filling up. If you don't secure your position soon, he'll retract the offer.' He had spoken to me, but out of the corner of his eye watched Jo - the intended recipient of his message. The professor excused himself as Jo's lip curled with anger, leaving me with her wrath.

'You said you weren't what they were looking for,' she hissed.

'I'm not,' I said, but I don't think she heard. She had already begun to rummage through her handbag. She pulled out a long, lilac purse and unfastened the clasp with such haste that it snapped off between her fingers. On the inside, in the transparent square pocket, Truman's coarse business card lay tucked behind a picture of me.

'I kept it because I was proud of you.' She peeled the card out and thrust it into my hand. I fished my phone from my pocket and dialled Truman's office number with Jo's glaring eyes following my every move.

'Hello,' I said when the receptionist picked up. 'My name is William Walters and I was asked to call by Peter Truman.'

The receptionist, Grace, told me in a honied voice she'd been expecting my call. I could hear her fingers stride across a keyboard as we spoke. She pencilled me in for a summer barbecue with the other graduates Truman had hand selected. I ended the call and smiled at Jo. She muttered something under her breath, which I wish I hadn't heard. She would never understand how draining it was to pretend to be happy all the time.

Out of nowhere, Alex grabbed me from behind. I turned and he clasped me in such a fierce hug I almost forgot he was mad at me. He greeted Jo with a rather camp *faire la bise*. Her annoyance with me dissipated. She skipped small talk and jumped straight into a conversation about his work, talking animatedly with him. It was as though *they* were friends, and I was just watching from the side-line. *Forever in the background.* She deserved a better grandson - one who could flood her with pieces of himself the way Alex could. No holding back, no hiding behind a wall.

'You haven't met Luke yet,' he said with oomph. Without invitation, he grabbed both Jo and me by the hands and led us out of the main hall. Caitlyn stood by the water fountain. It was impossible not to notice her, even with the swarm of students around the courtyard. She was with Luke, laughing at something he'd said. Alex took us straight towards them. In the short walk, I envisioned talking to her about the ceremony. Would she hug me on introduction or simply smile in recognition? When our eyes met, would she yearn the same way I seemed to need her?

But we didn't make it that far.

Jo fell. Or tripped. Or fainted. I watched it happen in painful slow motion. A noise escaped her - the wail of a terrified animal whose life is in danger. She clawed at her chest as though there was something under her skin she couldn't stand, something she needed to rip out. Beads of perspiration covered her taught face. Her hair mangled where it met her sweat. In her writhing, her head smacked the concrete. It was loud enough for the sound to rip through the gathering crowd and silence everyone. Professor Hall appeared from nowhere, and showing no signs of distress, he twisted Jo into positions which couldn't have been comfortable. He screamed at Luke—the first person he saw—to call an ambulance. My vision blurred as my eyes filled with tears. Luke whipped his phone out, called for help then shoved it away. Alex leaned into him for security. I couldn't stand it. Couldn't take the leering eyes on me. Couldn't handle the pressure to do something, *anything*. I needed the world to stop, to shut up and let me think. Caitlyn appeared beside me. She put her hand in mine, as a friend might have. I'm here for you, she was saying, and it meant everything to me. It was all I'd wanted. But not like that.

Sirens wailed in the distance as the ambulance raced towards us. The louder they grew, the more Jo inched towards death. With every heartbeat she faded away. *It was too late.* I dropped Caitlyn's hand and crouched beside my gran, begging her to stay alive. Her skin had turned an awful shade of blue, the colour of squished blueberries, the kind that stains and can never be washed out. I didn't know much about the human body, but I knew there was no coming back from that.

4

Absence

Over and over again the paramedic hit Jo's chest. Each time her body jolted in rejection. He strapped a small yellow device to her and repeatedly put his ear from her chest to her mouth. I assumed he was checking if she was breathing but I grew more and more impatient, wishing they'd just take her to hospital.

The paramedic kneeling over Jo called over to the one who had driven. The world fell silent as she darted around the ambulance to grab a stretcher from the back. The medics danced around each other in perfect choreography as they strapped Jo onto the board. They lifted her inside with ease, as though she were a doll and I couldn't help but wonder when she had gotten so light, so frail. Before I jumped in, I looked out to the crowd of students and lecturers and parents and grandparents watching my every move. Each of their faces filled with fear. I wished they hadn't seen the pain spill from my body, but I couldn't have stopped it even if I tried.

I'd never been inside an ambulance before. I expected a cold, metallic, transportation box - not dissimilar to a coffin. If Jo opened her eyes, she'd have gathered she was in a mobile hospital from the built-in medical equipment, defibrillator pack and spine board. Oddly, a comforting place to be. Jo, reduced to cargo on its way to its destination, rattled and jittered as we darted through traffic. Swaying involuntarily as we changed lanes, I fixated on the oxygen mask covering her mouth and nose. *Was she clinging onto life, fighting for another day, or had she already given up?*

'I'm not ready to lose you,' I said. My words came out as a choke. How was I supposed to do anything on my own when she had always been there, looking after and taking care of me? I gave her hand a small squeeze to let her know I was still there. I should have understood wanting to give up the fight more than anyone, but I decided in my own selfishness that if she left me like that, I wouldn't be able to forgive her.

The ambulance pulled to a halt at the hospital and when the paramedics opened the doors light flooded the small, rectangular space. I jumped out, catching my feet on my robes but managed to balance myself before I fell.

Wasting no time, Jo was carried inside. I stood in agony as triage nurses pricked and prodded her under luminescent lights. She was wheeled away from me without so much as a warning. My heart cracked, and even though it was buried in my chest, that didn't stop it from displaying on my face. A nurse, a mountain of a man, made his way to me and rested his hand on my upper back.

'She is in very good hands,' he said in a thick Nigerian accent. 'We will update you when we know what is going on.' He looked at me with the compassion only a nurse could possess before walking away without another word. The waiting room was desolate. I took a seat on an uncomfortable faux leather chair, but I wasn't alone for very long.

Alex—always one to make an entrance—burst into the waiting room with Caitlyn and Luke in his trail. They took it in turns to hug me. Caitlyn's idyllic touch gave me the warmth I'd learned comes with friendship.

'I'll take your robes back,' Luke said, motioning at them. Caitlyn and Alex had already disrobed. I took my own garments off and passed them to Luke with a muttered thanks. He gave Alex a small kiss on his forehead then left.

'You guys shouldn't be here,' I started, but Alex held his hand in the air to cut me off.

'She's your gran, of course we're here,' he said. I didn't argue. Said nothing. Jo would hate that he'd used the word gran. But I suspected he hadn't come for her. I think he came for me.

And I needed my friend.

Caitlyn said she would buy us coffee then wandered off, leaving Alex and me alone together.

'I'm really sorry,' I said, and folded myself so that I sat cross-legged on the chair. I fidgeted with the hem of my jeans, unable to bring myself to look at him. I couldn't help but notice the sharp way he shot his head to look at me.

'What for?'

'We got low grades in Professor Hall's presentation,' I said, wondering why he was making me explain myself. 'I know you wanted at least a seventy-five.'

'Oh, that's not important,' he replied. 'Professor Hall never gives excellent grades. He's been criticised about it for years. There's been enquiries and everything.' His nonchalance killed me. If he hadn't expected a top grade, then why had he pushed me so hard?

'I thought you were mad at me,' I said.

'Mad at you?' he asked with a coat of genuine confusion. 'We probably got the highest scores in the class.' He dismissed my concern, told me he'd lost track of time between work and Luke then apologised for not texting me. When he said he'd make more of an effort to keep in touch, I remembered he'd called me his friend once before. I thought it had been in jest, but friendships grow from acquaintanceships, and by showing up to the hospital, I knew he saw me as a true friend.

Caitlyn returned with our coffees. She dished them out, and as we waited, she nervously tore at the bumpy cardboard sleeve around her cup.

'I wonder how Luke's getting on,' she said. I suspected she only wanted to break the silence between us, rather than air her concern for her cousin, but then she added, 'he hates being in hospitals when he doesn't need to be.'

I opened my mouth to ask her what she meant, but the nurse came back into the waiting room carrying a clipboard, drowning it in his massive hands. How much time had passed? It didn't seem like any, but it also felt like years.

'William Walters?' he called.

Caitlyn and I stood. Alex, who had been pacing around the room, joined us. We made our way towards the nurse, both hope and dread pulsing with each step.

'Your grandmother is awake,' the nurse told me. His words hung in the air for a second. 'She has a severe case of pneumonia, but she is stable. Her left lung has collapsed so we have given her steroids.'

Alex and Caitlyn shared my relief. I hadn't realised how terrified I'd been; I'd expected the worst. My hands shook at the news. 'We will keep her overnight for observation,' the nurse said.

I looked to Alex for answers. The blank expression on his face told me he knew as little as I did.

'Then what?' Caitlyn asked.

'I am hopeful we will be able to release her in the morning,' the nurse said. I had an overwhelming urge to hug him. He focused on me. '—We can not get ahead of ourselves. She has a long, uncomfortable journey ahead. Tell me, are you living at home?'

I hesitated. A million thoughts passed through my head in the shortest space of time and I came to a crashing conclusion. *Truman's offer would have to wait.*

'I will be.'

'Good,' he said. 'She needs rest.' He winked at me as if we were a part of a secret club and told me I would have to meet with advisors the next day to discuss preparation for home caring and weekly visits. I swallowed a small lump in my throat and nodded, feeling somewhat relaxed for the first time that day.

'I'm sorry I spoiled your graduation,' Jo said as we walked into the ward. Only one other bed in the room was occupied; another older lady slept soundly by the window.

Jo winced as she pulled herself into a seating position for us. It looked impossible, but she managed it. I'd have given anything to trade places with her. Seeing her so weak and feeble was torture. She didn't deserve to feel pain, to be so close to death. And though she didn't show it, there was no doubt in my mind she'd be furious and mortified that Alex and Caitlyn were beside me - nobody had seen her so vulnerable, so undone. I perched on the end of her bed, clasped her hand in my own. She was nothing but bones under a thin veil of flesh. Why hadn't I noticed before?

'You should be out celebrating,' she said.

I protested, said I'd rather be with her, but it was futile. I would have told her I didn't feel much like celebrating, but she'd blame herself. With waving hands, she shooed us away, apologising again to Alex and Caitlyn for having ruined their day.

'You didn't ruin anything,' Alex said kindly, even though I wasn't sure it was the truth. Caitlyn agreed, introducing herself as my friend. The rhythm of my heart danced. Called a friend on a second occasion in such a short space of time and by Caitlyn, no less. I knew it wasn't wholly accurate, I knew we weren't friends. But it was something. *It was a start.*

'Visiting hours must nearly be over,' Jo said, begging me with the most subtle look in her eyes to leave. I gave her hand a tiny squeeze to show I got her message loud and clear.

'You're right,' I said definitively, and then turned to my *friends*. 'Let's go.'

I gave Jo a kiss on the forehead and told her I'd be back in the morning. Alex, Caitlyn and I meandered back to the waiting room where Luke sat patiently in an armchair, scrolling through his phone. Alex asked if I wanted to join them for a late lunch, but I said no. A small part of me wanted to, but I'd only dampen their spirits more than I already had. I only convinced them to take off without me when I told them I'd rather be alone. That was a lie. There was nothing more I wanted than their company. I appreciated having them around, enjoyed their sympathy, their hugs, and their warmth. But I couldn't take up any more of their time. I hadn't earned such a level of friendship – not yet, but I promised myself I would.

There was a chill in the air the next morning. I walked to the hospital regrettably not wearing a hoody. My t-shirt flapped gently with the cool breeze of the early summer wind. The automatic doors opened for me and I walked into the tenderness of the building, welcomed with a blast of warm air from the overhead heater. I retraced my steps along the labyrinth of corridors to Jo's ward, remembering it being on the second floor, past the reception desk and the third door along but I'd made a mistake. The ward was empty. I walked the length of the corridor, popping my head through each open door but Jo wasn't behind any of them. There was another ward at the end of the corridor, but none of the patients were my gran and the room was a different shape. When I walked past the reception desk twice, the woman behind asked if she could help me.

'I'm looking for my gran,' I said.

She looked at me as though I'd spoken a different language.

'Her name is Josephine Walters.'

She typed Jo's name into the system one finger at a time, but paused to throw me a sympathetic smile with a small sigh.

'The computer's just frozen,' she said, clicking the mouse button an unnecessary amount of times. I spun around, questioning whether Jo was on the second floor after all, and thinking I'd check the floors above, and below, when I bumped into the nurse from the day before. I grabbed his trunk of an arm, only then realising how worried I'd become.

'Where's my gran?' I asked, my voice filled with the panic of a lost boy.

The nurse studied me for a second. I read his name on his ID badge dangling around his neck. Tunde. The woman behind the desk, a mouse in comparison to him, remained silent, watching us both with terror in her eyes.

'Josephine Walters?' He spoke entirely on an exhale. I nodded sharp enough to burst any balloon of hope inside me.

'Come with me,' he said. I found his voice both gentle and soothing.

He led me into a small pastel blue room decorated with two dirt-brown armchairs. Between them, sat a coffee table with a bouquet of spouting from a cheap-looking vase. The sweet smell from the flowers brought the room to life. He offered me a seat, but I said I'd rather stand. His eyes were those of a manga character - so lively and animated, speaking volumes. When he frowned, they mirrored the sadness floating throughout the hospital.

'I am afraid your grandmother did not make it through the night,' he said. Gentle, but matter of fact. He paused for a moment, either to lessen the blow or let the words sink in. Then as though it would help, he added, 'she went peacefully.'

I shook my head.

'You've clearly made a mistake,' I said bluntly. There was no way she was gone. I was in the wrong ward, and he had informed me of the wrong death. The *other* woman in the ward had died. They had obviously moved or discharged Jo and got confused. I left the box of a room and walked along the corridor. The nurse called after me, but I didn't want to hear him. I quickened my pace until I was almost running. Ahead of me came the metallic clangs of an elevator so I sped up even more. When the doors opened with a ping I jumped inside. Frantically, I pushed the button for the third floor then repeatedly pushed the doors closed button until the elevator obliged. The nurse had made a horrendous mistake. Furiously, I shook my head at the incompetence. How does a hospital lose track of a patient?

I stormed along the third-floor corridors, which were almost a mirror image of the second floor, except busier. Each ward and room were fully occupied, but none of them held my Jo. As I walked, a hollowness grew inside of me like a virus, filling a growing void. I only lapped the floor once before I made my way back to the elevator. This time, I pushed the button for the first floor. The doors slowly closed and I stood lonely in the lift fighting back tears. Letting them fall would be a sign of acceptance. And I didn't believe it. *Couldn't believe it.*

It turned out the first floor was a children's department, so I knew instantly Jo wasn't there. A nurse asked if she could help but I was beyond any help she could have given so I turned away from her and ran down the stairs, taking them two at a time. I didn't stop running until I got outside and even then, I jogged to the bus stop.

As I waited, I willed the next bus to arrive, to take me as far away as possible from the hospital. Jo didn't pick up her mobile or the landline but that wasn't entirely unusual. The bus arrived and carried me across town. I pushed the stop button so hard the tip of my finger bent upwards, sending a shearing pain across my whole hand.

Jo's cottage lulled in the early afternoon glow under the shade of a nearby oak tree. The chimney, normally smoking, sat still and lifeless. As I walked the path, a willow, weeping, bowed down to me in the wind. Jo's absence was terrible and evident: the cottage had never looked so depressed before. I unlocked the door and called out her name to the shadows.

'Jo?' I said again, searching for her in each room. It felt wrong to turn the lights on, as though there could only be darkness without her, but even in the shadows I still knew my way around. When I reached her bedroom door, I froze. The handle was cold, as though untouched for years. The door creaked open with hesitance as I pushed it wide. I couldn't bring myself to go inside. Her yellow bedsheets were untouched. Each pillow plumped and propped. Her hairbrush lay upside down on her vanity unit, long silver hairs poking in all directions. Her book was spread open on the page she'd been reading. The clock on the wall still ticked. Sharp pains burst inside my chest. It felt like pieces of barbed wire had lodged under my skin, tearing me apart. The house was too quiet. I wanted to scream; to fill and break the silence. I pulled my phone from my pocket. The screen was still cracked, and when I pushed my finger down, even gently, I could hear glass crunch underneath, but still it glowed with life. I had three missed calls from an unsaved number. Local. Landline. I didn't need to search online to know it was the hospital. Instead of calling them back, I went to my contacts and tapped on the first person I could think of, even though I had no real reason to call him.

When I heard his voice, the first tear fell. I choked on the words which congealed in my throat. Telling him would mean admitting it had happened. *Impossible*. But my tears fell and my grief poured through the telephone revealing more than words ever could.

'William,' Alex said. He understood.

I stopped crying long enough for him to ask me where I was. I let out a long quavering breath, and a bubble of snot blew from my nose which I wiped away with the back of my hand.

'I'm at home,' I said, 'at Jo's.'

'We're coming over.'

I was grateful he said that, because I needed him more than ever.

Jo was gone, and I had nobody left.

5

Jo's Secret

Growing up, I imagined Jo's death more frequently than my own. I didn't want her to die, it was just a daydream which naturally played in my head from time to time. Often wondering how I would react, if I'd cope, what I'd do. I never thought I'd feel as empty and hollow as I did when it happened, never imagined I'd be so lost.

I don't know if they rang the bell or if they just let themselves straight into the cottage, but Alex, Luke and Caitlyn found me lying on the floor outside of Jo's bedroom.

'How are you holding up?' Luke asked. Alex hit his arm but I suspected Luke already knew it was a stupid and pointless question. If I had words, I would have told him I was dumbfounded. *How could Jo just leave me?* I'd have said I was embarrassed that Caitlyn was seeing me in such a state and maybe I'd even have thanked them for coming. But I didn't have words; I had mumbles and strings of broken sentences.

'I'm sorry,' I said eventually. 'I don't know why I called.'

'You don't need to be sorry,' Alex replied. He dropped to the floor, and crouching beside me, he stroked my arm. Instead of flinching like I normally would have when I was touched without warning, I welcomed the warmth of his skin on my own. Luke said he'd make us tea and left the hallway. Everything broken can be fixed with tea, apparently. *Except for me.* Caitlyn eyed the open bedroom door and pulled it shut so that I couldn't see inside anymore. But all I wanted to do was look, to pretend things weren't real.

'You have a lovely home,' she said. I suspected she just wanted to say something, rather than nothing. I wanted to thank her for trying to be nice, but couldn't find the words, so I met her comment with a lifeless smile. Usually Jo's cottage simmered with life, but that day it was cold as frost. I wished Caitlyn had seen it *before*.

Luke served tea in the living room, having made himself welcome to rummage the kitchen cupboards for everything he needed. Caitlyn picked up the cashmere throw carefully folded on the armchair and wrapped it around my shoulders as I sat, then excused herself to go to the bathroom. Luke took a seat on the armchair and Alex nestled himself on the floor, tucking himself between his boyfriend's feet. The intimacy made blood rush to my head. Alex asked me what happened. I told him everything in painful detail, solidifying the events in my memory. He listened carefully, hanging on my every word.

'Where's Caitlyn?' Luke asked a few moments after I finished talking. We exchanged blank faces, then got up to search for her. She was in the toilet on her hands and knees, scrubbing the floor.

'Were you sick?' she asked me. I blushed, looked for somewhere to put my hands but couldn't find anywhere. I forgot I'd thrown up.

'I'm so sorry, I—'

'It's okay,' she interrupted. 'I've cleaned it up. Most of it was in the toilet, but you missed a little bit.'

I shook my head slightly then shoved the tip of my thumb into my mouth, bit away what was left of my nail. My eyes turned glassy. *Why did Alex have to bring her here?*

Luke clamped his hand on my upper arm, looked me in the eyes.

'C'mon, mate. You need some rest.' He spoke with authority and led me back to the living room where I sat on the couch again. 'Have some more tea.' Obediently, I brought the cup to my lip and took a sip of the lukewarm drink, simultaneously wishing I'd never called Alex in the first place, yet hoping they'd never leave: I yearned for their peaceful company forever.

I lay down, and for some time fought the urge to close my eyelids. Their voices lulled around me. I hadn't slept well the previous night, counting hundreds of imaginary sheep. The harder I tried to stay awake, the more my eyes wanted to shut. So when I ran out of fight, I let myself fall into a dreamless nap.

I didn't wake until it was dark outside. I wiped the sweat from my brow and checked the time on my phone. It was still early evening, but my heart raced at the thought of being alone in the dark. The cottage was no longer sweet or homely, but rather dank and eery. Metal clanged in the kitchen so I crept from the sofa and tip-toed across the floor, stopping just short of the door. I peeked through the crack in the frame. A pan lay on the floor. Luke picked it up, gave it a wipe and found its home in the cupboard then returned to the dishwasher which sat open, almost empty. Another task Jo hadn't gotten around to completing. The cottage was full of them, like it's waiting for her to come home.

Alex stood with his arms folded over his chest. His shoulders jolted as though electricity were passing through him. Tears slid down his cheeks and fell onto his t-shirt, leaving behind small wet stains but he didn't seem to notice or care.

'It's just so sad, Luke. I can't do this,' he sobbed.

'We *can* do this. He's your friend and we'll be here for him as long as he needs us,' Luke said. They shuffled sideways and I could no longer see them, but I imagined Luke wrapped Alex in the safety of a hug.

'It's breaking my heart to see him like that. And I don't know what to do. Or say. We can't be what he needs.'

Alex's tears came pouring out of him and I suddenly felt pangs of guilt shoot through me for being the reason he was so upset. I never wanted to burden anybody with my pain. I hadn't asked for any of it - for friends, for death, for life. It had all just happened.

'How was your nap?' Caitlyn asked, taking me by surprise by coming into the living room from the adjacent door. I quickly turned to face her, hoping it wasn't obvious I'd been eavesdropping.

'Okay,' I said, my voice broken and groggy. 'What've you got there?' I nodded to a diary she clutched in her hand. Before she could answer, Luke came into the room to ask if we wanted tea. I didn't particularly, but everybody else was having one, so I did too. Caitlyn offered to help, following Luke into the kitchen. Alex came into the living room, as though I couldn't function being awake and by myself. Maybe I couldn't.

'She was alone when she died,' I blurted. That was the worst part. The guilt I felt kneaded in my stomach. 'I wasn't there for her.' Unlike me, she'd have hated being alone. It would have killed her. I buried my head into my hands, wondering how things could ever get better.

'It's okay,' Caitlyn said through a comforting hush.

'I know. I know she's in a better place now, but my heart hurts.' Instinctively, my hands came to my chest. 'It hurts so much.'

'There's no pain like being left behind,' Caitlyn whispered, giving me a hug. 'You'll get through this. We're here for you.'

Time passed, but I remained frozen in it. Unable to comprehend or process the depth of loss. Death, along with Alex, Caitlyn and Luke lingered in the days preceding the funeral. Each of us affected in a different way. Luke took charge of the situation, arranging flowers and trailing through Jo's phone book to contact her friends, ultimately organising the whole affair. Caitlyn, who had never even met Jo, shed tears of sorrow, filling her time sifting through Jo's old trinkets, books, and photographs. Alex spent his days making endless cups of tea, some of which, never even got drunk. Without Jo, the cottage remained a shell of itself. Sadness drifted through the vents, blanketing us with the emptiness she left behind. If the cost of losing someone you love was the pain I felt in the weeks following Jo's death, then I never wanted to love anybody or anything again.

On the morning of the funeral, Caitlyn told me I looked handsome. She dusted fluff from my suit jacket and asked how I was feeling. What was I supposed to say? Deeply depressed, because the last branch of my family tree had snapped from the trunk. Embarrassed and shameful, that I'd relied on people I barely knew anything about four months ago to get me through the toughest period of my life? Confused, by the conflicting emotions swirling in my head? In the end, I simply shrugged. My silence forgiven. It saved me from lying, from pretending I was fine.

Jo's friends arrived at the cottage, each of them wearing black dresses, black trousers and black shirts. It was already an exceptionally miserable day; I didn't understand why we had to wear such depressing clothing. When I was a child, those were the sorts of questions I would openly ask Jo, before I'd grown secluded in myself.

I would never ask her another question again.

To nobody's surprise, I broke into a fit of tears when the hearse arrived. Her casket, so small, so delicate, lay on display in the back, decorated with the arrangement of flowers Luke had chosen. There were no words to thank him for taking the load from me, but he was the kind of person who wouldn't look for them anyway. In a mumble, I asked him to ride in the funeral car with me. Alex and Caitlyn joined us, along with one of Jo's older friends who I had met only a handful of times. She sobbed the entire journey, blowing her nose on a teal-coloured handkerchief. Caitlyn sat with the same pink leather-bound diary I'd seen her previously hold.

'What is that?' I asked.

She searched for what I was looking at, as though she'd forgotten it was there. She blushed, stole a glance around the car.

'I'll tell you later,' she said. I nodded solemnly, rested my head against the window, willing the day to be over.

The crematorium sat on the outskirts of the city, surrounded by neat and well-kept gardens. We drove through the jungle of hedges encircling the car park and my heart broke all over again. There were a lot of empty spaces.

If I'd been the one to die, how many people would have shown up to my funeral?

The vehicles in attendance were parked—*abandoned*—in unforgivable angles so the limousine we rode in had to twist and turn to navigate the space. When we saw the building, Jo's friend sobbed harder and louder than she had before. Alex offered her a tissue. Jo had been to a number of funerals across my life. *It was simply her turn.* I sobbed then, too. Because what was the point in it all? We live and we die. What happens in between is just a discombobulated knot of events.

As mourners gathered outside, their sobs became one. A horrendous noise which filled the air. I didn't recognise the names or faces of those who had come to say goodbye, people and memories pulling out of focus. Like a child I stuck by Luke's side, temporarily stealing him from Alex. Neither of them seemed to mind. He had guided me through the planning with enough knowledge, comfort and safety that he had become a security blanket of sorts. Maybe I'd have been embarrassed of that if other emotions hadn't got in the way.

'Are you sure you don't want to do it?' Alex asked. Bearing the weight was unimaginable. Jo had raised me to climb mountains, not carry them. So Alex headed off, disappearing through the crowd. Caitlyn joined my side, still clutching the diary. Again, I asked her what it was, but the funeral director appeared and my question was lost in commotion as Jo's friends shuffled around. People parted ways for Alex, who appeared with five older men I'd never seen before. They carried Jo's coffin on their shoulders, and strode inside the crematorium. I followed with Caitlyn and Luke, and Jo's friends trailed behind. All of us marching to the sound of a tragically dirgeful song. I took my seat in the front row.

'I never asked her what my dad was like,' I said to Caitlyn who sat beside me. She turned her eyebrows upwards as she waited for me to continue.

'I hated bringing up my parents because it always made her so doleful,' I returned my focus to the coffin. 'And now, I'll never know.'

'I think you'll like what's in here.' She patted the diary she'd held onto so dearly. Up close, I could see the leather had been beaten by time. Some of the pages had yellowed and curled at the corners. They were held shut by a broken copper clasp. I wanted to take the diary from her, but it wasn't the time.

'I'm glad you're here,' I confessed. 'I'm so grateful to you and Alex and Luke. I honestly don't know how I would have done it without you.' She squeezed my hand in three quick successions, in time with the beat of my heart.

The wake followed. We reserved the bar at Jo's favourite golf club. One of her preferred past times was to sip coffee on Sunday mornings and watch golfers tee off. Against my expectations, the bar filled with strangers who wished nothing more than to share their sadness and their stories with me. Each of them concluding with a caring or sympathetic touch. I smiled, and nodded politely, hoping nobody would be able to tell that I wanted nothing more than to just go home and curl up in bed.

My feet struck the floor as I crossed the dimly lit room, hoping for a break from playing the role of heartbroken grandson for just a second. No two chairs were the same, so I took a seat on a chipped wooden stool at the end of an unoccupied table by the fireplace. I realised instantly why the table had no takers. The fire crackled and spat, sending bursts of heat towards me. I wouldn't be able to sit for long - I could already feel sweat coming on.

'Bought you a drink,' Caitlyn said. Her and everyone else. I wished she hadn't, but I took the glass and she took a seat. Her eye travelled to the mural of Jo's life above the fireplace. A collection of images compiled to showcase the highlights of Jo's life.

'I didn't even know you were making that,' I said, 'shows how unobservant I am.'

'You've been preoccupied,' she said. 'It didn't take long.'

'Everybody loves it, you know?' I said, which was true, everyone who had spoken to me had told me how wonderful the collection of photographs were. They'd commented on my artistic eye. It didn't seem appropriate to admit that I hadn't been the one to construct the masterpiece.

'I didn't know she did half of this stuff,' I said, then I took a sip of the drink she bought me, even though I'd already had more than enough. Cheap gin and slimline tonic. I despised the dryness which followed.

'She lived quite the life . . . ' Caitlyn trailed off, studied the photos on the wall in silence. *Jo swimming with sharks. Jo proudly boasting a trophy. Jo beaming, ready to jump out of an airplane. Jo holding my father in her arms . . .*

'May I?' I pointed to the diary in Caitlyn's lap and without permission, peeled it from her. It was heavier than I thought it would be, as though carrying the memories of my grandmother had given weight to the pages. I ran my fingertips over the leather cracks, certain I'd never seen it before. I opened the first page and found her immaculate penmanship.

LIFE IS A SERIES OF ADVENTURES AND IF WE CLOSE THE BOOK EARLY, WE MISS THE BEST ONES. DON'T FORGET TO LIVE.

On the next page, she'd written a bulleted list. Many of the items had been scored out by thin, straight red lines.

'It's a bucket list,' Caitlyn said.

'What?' I asked.

'A bucket list,' Caitlyn repeated. 'It's a collection of experiences and accomplishments she wanted to achieve in her lifetime,' Caitlyn explained, confusing my question as a lack of understanding.

I flicked through the pages, each of them filled with an adventure Jo had been on during her time on the planet. Each one adding depth to the woman I never knew.

'I didn't know she could rock climb,' I said. *But what I meant was, I didn't know her at all.* Returning to the first page, I ran my finger down the list, stopping only on the last item: see William graduate. I slammed the book shut and thrust it back across the table. She'd gone from swimming with sharks to wanting to sit in an audience. Centre stage to background. All because of me. She'd changed her dreams. And for what? *To raise ungrateful, unpleasant William who wanted nothing more than to prematurely end himself.* I picked up my drink and downed it in one. Caitlyn stared at me with wide, needy eyes, not understanding the pain in my heart. I gave her a shrug, hoping to let her know it wasn't her fault, then left the table, left the room, and stood outside by myself. Who was the author of that diary? Not the woman who had raised me, that's for sure.

'William, what's wrong?' Caitlyn asked. I liked that she'd come after me. I faced her despite the tears streaming down my face. I wanted to blame the alcohol for me being so upset, but I couldn't hide the fact that the diary was the real trigger. Luke and Alex approached, slowing their pace when they saw my dismay.

'I didn't even know her. This life, this whole life,' I grabbed the diary back from Caitlyn and waved it in the air. 'I didn't know about any of it.' Flipping through the pages, I found a piece where Jo described one of her summers. 'She worked in a zoo. She flew over the North Pole. How do you even do that? There's a whole life in here and it all just came to a halt. She stopped—'

'She did not stop living because of you,' Caitlyn said, like she'd read my mind. I grew embarrassed, aware of my theatricalities. I hadn't been so passionate about anything before and I didn't know what to do next, so I peeled Alex's drink from his hand and took an initial sip. He didn't seem to mind.

'Her priorities changed, that's all,' Luke said. He had a mysterious way of calming a situation down with his rustic voice.

'But why didn't she ever tell me?' I asked, searching their faces for a clue. Alex and Luke exchanged glances. Caitlyn simply shrugged.

'I don't know,' she said. 'I don't know.'

I drank the remains of my drink and turned away from my friends.

A gentle wind came, sweeping the trees and making the grass bow in the distance. How I wanted to be carried away with the gust.

'I'm going to be sick,' I said, and ran off.

And that's the last thing I remember from that day.

6

The Bucket List

'But you promised,' Caitlyn whined.

'A drunken promise doesn't count,' I said.

Two weeks had snailed by since the funeral. We'd gone from speaking every day to infrequent texts which she blamed on her new job behind some bar I'd never heard of before. She went for the interview and got the job on the spot. Since then, she'd worked long, unsociable hours every day.

'Why not?' she asked, stubborn as a child.

I studied her as she unfurled her picnic blanket across the grassy meadow. Her dangling earrings jangled as she moved, brushing against the cotton of her *Louis Theroux* t-shirt. She plonked herself down and plucked pieces of fluff from the blanket, discarded them to the side. Heartbroken that Jo hadn't finished her bucket list, Caitlyn wanted to finish it on Jo's behalf. When Luke pointed out that we'd never finish by the time summer was over, Caitlyn insisted we at least try.

Her hair fell out of place. I battled the urge to brush the strands away from her eyes, and instead unearthed a blade of grass which I snaked between my fingers. She dug into her backpack and pulled out two Tupperware boxes, one held crustless sandwiches and the other an array of summer fruits.

'Money,' I said. Choosing to ignore me, she unclipped the plastic lids and offered me a sandwich. On cue, two pigeons arrived, eyeing up our food. I picked tuna-cucumber with one hand, and shooed the birds away with the other, secretly hoping Caitlyn would keep pushing.

'It's not exactly a trip to the Bahamas,' she said.

'We're too busy. Plus, you have your new job. . .' I trailed off, officially out of excuses. 'Speaking of which, how is that going?'

'Don't change the subject. It's going fine, though. Since you asked. I can tell you all about it on the way to the Isle of Wight. I'm not working this weekend. Are you free?'

I remained quiet; defeated by her ability to combat every flimsy excuse I had given her. In my silence, I studied a small blackbird, darting around on an overhanging branch. The worst had happened, but things weren't awful. The sun was beating down, Caitlyn was fighting to spend time with me, and I had people who I could call friends.

'I'm free,' I said, and against myself I broke into a smile.

With an excited squeal, she threw a grape at me which landed in my lap.

'We'll invite Alex and Luke and make a day of it,' she said.

I plopped the grape into my mouth and asked her if she'd been able to apply for any graduate-level jobs yet.

'Honestly,' she sighed, 'that feels like a loaded question. Everybody's on my case. I haven't,' she said with a dramatic eye roll. She took out her phone and shuffled towards me. Almost in my arms, but not quite, I could smell the sweet perfume she wore. The rosy undertones cloyed my skin.

I let out a small gasp after catching sight of her screen.

'Caitlyn, it's a three-hour train ride.'

'So?' she asked.

The tickets were expensive, and Caitlyn was working twelve hour shifts just to get by. I thought about that for a moment as she navigated through options on the screen. With the money my parents left behind, the security of the cottage and the minor fortune I'd inherited from Jo, finances weren't something I had to worry about. I slid another grape between my lips suddenly feeling guilty for not having paid for the picnic food.

'I'll get the train tickets,' I said.

Naturally, she protested, but I wouldn't let her finish. I made a show of pulling out my own phone and loading the booking app.

She called Luke and from her reaction, I could tell that he and Alex were free to join us. She unfolded a plan to him over the phone, even though we hadn't made one and I wondered how, if it was so easy to make friends, why I hadn't had any until then.

* * *

I arrived forty-five minutes earlier than scheduled on the Saturday morning. Sitting on the uncomfortable platform bench, I watched trains come and go, all the while yearning for the thrill of a deep, powerful horn to blast in passing. Trains fascinated me. I found headlights tantalising and loved the exhilaration as they sped by. But my favourite thing about them was the tracks underneath. I loved the seductive pull of the sleepers. I always found myself drawn towards them. If I just put one foot in front of the other and did it again, and again, then there would be nothing left. No more William. No more problems.

Pulling myself from those self-destructive thoughts, I decided to fill the rest of my time by pacing the slabbed grounds outside, and tried to come up with friendly, entertaining conversations in my head. In her usual carefree fashion, Caitlyn arrived with only eight minutes to spare. She hopped out of a Range Rover and waved goodbye to the driver, a short-haired, stern-looking woman who eyed me suspiciously. I assumed she'd come with Luke and Alex, but she showed up alone. She walked towards me.

'My mum came to visit me last night, and stayed in the Hilton,' she said, even though I didn't ask. She hugged me and continued, 'she's heading home today, so dropped me off on the way.'

'Are you close?' I asked, remembering that she'd cancelled on Luke because of the argument she'd had with her mum.

'Yeah,' she said. 'We're really close. When my dad left, I was all she had really.'

'I'm sorry.'

'You don't know what happened?' She asked. I shook my head and she motioned at me to sit on the bench with her. The train pulled into the platform and a swarm of people clambered out.

'I thought Luke might have told you. My dad ran away with his mum—they're obviously not the related ones—apparently they'd been having an affair for years before it all came out.'

'Oh wow,' I said. I couldn't imagine the pain of watching a family tear apart. In some ways, it seemed great that it was always just Jo and me.

'Have you spoken to your dad since?' I asked, not sure if it was an insensitive question or not. Caitlyn nodded.

'I met with him the first time a few weeks ago, just before exams but it was a mistake. I realise now I can't forgive him for leaving. They were all really close you see, the four of them, and it kind of broke my mum afterwards. She acts like she's made of stone, but actually, she's a big softie inside, especially when it comes to family. That's part of the reason she was visiting, she wanted to see Luke, because of his—'

Her phone rang, cutting her short. She pulled it out of her coat pocket and flashed me the screen.

'Speak of the devil,' she said, and accepting the call, pulled the device to her ear. The train doors shrieked and closed. I grew anxious that the train would leave without us.

'You can't make it,' she said in a rather passive tone. 'You still have time,' she argued. *They didn't.*

Ending the call, Caitlyn grabbed my arm and told me to run. Without having time to question her, I was yanked along. She slammed her fingers against the button on the side of the train and the doors slid open. We hopped onto the carriage and the shrill warning of the doors shrieked again as they slammed shut.

'What just happened?' I wobbled as the train pulled out of the station. Caitlyn grabbed onto both the handrail and me. With a quick head flick, she pointed towards empty seats and as we sat she said, 'Alex and Luke cancelled. Luke's not feeling great and has to go to the doctor.'

'So you thought we'd go without them?'

'We already had our tickets. Plus, why should my day be ruined because Luke has a headache?'

I twisted away from her, afraid my lips would be forming into some sort of revealing smile, and looked out of the window. Wilderness passed in a whimsical blur as the train picked up speed. A cocktail of emotions stirred inside of me – a shot of confidence flavoured with excitement and shaken with nerves. With no idea of how we would fill the journey, I imagined myself being funny, cracking jokes and making her laugh. It would be as though we had been friends for years, but she was the one to fill most of the ride with conversations. She talked about the scenic landscapes we travelled through, other passengers on the train, and exciting events from her week. I wasn't very good at starting conversations - I struggled to grasp which thoughts to put into words and which ones to keep private. In response to the silence I gave, she rested her head against the window and watched the countryside go by. The open fields matched her leaf-green eyes. Some people are empaths, can match the mood of those around them. Caitlyn's eyes were like that: they changed with her surroundings and her feelings. Wispy ideas floated around my head until they created something whole in my mind – a plan, or scheme, that would make her happy. When she caught my eye, she squinted, questioning me without even opening her mouth. I shrugged gently, and a little laugh escaped. We could, it appeared, communicate without speaking.

The train crawled into the platform at Southampton station. We departed and walked through thick, sea-salt air towards the docked Cowes ferry and boarded the massive ship which would carry us to the island county. Caitlyn, ahead of me, climbed to the top deck to watch seagulls follow in the ship's wake. Usually, I despised when people take picture after picture on their phone, watching life through a lens, but I couldn't hold it against her. As she snapped away, I admired how happy she looked, blissfully unaware that I was studying her. The ferry reached the isle, the trip not lasting as long as I'd have liked, and despite the summer sun beating down on us, there was a chill in the ocean breeze. I realised, as I waited for the gate to open, it would be the first time I'd ever set foot outside mainland Britain. I jumped onto the dock with two feet held firmly together to mark the occasion. Caitlyn laughed and humiliation rocked from the balls of my feet all the way to my cheeks where my torture displayed itself for her to see.

We made our way from Ryde to Shanklin Beach by the Island Line, the small, reliable train reminiscent of its much older cousin, the London Underground, only to discover that Shanklin Stables were several miles away from the beach. I learned the hard way that planning and organising were not Caitlyn's forte. So we trekked, following the map on my phone. Sharp smells—a mixture of dry manure, ammonia, and wet fur—told me we were approaching our destination before a row of tattered roofs with missing shingles came into my line of vision. The bricked stable basked amongst meadow flowers and grassy fields. Behind, lay an old Victorian estate. The horses whinnied and nosily watched our movements as we approached. Straw shuffled under our feet as we walked through.

'Reminds me of home,' Caitlyn said. I hadn't pictured her to be a farm girl. *Actually, I'd given little thought about her past.* I didn't get the chance to ask because somebody announced themselves by clearing their throat behind us. It was a middle-aged woman wearing tight equestrian attire.

'Hello,' Caitlyn said. I was grateful for her confidence, her ability to control social situations. She was always happy to take the lead. 'I called earlier in the week. We have a booking under Donoghue.'

'You're late.' The woman spoke with the earnestness of a schoolteacher. The trace of an undistinguishable accent lined her speech.

Caitlyn nodded sullenly.

'Sorry,' she said. 'We got a little lost.'

The woman accepted our excuse with a reciprocal nod. The lopsided chestnut-bun atop her head threatened to fall. Her name, she announced, was Melissa. Caitlyn introduced us. If I didn't speak soon, then I never would, but I couldn't think of anything valuable to add. Melissa enquired about our horse-riding experiences and again Caitlyn answered for us. That may annoy most people, but I liked the way she was our combined voice. Melissa talked us through the horses and the route, said she'd lead the way and told us there were no other bookings for the day. That meant we had free rein, as it were. We moved to a part of the stables filled with riding gear. Her eyes scanned our bodies as she silently sized us up.

'Is there an occasion?' she asked.

Caitlyn explained the events which led us there in painful precision. I grew hollow hearing them. I missed Jo so much. Fragile, like I could break at any moment, I blinked away tears. Melissa nodded, paying no attention to me. She didn't ask any questions afterwards, just poised her hands on her hips impatiently as we changed into our riding gear.

Regardless, I dressed slowly, thinking I'd made a mistake, tried to move on too fast. Life never stopped. Not for one second. *How could it be so unforgiving?*

Previously, I had suspected Caitlyn would look amazing no matter what she wore. Seeing her in riding gear confirmed my theory. I was grateful there were no mirrors in the barn, certain I'd look nothing short of ridiculous. Melissa treated the horses with a warmth she could not give humans – though I couldn't fault her for trying. She told me I would ride Pepper, a timid old beast, great for beginners, but inaptly named since his bristly hair was the colour of tree bark. Caitlyn would ride Snowflake – a magnificent white horse with a thick mane trickling down her long neck and woodland eyes which sparkled in the same way as Caitlyn's.

'And I'll be riding Gypsy-Heart,' Melissa declared. When the horse in question neighed, it made me wonder how much of our interactions the creatures understood.

I was told to greet the horse with confidence. At first, I thought that was a joke, but Melissa's sombre face told me it was not. I had a better chance of conjuring the Devil himself than feigning confidence. I weighed a mere nine stone and Pepper bore impressive and intimidating muscles under his skin, so I was in no position to mock him. With utmost respect, I offered him the length of my arm and the back of my hand and waited in anticipation. And hope. The horse sniffed. Ever so slowly, he took one careful step forward, fixated on me with a hypnotic stare. I couldn't help but wonder if that was what Jo had envisioned when she added it to her bucket list.

Mounting Pepper was easier than I'd first anticipated. He stood patient without making a fuss. I couldn't say I'd be so understanding if another species threw a saddle over me and climbed onto my back.

Horse riding, I found, was an extremely pleasant experience. Admittedly, when Pepper transitioned from a walk to a trot, I worried I was not in control, but I adapted quickly, bounding through the thicket of trees. The air was light, breezy. It seeped into my pores. I was at one with nature. Being at least a head higher than Melissa and Caitlyn, I had to bow frequently to avoid stray branches and sand-coloured leaves from hitting me in the face. Beneath Pepper's hooves the ground was compact with crushed foliage and solid muck. We trotted into a clearing where the sea lay ahead of us. A crystal promise of infinite freedom. Screams escaped me as Pepper excitedly increased his speed, effected by the salt air in the same way a child would be by sugar. We passed Snowflake and Caitlyn, then Gypsy-Heart and Melissa, who was shouting at me; uselessly telling me to grip the reins and take control of the situation.

I imagined Pepper halting abruptly and myself flying over his head, snapping a rib or breaking a leg with a bad landing. Or worse, me lying on the ground and Pepper stomping all over me. To stop myself from falling, I pulled hard on the rein and bowed my head towards Pepper so that I was closer to him.

In the tall grass, the other horses tried to overtake, but Pepper galloped too fast for them to keep up. There was an unfamiliar warmth inside me, one I don't think I'd ever experienced before. I suspected it was the feeling of a thrill. *I was enjoying myself.* The rush was exhilarating. Laughter bellowed from me as Pepper bound into the water, splashing around like a child.

Melissa approached sombrely with a face of stone. Pepper made into a trot along the water, but Melissa's rigid voice cut through the air, killing fun on the spot. I almost apologised, but Pepper hung his head in shame, and I realised it was him she was telling off, not me.

'I am so sorry, William. I don't know what's gotten into him,' she said. In the no-blame-no-claim age we lived in, I understood her concern not to be for my welfare, but for her business. 'Are you okay?'

'I'm . . . *great.*'

Though she was disapproving, her lips formed a smile. She understood the rush.

'Are you all right?' Caitlyn asked when she caught up with the less mischievous Snowflake.

'Never better,' I said.

Pepper was sheepish the whole way back to the stables. Like a dog, he held his tail between his legs. Melissa wouldn't hear of my refusal to come in for tea, since getting soaked from Pepper's splashing, and brought us to the drawing-room of her estate. The floors were rough wood, probably original, I thought, as one board creaked under my weight. Caitlyn studied the walls, lined with rows and rows of books. By the window, there was a small coffee table and a plump purple sofa. Melissa brought me a heater to sit in front of so I could dry off, then disappeared from the room.

'I'd love to have a library in my house someday,' Caitlyn said, spinning around.

I collapsed onto the sofa and watched her. My body was unprepared for the physicality of horse riding. Then a thought came to me. I burst out laughing, and my sides ached. I buckled over and laughed even harder.

'What's so funny?' Caitlyn asked.

'Jo would have hated horse riding,' I said, and Caitlyn joined in my burst of hysterics.

We calmed and Caitlyn rested her head on my shoulder. 'Who knew it would be so exhausting?'

Caitlyn sat upright, pulling away from me when Melissa came back into the room carrying a tray of tea and biscuits. She told us to stay as long as we liked but the offer seemed forced; her smile told me we should leave as soon as I was dry.

I nodded, reminded myself to enjoy the moment, the company and the view. The garden on the other side of the window sat in tranquil serenity. In the distance, the sun sank slowly into the sea. A picture; perfect enough for a postcard.

'Beautiful, isn't it?' Caitlyn said.

'Yeah,' I agreed, but I wasn't talking about the view outside.

Darkness had fallen when we left Melissa's estate. The sea air was noticeably colder, and an unwelcome breeze nipped at our exposed skin. Stars glittered in the sky above and around us, and in that moment it felt like we were the only people in the whole world. Using the torch function on her phone, Caitlyn led us along the rocky, uneven paths. We were starving, having skipped lunch and decided we would eat in the first place we came across on the way to the port.

The Island Bay was a distance away, standing small and rickety on the edge of the pier. Nothing short of quintessential, the place was perfect. A small bed and breakfast with a tiny restaurant attached.

We were the only diners which gave the owner unspoken permission to spill the history of the Isle. Earlier that morning, Caitlyn had warned me not to pester locals about island ghosts, but she couldn't help herself and asked the owner about the folklore. He served facts with our dinner as though he'd swallowed a history book. The whole affair would have been romantic, if it weren't for the candle between us being a diminished tea-light and the single rose being made of plastic. At least, we agreed, the fish was fresh and delicious.

Afterwards, as we meandered to the port, I debated whether to reach out and grab her hand but ultimately decided against it. A rejection would set our fragile friendship backwards and I was pleased with where we were. All in good time, I told myself.

We walked down cobbled sidesteps, carefully footing loose pebbles and broken stones. Clouds had rolled over the moon and stars, making light sparse by the water. On the road to the dock, there was a sign. My stomach sank before we reached our destination. I did a double take, trying to convince my beating heart that I was mistaken in what I'd just read.

'Caitlyn,' I said, failing to hide the distress in my voice.

'What?' she asked, no hint of alarm in her tone.

I pointed to the sign she wasn't seeing, waited anxiously for her to catch up.

'Oh,' was all she said when she read that the last ferry had already departed. Panic coursed through my body like a virus. Caitlyn approached a greasy-haired teenager standing on the docks. He wore a fleece with the ferry's insignia embroidered on his chest and was closing the dock gates. I followed her, wishing the kneading in my stomach would stop.

'Isn't it too early to have missed the last boat back?' she asked. Her casual nature was painful.

'We had to cancel the service for the night because of the storm. First one back is in the morning.'

'What storm?' she asked. Answering her query, the sky crackled above us.

'That one,' he shrugged.

'Is there any other way to get to London tonight?' Caitlyn asked.

My breaths came short, rapid and wheezy because I already knew the answer. My body refused to intake any air as my nostrils threatened to close.

'No,' he said and padlocked the gates shut. He looked at us expectantly, as though we would have more questions to ask him. Then he studied Caitlyn, like it was the first time he'd really seen her. His eyes trailed down her body. Inwardly, I cursed at him. More so, I cursed myself for letting us risk the last ferry home. My body betrayed the part of my brain which told me to play the situation cool. *As if I'd know how.*

'What are we going to do?' I asked, my fingers involuntarily grab the zipper on jacket. 'We're stranded.'

'You need to calm down,' Caitlyn said as she walked away from me. 'We're not *stranded*. For a start, we've literally just left a bed and breakfast.'

The situation didn't sound so dire when she highlighted that. I nodded, still jittery, and mentally saw the healthy figure of my bank balance, certain I had enough to pay for us for the night. But it was still money I hadn't planned on spending, and that made me all the more annoyed with myself.

'Come on,' she said, unable to mask her frustration, retreating back the way we came. We were welcomed back graciously and when Caitlyn explained our misfortune to the owner, he took pity on us and offered us a complimentary bottle of wine. There were only three rooms in The Island Bay. One contained two single beds, which I volunteered to take, thinking I could push them together. The other homed a double bed, which Caitlyn gratefully accepted the keys for, and the owner was the permanent occupier of the third room.

'That was nice of him to give us a bottle,' I whispered as Caitlyn unlocked her bedroom door. She made a noise of acknowledgment, clearly hating that I'd panicked in the first place, then walked straight into her room. She gasped, threw her hands up and ran to the bed. I followed inside, having to bend my head to enter. A small part of the roof gave way. Rain and plaster poured from the ceiling, landing in a heap on the bed. The sheets were drenched and stained. Caitlyn looked at me, peeled the key from my hand with a grunt, then made her way to my room. It was compact, with the two single beds separated by a rustic table between them. The floor was uneven with a dip by the door and rancid floral wallpaper peeled in places where it met the ceiling. It was also uncomfortably warm; but it was dry, and it would do.

'It's cosy,' she said. Her sarcasm thicker than the woollen blankets resting on the beds. With a smirk, she said, 'at least this one doesn't have a water feature. And you better not snore.'

Any tension that had risen between us had dissipated and we both laughed at the ridiculousness of the situation. I imagined, in weeks and months, or maybe even years to come, we'd still be laughing - our intimate inside joke.

'Wine?' she held the bottle of Sauvignon Blanc into the air. I wrinkled my nose as if the only answer wasn't yes and nodded.

'Come on then,' she said, leading the way back to the restaurant. She told the owner about the ceiling and asked for the glasses we'd forgotten to retrieve earlier. Instead of heading to the room, she wandered outside while the owner rushed to assess the damage.

The storm was in full blow, but the rain pelted downwards instead of sideward, so we sheltered on the porch. We sat in the vacant rocking chairs, looking out at the sea. The owner popped out with blankets, apologised for the misfortune, then disappeared back inside, keeping himself scarce. It disappointed me when Caitlyn pulled her phone out of her pocket, as though my company wouldn't be enough to satisfy her. Catching wind of my emotion, she tucked the wine glasses between her legs, flashed me the screen and told me she would text her mum to update her on our escapades. I thought of the stern woman I'd seen that morning, and tried to picture what kind of person she must be, to have gone through everything she'd gone through and still be a rock for Caitlyn. It gave me a new appreciation for Jo, and I tried to imagine her there with us, but couldn't. Caitlyn pocketed her phone and poured the wine freely. We toasted to Jo, and to our precious and meaningful day.

As I stared at the sea, I remembered I'd promised myself to live only until after graduation. That had come and gone and I hadn't even noticed, or thought about suicide at all. *I'd been so busy living I forgot I wanted to die.* Everything had changed. I watched the waves fold into themselves. There was an entire world out there and a whole life ahead of us.

'Caitlyn,' I said slowly, 'would you change anything if you could?'

'I'd be prettier, more confident,' she said. That wasn't what I'd meant and her answer took me by surprise.

'Really?' I said, 'but you're beautiful.' I spoke without thinking and instantly regretted it. I hoped the rain would hide my reddening cheeks.

'Thank you,' she said. *No fighting. No arguing. No telling me I was wrong.*

'What about you?' she asked.

Everything.

'I'd be more confident,' I said truthfully. No need to think it over. The rain eased and as though the silence between us calmed the storm, the clouds overhead turned lighter, like the dirty water they held had been wrung out.

'Promise me something, William?' she said, meeting my eye. I clenched my fists, the suspense killing me. I made a noise, encouraging her to continue.

'You're so sweet,' she said. 'Promise me you'll never change.'

She took me by surprise, hitting me with a force I hadn't expected, and the world spun. To steady my head, I focused on the moon which began to reveal itself in the black clouds and let it anchor me. So much for the storm, I thought, and then realised I hadn't spoken yet.

'I promise,' I said, sounding so confident I almost believed myself.

'Do you think Jo would have enjoyed today?' Caitlyn asked, her voice as distant as the stars. I nodded, but she didn't see.

'She'd have loved it,' I said. 'Especially the part where we got stranded.'

I wished my first reaction had been to love it too, to see the adventure in the day, instead of worrying. There was a parallel between Jo and Caitlyn; they both had an ability to have fun in most dire of situations.

7

In The Air

August arrived with a slight chill in the air. I sat patiently in the Audi A3 I'd rented, the heating blasting at my face. Long after dusk, but not quite dawn, the streetlights glowed in the dark, illuminating the road ahead. Caitlyn came timidly out of the modest house she rented and locked the door behind her. Despite the morning chill, she only wore a shell-pink dress with a cardigan draped over her shoulders. The image of a 50s housewife born in the wrong decade.

'Good morning, William,' she said, getting into the car.

Over the past few weeks, our greetings had become warm and friendly - no longer a questioning glance or a hollowed silence, but a warm exchange between friends. We'd moved beyond needing a reason to talk or hang out, which meant the whimsiness of completing Jo's bucket list had gently fallen down our list of priorities. She'd call me when she felt like it, and we didn't need Alex or Luke to be present. For me, it was unknown territory. Everything was all so new, and I was feeling brave.

'Morning,' I returned.

'Are you going to tell me where we're going yet?' she asked, a sideways glance thrown my way. I pursed my lips and shook my head playfully. She should have known I wouldn't give in so easily. I stuck the car in gear and pulled away and she turned the radio up. As we drove, she occasionally sang off-key and a little out of tune, but the smile on her face told me she had fun regardless. For the most part though, we drove in a comfortable silence which neither of us seemed to mind. Along the way, the sky transitioned from an inky black spill to a lilac pool which stretched across the expanse of the world.

'We're almost there,' I said when I caught her eyeing road signs.

'Almost where?' she asked.

'If I told you, then it wouldn't be a surprise anymore.'

I nodded at the window on her side of the car. 'Look.'

She followed my line of vision. The entrance sign was on my side and in her desperation to know what I was telling her to see, she missed it.

'What?' she asked.

'I thought I saw a bird,' I lied.

'I think I know . . . but surely not?' she said, more to herself than to me.

I didn't reply for fear of giving anything away. I turned the steering wheel and drove onto a dirt road. Ahead of us lay nothing but open fields. The sun had risen, casting golden rays across the sky for miles. For a moment, we appreciated the serene beauty. Then I told her we had arrived. She made a noise to display her dissatisfaction. A dirt road and an empty field weren't her idea of a fun morning out. Everything was going as planned. I parked the car by a lone sycamore tree and when I took the keys out of the ignition she grabbed my arm.

'This isn't where you kill me, is it?' she said.

'Nah, I do that later,' I joked. 'After.'

'After what?'

'You'll see.'

She projected a laugh which filled me with confidence. I grabbed my bag from the back seat and climbed out of the car. I expected her to complain but she didn't. Instead, she walked around to me, throwing glances across the vast empty field.

'What's in the bag?' she asked.

'It won't make sense until you see it. . . it's rather unusual,' I said.

She pulled a puzzled face but didn't question me further and followed me across the field. My ankles got wet as the morning dew transferred from blades of grass to my skin. Accidentally, our strides fell into synchronisation. In the rhythm, our hands brushed occasionally. I wondered if she noticed too. She pointed to something in the distance; our destination: A small brown blur. I smiled and nodded, still giving nothing away. In hindsight, I could have parked closer without revealing the mystery. Eventually, the blur grew definitive, turning into a rectangular shack. Behind it, hidden by deceptive angles and rows of trees and hedgerow, stood a domed building made almost entirely of glass. As we neared, signs, posters and the multiple sheets of material strewn across the field like carcasses revealed the surprise.

'Shut-up!' she said. 'We really are going for a ride in a hot-air balloon?' Excitement littered her expressions. I nodded, proud of myself.

'Another one from the list,' she smiled as realisation dawned on her. We hadn't really discussed the list since we returned from the Isle of Wight, having made the adventure our own as opposed to living out my grandmother's fantasy. Regardless, the sentiment seemed to mean as much to her as it did to me.

'Another one from the list,' I repeated, so quiet it was almost to myself.

A squat of a man came out of the shack, closing the wooden door firmly behind him. His yellow high-visibility jacket glinted as he moved.

'A'ight?' he called to us with a wave. When we got nearer, he added, 'You took a long way for a shortcut.'

He motioned towards the domed building with his hand. From this vantage point we saw a small car park beside it. The adjoining road was the intended way to enter the site.

'Hello,' Caitlyn said with fresh enthusiasm she reserved for strangers.

'Flyin' today?' he asked, and without waiting for an answer cupped his hands over his eyes and looked into the sky. 'Beautiful day for it.'

'Yes,' Caitlyn said. 'It is a beautiful morning.' She was chirpier than I was feeling. Seeing the balloons strewn across the field made my stomach churn. So much could go wrong . . . I imagined the canvass getting bigger and bigger until it popped like a . . . well . . . *a balloon*.

'I'm just about to blow 'em up. You're a tad early. Go inside an' get a coffee an' a bacon butty.' He nodded towards the domed building. 'Tell 'em Tom sent you.'

Caitlyn thanked him and turned to walk away.

'Give me half an hour,' he said as he checked his watch.

'I had a bit of an odd request . . .' I said slowly. Looking from Caitlyn to Tom, hoping he wouldn't spill my secret. 'I emailed about it.'

'Oh, you're the one who—'

'That's me,' I said.

'Well, I really should say no, but so long as you don' tell anyone then I don' see why not.'

'Thank you,' I smiled. Not as zealous as Caitlyn.

The coffee shop was on the second floor and as we climbed the stairs, Caitlyn pestered me about my request, inquisitive as ever. *All in good time.*

Against Tom's recommendation, we didn't have bacon butties. In place, we enjoyed coffee and a croissant each. From our seats, we spied him working hard below. The balloons rose like lungs as they filled with air, coming to life.

When he finished, he took us to an empty room where we sat through a tedious introduction video and a safety presentation before we were taken back to the field. We stopped sharp at the first of the balloons.

'She's a beauty,' he said, looking to us for agreement. The material was oyster-blue with gold spirals strewn across. He opened the wicker basket, and motioned us in after him, elevated, it seemed, by our company. It was as though he hadn't done this a million times before. A dangerous thought snuck into my head. *What if he had never done this before?*

He fiddled with mechanics in a trinket of a box and a blast of flame erupted into a device which looked like a funnel. The thoughts which crept into my head refused to leave. They burrowed into the folds of my brain and convinced me I would fall from the sky. Caitlyn grasped my hand, grounding me, then shook with fright from the roar of flames, but converted her energy into a small excitable dance. I wanted Tom to see that Caitlyn had chosen to entangle her fingers around my own, to know I could be with someone as beautiful as her, but he was too busy fumbling with the intricate parts of the machinery to notice us. It didn't matter, though, because it was enough just to have her need me.

He asked if we were ready but didn't wait for an answer before he tugged a thick rope and knotted it into place. With a mighty breath, the balloon rose from the ground.

We joined the clouds and looked down onto the world. I left my body, turned into a falcon and soared across the sky. Up there, things were so simple, so clear. It was as though worries couldn't exist so high up. Around us, the sun beamed on hilltops leaving behind glossy rays which streaked the valleys beneath. The heat from the burner was so intense that sweat dripped from my brow. I wiped it away, hoping Caitlyn didn't see. Her stare was fixated on the view, her mind preoccupied with the beauty of the world. I wanted that moment to last forever.

'Whenever you're ready, Tom called to me, 'now's a good a time as any.'

I nodded to show I'd heard, then dug inside my backpack and took out a ceramic pot.

'Is *that* . . .?' Caitlyn asked.

I nodded again and twisted the lid off, let it drop it to the floor. I stuck my arm out of the wicker basket, as far as I could reach and craned my wrist so the pot leaned at an angle. My grandmother's ashes shifted in the urn and poured freely into the sky. Jo took flight, catching the wind. Instead of rolling down my cheek, my tears streaked across my face. I hoped it was everything she wanted it to be.

The sun and the wind dried my tears as I whispered my final goodbyes. At long last, Jo was at peace, and even though her body had been reduced to ash, the balloon felt lighter somehow, like she was moving on. I learned that day that happiness is measured not by the things we have, but the things we leave behind.

'That was really sweet,' Caitlyn said as we descended. Her snowy skin glowed under the dwindling flame. She leaned into me with a hug and I was certain she would feel my heart pound inside my chest. In the intimacy, I had an intense desire to plant a peck of a kiss on the crown of her head. I suspected she would have liked that, but something inside me told me not to, told me it wasn't a good idea. So, I did nothing instead. But that didn't matter, because I finally knew what it felt like to be alive . . . *and I enjoyed the feeling.*

Summer baked on. Week after week, I met with Caitlyn, Alex and Luke, usually doing things I'd never done before - like taking road trips out of Oxford, practising chipping shots at the putting green and spending lazy days in the park. Enjoying every moment, I longed for the stretch of days to last forever, but the season was ultimately finite, and I knew it was coming to an end. On an especially hot morning in the last week of August, I dressed in my suit and caught the train from Oxford to London. It seemed like a lifetime ago I'd called Truman's receptionist to schedule the barbecue with him and the other graduates he'd selected for the year's intake, but the day had finally arrived.

The event was at his house, nestled on the outskirts of London, surrounded by quintessential woodland, and fences that stretched on forever. Unable to drive closer, the taxi I'd gotten from the station dropped me off half a mile away from his home. I buzzed the gate and when it swung open, I walked through. Like something from a fairytale, I followed the path until I reached a glamorous building tucked behind the edge of a forest.

An excitable middle-aged woman with bouncing red hair came at me in long strides and shook my hand. I recognised her indistinguishable voice from the phone call I'd made months before. Her name, she told me, was Grace. Truman's receptionist. Standing tall and slim, she looked more like a model than a law secretary, nothing like I'd pictured at all, but still it was nice to put a face to the name. I hid my preconception and my nerves under a smile and introduced myself.

'He lives here?' I asked.

'Just in the summer, or on bank holidays,' she said, as she led me around the side of the house, 'usually he stays in his Pimlico flat for an easier commute.'

Truman's holiday home was constructed entirely of glass panels. Inside I could see a marble kitchen, hanging chandeliers and wide-open spaces, indisputable signs of money.

'Walters,' Truman called as we turned into his back garden. There were a handful of other younger people, all dressed slick, and a few older people who wore the casual outfits of the upper-middle class. Truman already had a beer in his hand and as he approached me, grabbed another in a single sweeping motion. He passed it to me and I took it with caution. Alex had pre-warned me not to drink too much, but it didn't seem to be as formal an occasion as I had previously feared it would be. I'd suspected at least another round of interviews or some form of impossible test, but the day really was just a summer barbecue. Truman placed his free hand on my shoulder and led me around the garden introducing me to the team as he went.

'And this,' he announced as we approached a blonde woman in a sharp red and black pencil dress, 'is my wife, Kimberly.' She shook my hand limply, smiling all the while. There was boredom beneath her eyes.

'I bought this house for her as a wedding present. Got an impressive deal from my own mentor, Antony Clarke,' he said, for what I imagined was the umpteenth time that day. She smiled sweetly and he leaned in for, what looked like, an unwelcome kiss on the cheek.

I weaselled away from them, finding a spot with other graduates Truman had picked for his collection. Against my expectations, none of them were first class students, but averaged Bs across their modules. I eyed Truman suspiciously, wondering why he wasn't bagging the best of the best for his firm, why he'd settle for a loser like me.

I ate with the group, engaging in small talk without revealing too much about myself, listening to their achievements with a smile and a nod. When I needed the toilet I made my way inside for the first time. The kitchen was stamped with architectural design, decorated and pristine as a show home. Grace stood at the counter, dressing a salad.

'Impressive, isn't it?' she asked, catching my wandering eye. I nodded, asked if she needed any help, but she didn't, she was almost done. Skimming polite conversation, I excused myself. Assuming my need, she pointed down the hall and I quickly shuffled away. Out of politeness, I kicked off my shoes and tucked them to the side. The hall was long and carpeted silver, the fibres plush under my feet as I darted towards the toilet, which happened to be engaged. My bladder pulsed impatiently.

A house so big would have a second bathroom. I didn't think it would be rude to have a look, so I ran up the spiral staircase taking them two at a time. When I reached the top step, I found a bathroom ahead of me. Suddenly, I felt I was breaking some unspoken boundary by being up there, so I rushed along, almost bursting when I closed the door behind me. I ran to the toilet and felt the sweet relief as the intensity of my needs washed away. Finished, I flushed then washed and dried my hands. Almost reaching the door handle, curiosity got the better of me. Beyond the free-standing bathtub, there was another door. It could have been a cupboard, but something told me to look. Slowly, I crept over and stole a glance inside. It was no cupboard. I stepped into an elegant but simple bedroom. A four-poster bed lay in the centre of the room and a mahogany vanity unit sat by the window. I picked up a plastic hairbrush and dropped it to the floor when I heard a sound. I rushed back to the bathroom as the other entrance to the room opened. My heart hammered in my chest. I was sure Truman would understand that I'd needed the toilet badly enough to explore his house, but it was a conversation I'd rather have avoided in the first place. I peeked through the door lock and saw the hairbrush I'd dropped sitting at an angle on the floor. Truman's wife, Kimberly, walked into the room, shuffling almost impossibly in her too-tight dress. If she noticed the brush, then she'd have known I was there. I closed my eyes and held my breath. Waited to be exposed.

'God. My husband certainly knows how to pick them,' I heard her say. I opened my eyes, ready to apologise, but she wasn't talking to me. Matthew, another graduate, stood in the room across from her, his shirt untucked and his feet spread apart. I continued to stare, unsure why they'd be together, wondering if the day was an additional test after all. I had to suppress a gasp when Kimberly lay her hands on Matthew's chest. She leaned into him and smacked her lips against his. When she pulled away, he smiled devilishly. Her fingers rummaged at the buttons of his shirt. She laughed meticulously as they came undone.

Certain he was unaware of Kimberly's antics; my heart broke for Truman. I couldn't stand to watch anymore, so I darted out of the bathroom. They didn't even have the decency to fully close the bedroom door, so out in the hallway I had to scurry past the open space and tip-toe all the way down the stairs.

I sat on a kitchen stool to put my shoes back on. Despite Grace preparing food, the counters were immaculate and clear of any clutter. Her presence in the kitchen undetectable.

Truman walked into the kitchen from outside, said my name with candour.

'Are you having a good time?' he asked.

I nodded, afraid to look him in the eye. Did he know? He couldn't possibly.

'What do you think?' he asked, pointing at where I thought at first, was upstairs, but realised quickly that he was gesturing towards the house in general.

'It's lovely,' I said. Certain it would destroy him if the news came from me, I bit my tongue. He told me again how he'd acquired it.

'It'd be nice to do the same someday,' he said. 'Would you like to see upstairs?'

'I'd rather see the garden again,' I replied, thinking on my feet. 'Tell me about the land.' I made my way outside. Always eager to tell a story, Truman followed.

After twenty painstaking minutes, Kimberly graciously walked from the side of the house looking a lot less bored than she had in the morning. Grace eyed her suspiciously. When Matthew stumbled out of the house, I excused myself from Truman, and made my way across the grassy expanse. I was mid-stride when Kimberly grabbed my arm with a vice like grip. Her hair was no longer in a tight bun and her skin glowed with the radiance of a pleased woman, but her eyes were what I focused on. Diminutive and beady, they dared me not to challenge her.

'I know that was you up there. I saw your shoes,' she said. Her mouth barely moved, but her eyes shot to my feet. The purple rim around the sole of my shoes were unique. I couldn't deny they were mine. 'If you value your future,' she continued, 'I suggest you keep your mouth shut.'

I was so shocked I couldn't respond. Her lips contorted into a sweet smile and she walked away. I watched as she wriggled her arm around Truman's. She gave him a peck on his cheek, all the while never tearing her defiant stare from me.

8

Unmasked

Summer ended with an unwelcome storm. Standing in Jo's lounge, I watched rain patter against the window for what would be one of the last times. The cottage would always be Jo's. Without her, it was a lifeless stack of mortar and brick. The memories etched in my heart would go with me wherever I went, so it didn't matter that I was selling up and moving on.

Headlights cut the barrier of night the weather had created. I held my glass in the air and noticed my suit was taut around the elbows. I would need to buy a new one before starting work. Spinning the contents of my glass around, the lone ice cube clanged against the sides and I downed the trickle of amber liquid. I navigated around the packed boxes spread across the room like a warzone and discarded my glass on the table then left the cottage, locking the door behind me. Without looking back, I ran into the rain and climbed into the taxi.

Alex pulled the door open as I paid and thanked the driver. I stepped out, into the rain, and he sheltered me with his *rainbowed* umbrella. We stood in front of a picturesque townhouse; somewhere I never would have guessed Luke would live.

'You haven't visited yet, have you?' Alex asked as he pushed open the teal front door. He missed the step inside but caught his fall.

We entered a long and narrow hallway, leading to carpeted stairs. A thin table sat against the wall, holding three bowls filled with trinkets and loose change as well as a vase of flowers. Above the table, hanging from the wall, sat an elongated mirror which Alex checked himself in. He moved strands of hair, making minuscule difference if any at all. As we ascended the stairs, Luke pulled open the door at the top, welcoming me inside his home with a smile and a hug. The air smelled of freshly laundered linen, as though he'd been washing clothes all afternoon, though I was certain he was the type to make regular trips to the dry-cleaner. I followed as they led the way to the lounge, an open-spaced room with large arching windows. From the abstract table to the curved lamps, each piece of décor looked like it had been carefully selected from an art gallery. I studied the glorious paintings hanging over the exposed brickwork walls.

'It's a Celle Don Ray,' Alex said, admiring one in particular. 'Do you know her?'

'No,' I admitted ruefully.

'She's one of Luke's friends. He's actually the inspiration for that piece,' Alex said. Between the parallel lines and blocks of colour, I couldn't see the resemblance, which I thought would be a compliment to Luke, but an offence to the artist, so I didn't say anything.

'Champagne, wine or gin?' Luke offered, and motioned for us to follow as he moved through the flat.

'Champagne,' Alex answered, as we entered the kitchen, his tone suggesting there was really no question about it.

We drank in the lounge. I sank into the couch when they invited me to take a seat and listened tentatively as they told inside jokes and anecdotes. When prompted, I told them about the barbecue and of Kimberly's threat.

'So you're going to keep your mouth shut?' Alex asked.

'Doesn't sound like he's got a choice,' Luke said to my relief. I worried they'd tell me I had a duty to tell Truman. 'If you tell him,' Luke continued, after taking a drink, 'and he believes her, then you're gone.' He threw a glance around the room. 'But if you don't tell him, then nothing happens. Seems like a no-brainer to me.'

Alex threw him a disgruntled glance. Luke shrugged back and took a sip of his champagne.

'You must tell him,' Alex said to nobody's surprise. 'Wouldn't you want to know?'

'On the contrary, I'd rather not.' I took a sip of my drink, finishing the glass, quite satisfied that I had done the right thing. After all, the affair really was none of my business.

'We're out of champagne,' Luke intervened. 'But there's gin if you want some.'

I nodded, grateful for a change in conversation. Luke finished his drink then made his way to the kitchen. Meanwhile, Alex rose and bounded across the room and opened a box neatly tucked in the corner. He pulled out the masks he'd insisted on buying for the party, even though I was certain nobody else would show up wearing any. In rhythmic steps, he skipped back to me, his arms flailing with exaggerated and dynamic swings. For a second, he studied the masks, deliberating over them, then tossed me a walnut-brown eye-mask with slick feathers like whiskers poking from the sides. Luke returned with our fresh drinks, then took his own mask from Alex. A full-faced oceanic piece with darkened eyes and a jewelled mouth, easily wearable to a *Día de los Meurtos* party instead of the end of summer masquerade-ball in Oxford. I made no comment. In contrast, Alex's mask was simple. It was violet and wispy and covered only a fraction of his face. He asked if I needed any help tying my own on.

'I need the toilet,' I said. 'So I'll fix it in the bathroom mirror, but thanks.' Then as casually as I could, asked when Caitlyn would join us.

'She's meeting us there with Nick,' Luke replied.

When Alex pointed out that the bathroom was the third door on the left, he robbed the opportunity to ask who Nick was.

Standing at the sink, I splashed cold water over my face. Caitlyn had been the one to find the ball and arrange the tickets, so it disgruntled me she wouldn't be joining us for pre-drinks. I hadn't asked her what her plans were because I'd just assumed she'd be coming with us since we'd done everything else on Jo's bucket list together. Still, I couldn't let it ruin my night, so I dabbed my face dry with the cotton towel hanging on the door and let out a deep breath. Already the effects of the booze were kicking in. Wishing I didn't need to drink to be fun, I tied my mask around my head tightly, disguising any fears I'd been clinging onto. With the fake exterior, I could be somebody different, somebody else. At the ball, I would ask Caitlyn to be my girlfriend. It would be romantic, if not a little tacky. There would be flowers there, hopefully peonies, her favourite. I'd pluck one and offer it to her as I asked. She would swoon into my arms. Yes, I could see it all, standing in Luke's dimly lit bathroom. Everything was going to be perfect, and I was finally going to be happy.

As I turned to leave, I noticed a white paper packet scrunched into a ball on the floor by the bin. Intrigued, I picked it up and unravelled it, folded out the creases. The recipient's name had been ripped off, but the universal green cross revealed I was holding a prescription package. I binned it as a memory surfaced, trickling through the alcohol-infused blur in my mind. *Luke and Alex walking out of the doctor's practice the day I'd gone for help.* Hastily, I opened the medicine cabinet and saw maybe a hundred prescription packages lining the shelves. Outside, I heard footsteps coming down the hall but I couldn't not know. In haste, and trying not to rustle the packaging too much, I stole a glance at the prescriptions. Drugs with long, complex names I'd never heard of before. All addressed to Luke.

I came out of the bathroom and in the hallway, bumped into Luke, who was leaving a room I assumed would be the master bedroom. He had a phone charger in his hand, and held it up to show he'd been retrieving it.

'Are you all right?' he asked.

'Yeah . . . are *you?*'

He nodded, and we walked to the lounge together. In the middle of the room, Alex was dancing with no inhibition. He'd switched Luke's background jazz music for his preferred chart pop. The speakers pulsed louder than they had before. Drink flew from the glass in Alex's hand, but he didn't notice or care. Luke joined him, and as I watched them from the door frame, my heart sunk. There had to be something seriously wrong with him that he'd need so much medication. Evidently, it wasn't only me who was good at pretending he was fine when he wasn't, because there they were, a perfect blend of merriment and frivolity when I knew one of them was very, very sick inside.

The ball was being held in the banqueting room in the Bluebird hotel. A small, independent, mansion of a place, hidden away from the life of the city. To get there, we ordered a taxi. On the way, we not-so-subtly swigged from a hip-flask which Luke hid in his jacket pocket. Alex had his hand nestled in Luke's. I wondered what that would feel like, to have someone else's sweaty palm nestling in my own for an entire car ride and not to be bothered by it. *Enjoy it, even.*

The car scrunched on gravel as we took the last stretch of the journey, through a narrow tunnel of bowing trees, and as the hotel came into view my stomach cartwheeled as I imagined Caitlyn waiting for us. I needed to stop letting my brain get to me and ask her out. I could feel in my bones that the time was right.

I stumbled out of the taxi, more drunk than I cared to admit, followed by Alex and then Luke, who paid the driver with an apology for someone's drunken behaviour. I must have misheard though, I thought, because we were all very civilised and fairly quiet during the ride. I told Luke I'd buy him a drink then sauntered away to find Caitlyn. Against my expectation, she wasn't waiting for us at the front door.

An illusion of confidence, I strode into the hotel lobby and scanned for her trademark blonde hair but it wasn't present in the blend of reds, brunettes and peroxides strewn across the room.

'There you are,' Luke said. He clamped a hand on my shoulder, as though to keep me at bay.

'Where's Caitlyn?' I asked, hiding no pretence. He shrugged, checked his phone and frowned then tucked it back inside his pocket. His nonchalance irritated me, but if I showed my impatience, then I'd reveal how I felt about her, so I buried it deep.

Luke showed our tickets to the hotel receptionist who eyed me suspiciously, though I didn't know why. A waiter approached, presented us with a tray lined with champagne flutes. We took one each and gave cheers. I took a sip and was repulsed. The drink was a nasty, cheaper version of what we'd enjoyed earlier. I stole a glance at Luke, but he didn't seem to mind the difference – he even looked like he'd expected it.

With growing angst, I guided Alex and Luke into one another, and when each was distracted with the other, I slid away unnoticed. I passed by masqueraders, wondering who they were with their hidden faces, and entered the ball room. Grander than I had imagined the event would be, I stood rooted to the spot. I'd envisioned a questionably organised party attended primarily by students letting off steam at the end of the school year. Instead, I found myself surrounded by an older generation of working-class types who were enjoying the escapism of their busy lives for a night. I tried to imagine my grandmother dancing under the candelabras, but even in her youth I couldn't conjure the image. Yet another activity I failed to see her enjoying. *Did I know her at all?*

To stop any alcohol-infused tears from trickling through I left the grandiose room and stumbled into a side bar, adjacent to the lobby. I stepped inside just as a furious woman launched a drink across the room. Missing me by mere inches, the half-full pint glass shot past and smashed against the wall beside me. Splinters of glass fell to the floor. The Guiness spattered the white paint, leaving murky trails of roasted-brown streaks behind.

'You're a psycho, Martha,' a burly man screamed at the perpetrator, and in his brisk attempt to flee the scene knocked into me.

'I'm sorry about that,' the glass thrower rushed to me. She slung a lanky arm around my shoulder. Her breath smelled of a toxic combination of coffee, cigarettes and cheap alcohol. 'That was my boyfriend, Marcus. He's been cheating on me with Kerry, hasn't he?'

Before I could respond to her rhetorical question, the barman told her she'd have to leave.

'Let me buy this chap a drink first. I did nearly take his head off there,' she slurred. The barman nodded and pulled out two shot glasses. He brought a bottle of tequila over as the woman, Martha, dragged me to the bar. With each step, the sequins on the arm of her dress scratched my neck.

'Chin up, Martha. He's scum anyway,' the barman said. He winked at me, as though we were part of a secret club. If we were, I didn't understand the rules.

'Aye, but he was *my* scum,' she said. Without warning, she knocked back one of the tequila shots and made a rasping noise, then stuck her tongue out in display, as though we wouldn't believe she had successfully swallowed the drink. She thrust the other into my hand, so I shotted it, but unlike her, I struggled to keep the rancid drink down.

'Martha, I'm going to have to ask you to leave. If Mario catches wind of the—' he pointed a thumb towards the stained wall, 'well, you know he'll be on one.'

Martha shrugged. Something told me her behaviour that night wasn't an isolated incident. Wondering how I'd gotten wrapped up in someone else's drunken drama, I wrestled free from her tentacle of an arm and made my way through crowds of people, continuing my search for Caitlyn.

There were no missed calls or messages on my phone, but that wasn't surprising - if she was going to call anyone, it would have been Luke. An irrational annoyance flared in me. We were supposed to complete Jo's bucket list together, and she was missing it.

My drunken legs carried me outside, away from the clamminess of bodies. The rain had dwindled into a refreshing hazy mist. I watched a taxi snake along the road, headlights carrying more people to the event. I squinted to make out the passengers, but it was too dark, and they were too far away.

Someone asked me for a light. I made a show of checking my

pockets as I spun around, even though I knew I didn't. With a vigorous head shake, I gave an overly sincere apology then slid into the shadows until the taxi pulled up. The doors opened and in brooding slow motion a long leg poked out. First, a scarlet heel hit the ground, followed by the body of an older woman wearing a ball gown. Flooded with disappointment, I took a final glimpse of the car park and made my way back inside.

I spotted her in the dark, from across the room, with Alex and Luke. For a moment, I stood idle, hidden in the drapes, drinking in the scene. Her arm slinked around the shoulder of a stranger, the same way the woman at the bar had leaned on me. A human claw. A mating ritual. I marched towards them in jealous and angry strides. They were laughing and swayed in time to the music, not caring that I was dancing on their fingertips.

'Caitlyn,' I said on my approach. 'Can I have a word?'

Unable to read my anger, she threw herself into me with a full-bodied hug. My irritation dissipated immediately. Only then, I remembered I hadn't plucked her a flower to present her with, but it didn't matter, I decided.

'You need water,' she said, and pulled me away.

She didn't stop until we were in a quiet space by the main doors.

'I want to ask you something,' I said, peeling my off my mask. The world swayed and to keep myself upright, I leaned against what I somehow thought was a pillar, but was actually a potted yucca tree. The plant crashed to the floor, sending soil and greenery everywhere. Caitlyn watched in horror as I scrambled to pick everything back up with jaded inhibition. Others stopped to watch the spectacle.

'William,' she intoned as I brushed my hands free of dirt. 'Are you okay?'

A gaunt figure emerged from the gathering crowd. There was no mask covering his sallow cheeks, no decoration over his down-turned eyebrows. He stood as tall as I did and seemed to look me up and down with a swift glance, mocking me with a twisting lip. Caitlyn pulled into him, as he wrapped his arm around her and kissed her forehead.

'This is Nick, my boyfriend,' she said to me, then turned. 'Nick, this is my friend, William, the one I was telling you about.'

Her words were a thousand needles pricking my skin all at once. *Her boyfriend. She had a boyfriend.*

'William, what did you want to ask?'

'It's not important. I was just wondering what type of tree this is?' I gestured to the plant I'd knocked over, and then picked up.

'It's a yucca,' she said.

I gave a nod and left the room, the lobby, the hotel. Outside, fresh air hit me like a brick in the face. The alcohol in my system threatened to erupt but I swallowed it down and leaned against the wall to steady myself. I watched Martha stampede across the car park, screaming and shouting, her long arms flailing above her head in bursts of fury. By the side of the road, the man I recognised as Marcus and a woman who I assumed was Kerry, were frantically ushering a taxi, glancing back at the rampant Martha.

'Don't you think you can run away from me,' Martha yelled. She peeled off her shoes and ran with them in her hands. Puddles splashed under her bare feet, sending thick sprays of water in all directions. Like a bowling ball, she ploughed towards them. The event was a show I couldn't stop watching. Marcus and Kerry managed to clamber inside the taxi. Martha was an unstoppable force, full of rage. From her cleavage, she pulled out a set of car keys, which she then dangled in the air.

Suddenly feeling a lot more sober than I had all night, I chased after Martha, calling her name. She climbed into a nearby Polo, started the engine and threw the car into reverse. I dived out of the way as the speeding car swerved in my direction.

With a bang and a crash, she drove full force into the taxi, causing it to veer into a tree. The bonnet of the Polo crunched like a packet of crisps under the impact.

I hadn't noticed the gathering crowd outside the hotel doors until Alex ripped himself from it. He pulled me off the ground, unable to tear his eyes away from the drama. The taxi driver got out of the car and hurled abuse into the air. Ignoring him, Martha lobbed curses at Marcus and called Kerry grotesque, obscene names. Punches, insults and high-heels thrown.

'Just be glad we're not as dramatic as that,' Alex joked. I nodded, but felt the sharp twist of acid shoot up my throat, so I turned around and let the tequila shot erupt from my stomach, along with the pretend champagne, the real champagne and the remnants of my undigested lunch.

The next morning—my last in Oxford—I lay in bed, procrastinated getting ready to meet my friends, instead fruitlessly searching online for the reasons Luke may need such an array of medication. It didn't help that I couldn't remember the names of the long, complicated names of the drugs I'd seen.

Afterwards, I sat in the Grove with Alex, Luke and Caitlyn. The dust had already settled, and my own drunken antics of the night quickly forgotten, overshadowed by the mess that was Martha; her actions made the front page of the *Oxford Mail*.

My friends wanted to commemorate the occasion with a celebratory and final picnic. Short puffs of wind ruffled my hair but brought a refreshing air that I gladly inhaled. The park was busy, but not as much as it had been over the last few weeks. Caitlyn rolled over, rested her head on my thigh, and I saw it instantly. The signs of friendship she had displayed the entire summer were just that: Friendship. I'd mistaken her kindness for flirtation, a titanic error on my part. But aside from that, she had failed to mention Nick, and I couldn't help but wonder why. Especially when she had told him about me.

'I don't think last night was quite what Jo would have wanted,' I said.

'No,' Caitlyn agreed. 'But it gave us a story to tell, and at least we went out with a bang.'

'How do you feel about moving tomorrow?' Luke asked.

'I'm fine,' I said. And I was. Indifferent, actually. 'We ruled this summer like it was our kingdom.' I only realised how lame I sounded when the words were out, but it was already too late to take them back. Caitlyn furrowed her brow, leaned her head further into me to look up.

'Does that make me the princess?' she asked, with a laugh.

'I thought that would have been Alex,' Luke jabbed before I could reply.

Alex hit him playfully and said, 'I'm nothing if not the queen.'

Caitlyn fashioned each of us a small crown from the leftover tinfoil she'd used to wrap her homemade sandwiches. The sun slowly sank, taking my heart with it. I'd had the greatest summer of my life, and I was the best version of myself when I was with her. But all things end. Smiling to myself, I deflated onto the blanket quite reserved. We hadn't finished the bucket list, but we had run out of time. There was nothing else to tie me to Caitlyn. It was time to move on.

9

Trifles

The following day I grabbed my suitcase full of clothes and my backpack filled with knickknacks and took the mid-morning train to the capital. I arrived at Paddington station at midday and at once blended into the whizz of the city.

By the early afternoon, I'd already met with an estate agent in Finsbury Park—the closest area to the city I could afford on my graduate salary—exchanged my deposit, signed my tenancy agreement, and settled into my one-bedroom flat, which, though small, seemed full of empty space. I stared out of the window, an imperfectly skewed view of the city ahead of me, ready for a fresh start.

Under gun metal skies, I made my way to work on the morning of my very first day. I shared the commute with weary-eyed teachers, groggy builders and slick businesspeople looking sharper than I ever could. My journey was filled with twiddling fingers and avoided eye-contact. When I arrived at London Bridge station, I conjured a hypothesis that there are so many exits that nobody knows just how many there actually are. Inevitably that day, I chose the wrong one. I rode the escalator, arrived at street level and willed my phone to find at least one bar of signal as I refreshed again. When the screen finally loaded a map of the surrounding area, I briskly followed the line of blue dots, narrowly dodging city-dwellers and fellow commuters as I darted between them.

Arriving outside the building, I checked the time and caught my breath. Nine minutes late. Not the end of the world. I opened the glass doors and walked inside. Blasted with the air-conditioning, my brow broke into a fresh sweat. I had nothing to wipe the perspiration away except for the sleeve of my suit jacket. In the lobby, my ID was checked by security before I made my way up the spiralling staircase at the end of the room, which led me to the firm's reception.

'William,' Grace said. Her eyes widened with fear, her lips folded into a forced smile. 'You're late.'

I fixed myself and smiled apologetically. I took in the features of the room as I strode across it. Plants, benches, and artwork lined the dove white-silver walls. Grace's desk was the dominating feature though, circular like a donut with her sat in the centre. There was no obvious way inside and I briefly imagined she was forever trapped answering phone calls and taking messages.

'I am, yes,' I confessed.

'Truman hates tardiness.' She eyed me up and down, then passed me a paper tissue. 'They're in the boardroom. The elevator is over there.' She pointed and I thanked her, told her I got lost but as I turned away, she called me back.

'He also hates excuses.'

The elevator doors opened straight into the boardroom. Twelve pairs of eyes stared as I stepped inside.

'Sorry,' I muttered to Truman as I tried to find an empty space around the table. He watched as I searched in vain.

'Pull up a seat,' he said, flicking his wrist to a stack of chairs piled against the wall. The metal legs clanged against each other as I peeled the top chair. Aware of the nuisance, I tried to shuffle quickly and subtly between two of the other graduates I'd met at the barbecue. I couldn't remember their names, and I was glad for that because they made feeble attempts to shuffle over and give me room.

'As I was saying,' Truman continued, 'you lot are no better than janitors. Just because you have a degree, doesn't mean you can strut around here like you own the place. Refuse a task by your mentors, no matter how mundane, and you're out. Late three times, and you're out.'

I nodded, hearing the message loud and clear. Day one and I was already walking on eggshells. Never again, I vowed, would I be late.

As if the humiliation wasn't enough, he set out to punish me further by setting me an impossible task; to review a twenty thousand-word contract for mistakes by the end of the week. I nodded, taking in my penance with a bitten tongue. Sourly, I thought it was no wonder his wife had cheated on him; she probably loved defying him in secret.

When I handed him the proof-read contract on the Friday morning, he read less than a page before he let out a long sigh. He looked at me over the rim of his glasses. His unforgiving features stained with disappointment.

'What exactly is *purisdiction*?'

'A typo,' I suggested slowly.

'You've changed the formatting to single-line spacing,' he said. His eyes trailed back to the sloppy piece of work.

'And there's another mistake.' He pointed to an apostrophe. 'Did you even make any changes?'

It was written by someone on the graduate class from last year yet he was treating the mistakes as though they were my own. I'd spent three years at university learning to argue, defend and justify my decisions but I knew I had to choose my battles carefully to win the war. I bit my tongue.

'Not vigorously enough.'

He picked up the draft and tossed the piece back to me, though there was a hint of surprise on his face. 'I want this to be perfect by Monday.'

'Yes, Sir.'

My peers had been photocopying and researching all week, their laughter reverberating the office walls. While they got to do real work, I spent my time editing a contract nobody would ever read. They wanted to celebrate the weekend by going to the pub and invited me to go with them. I turned them down, opting to tell them I had plans instead of revealing that Truman wanted a tighter version of the work I'd already submitted.

I called Caitlyn that night, but her phone rang straight to voicemail. I hung up, wondering if she was working or spending time with Nick. I couldn't help but question if I hadn't left, would we be doing something together? I rang Alex next, but he didn't pick up either. He texted me immediately, saying he was at the cinema with Luke, and that he'd call me later. Neither of them got back to me.

I carried myself to the off-license and bought a pack of beer, then took the long way home. In the short time I'd been in London, I'd learned how to blend into crowds. I found I could disappear in ways other cities would never allow.

Back in my flat, I drank my bottled beer as I re-read and edited my work. Trying to spot the mistakes which had annoyed Truman, all the while growing irritated at how stupid I'd been. By the time I finished, it was late, and I'd swigged my way through the entire pack. I was drunk.

The weekend continued to trudge along, bringing fresh bouts of rain and a sharp decline in temperature. Regularly, I'd look out of my window wondering if that was as good as life was ever going to be. Already, Alex and Caitlyn were ghosts, remnants of a past and fleeting existence. I was worse off for knowing them. They had come into my life and showed me what it meant to have friends, companions, but then disappeared as quickly as they came, and left me with nothing. I was alone again.

My loneliness didn't consume me, but became a part of me. It manifested itself into a shadow who would follow me around, hold my hand, haunt me. A constant reminder that nobody cared. In the past, I'd been grateful I didn't have a group of friends because I hated small talk and arranging meetings, but I grew to look at crowds of people as something I longed to be a part of.

On the Monday morning, I fastened my freshly edited work together with treasury tags and slid it into my satchel, then made my way to work. Arriving before everyone else—a habit I'd fallen into after my disastrous first day—I slid the contract into Truman's pigeonhole then made my way to my desk where I reread information on the cases I'd already been working on.

In the early afternoon, the hum of the office chatter died. Truman had made an appearance. I caught sight of him, walking towards me, my work by his side. He dropped it with a thud onto my desk.

'That's better,' he said. I met his intense stare waiting for something more than never came. He turned on his heel and marched away.

At the end of the second week, when I stood in the canteen and the coffee machine reluctantly spat a cappuccino into my mug from the overused nozzle, Matthew approached. He flashed me a charming smile, reminding me of his Cheshire-grin when Truman's wife sunk into him. He really was a peacock of a man, I decided, as he picked an apple from the fruit bowl and bit into it. I watched his spittle fly across the counter.

'I reckon he tortures people on purpose, you know.' He leaned against the wall with the confidence of a manager, not a freshly plucked graduate. 'The way he embarrassed you last week and made you edit that contract. He made Sasha cry yesterday. He'll get what's coming to him.'

I didn't particularly want to talk to Matthew, so I made a noise to show I'd heard him and sipped my coffee. It was so hot I scolded the roof of my mouth and could feel a blister bubble instantly. Unwilling to show pain or discomfort, I smiled and made to leave the room.

'A few of us are going for a drink tonight. You should come.'

I could think of several things I'd rather have done, but the real alternative was sitting at home alone on a Friday night with no one else to talk to, and I wanted to do that even less.

At the end of the long day, I met with Matthew and the other graduates and we made our way to the pub around the corner from the office. We crammed around a small table and as we drank discussed the progress of our first two weeks. With my tongue, I poked the fresh blister on the roof of my mouth. The discomfort an addictive form of torture.

'I still can't believe he made you cry,' one of the girls said to another, who I assumed was Sasha. I made a mental note to make more effort to learn their names.

'I think he does it on purpose, you know, treats us horrible to keep us in place,' chimed Sasha. They met her belief with agreeable murmurs.

'You know why he hired us, don't you?' Matthew asked the group boldly. 'We're all second-class graduates, yet he supposedly wants nothing but the best for his firm. He chose us because we'll always be good, but we'll never be better than him.'

The way he said it sounded like it was a bad thing, but I was one of the few people in my class to have secured a job before I graduated.

'Oh, I hope nobody minds,' Matthew said, after forcefully swallowing beer. 'My fiancé, Jane, is meeting me here.' He gestured to a woman approaching the table.

'Fiancé?' I spat as I turned around. 'I didn't know you had a fiancé.' I tried and failed to make my shock more subtle. Truman's spouse, Kimberly, was a bored housewife; her cheating seemed natural to me, but Matthew's infidelity on his doting wife-to-be was unjust and unfair.

The woman in question, Jane, burrowed herself into the group around the table, right beside me. She wore flat shoes and an off-white blouse tucked into a long, moss-coloured skirt. There was minimal, if any, make-up on her face. Not the type I'd imagined Matthew to settle down with. Nothing like Kimberly.

'Seven years strong,' Matthew said. He held up his pint glass in a toast to himself.

'Eight,' Jane corrected playfully. He brought himself around the table and kissed her cheek, only to receive a chorus of support from the group.

'Eight years. . . so you were—'

'—Childhood sweethearts.' Jane placed her palm flat over Matthew's chest, showing off the tiny diamond encased in the ring wrapped around her finger, and nodded. 'He proposed after graduation.'

Matthew announced he'd buy her a drink and took off to the bar. My colleagues welcomed Jane into the group. I thought about my graduation, how it should have been so many wonderful things, but was the worst day of my life. I took a swig of my drink, then another and another, hoping to bury the nagging agitation rising from my gut. I wished I'd never seen Matthew and Kimberly together. The knowledge was a burden I hadn't asked for, a heartache Jane certainly hadn't envisioned when she'd said yes. It wasn't my place to tell her. The information would ruin her. Or would it save her from wasting a lifetime with a chauvinistic, arrogant twit of a man?

I took another swig of my drink, draining the glass.

'Slow down there, champ,' Matthew nodded towards my drink with a smile when he returned. He passed Jane a small rock-glass which she examined with irritation.

'A single?' Jane asked with an unimpressed furrow of her brow.

'It's what they served me,' Matthew Shrugged. 'I'll get you another soon.'

When one my colleagues pulled a packet of cigarettes out and announced he was going for a smoke, Matthew asked Jane for permission to go. She rolled her eyes and gave approval.

I debated leaving then, but Jane finished her disappointing drink and said she'd come to the bar with me to get another. A double this time, she added with a wink. She told me about her own work, and how happy she and Matthew were, and I felt my intestines twist and pull. I thought I was going to be sick.

'You don't look so good, are you okay?' Jane asked. I shook my head.

'He's cheating on you,' I said.

Releasing the information was like taking a breath of fresh air after a hefty fumigation process, but still I clasped my hands to my mouth and clenched my teeth in regret. My tongue pressed on the blister on the roof of my mouth, which burst with a small explosion, one which left a rancid, metallic taste behind. Luke had said the affair was none of my business when we discussed Truman and Kimberly. What made it my business with Matthew and Jane? Alex had said it was better to tell them, but I still didn't feel good. Jane dropped the empty glass in her hand. Her shoulders shuddered and her hands shot to her face.

'I'm so sorry,' I said, but she didn't seem to hear.

'I knew it,' she said. She shook as her pain and shock evolved to anger. 'I knew it.'

Matthew caught sight of his upset fiancé, as he returned, and marched towards her.

'You are scum,' she screamed at him, then stormed away.

He looked at me, but I couldn't meet his eyes. He ran after her and I decided all too late that I'd made a mistake which was impossible to rectify. Sasha approached me with intention. I wanted nothing more than to go home, crawl into bed, and never face the world again.

'What did you say?' Sasha demanded.

'I told her he cheated on her.'

Her face dropped and she bit her lip. 'Why would you do that?'

Her reaction gave me answers to questions I'd never asked. 'With you, too?'

Before she could answer, I walked away. Better to have no friends, than bad ones, I thought. A sacrifice I would happily make.

Outside, the night air was cooling. Jane was alone, walking away from Matthew. He stood in the street with his hands held to his head. When he saw me, he swore and hurled abuse at me. He marched over, then swung his fist in the air, which collided with my eye. His flesh sunk into my socket as a sear of pain flashed across my entire face. Dumbfounded, I couldn't move. I'd made a diabolical decision in my tipsy state and that was my punishment. Forgetting about me, Jane marched off and Matthew ran after her.

I walked home wondering why everything kept going wrong. In time, the grotesque yellow and purple bruise around my eye would fade, but the person I had become would always be there, underneath the scarred tissue. I wasn't sure I liked who he was. I'd lost friends before I even made them. I knew in my heart it was time for things to change.

10

The Rusty Fox

The move to London was meant to be a fresh start, but I quickly fell into old habits. Phantoms plagued me daily. I heard my phone ring only to learn it hadn't rung at all. I saw shadows of people in the street that I once knew, only to realise I chased after strangers. Sometimes I felt the ghost of a touch then remembered there was no one around.

I researched the doctors at my local practice and booked an appointment, promising myself I wouldn't shy away from dark truths: I'd explain in brutal honesty just how low I'd felt.

Arriving at the practice early, I signed in and made my way to the waiting room, an open space with only one other patient sitting in the pastel seats. In avoiding her stare, my eyes travelled around the room. Blu-tack stains smeared the walls and a water cooler glugged in the corner. A TV flashed snowy static and the floors were scuffed with abstract patterns.

'You're staring,' she said.

Her voice was deeper than I imagined it would have been, as though she coaxed her words with nicotine. She snapped a bubble. Pink residue stuck to her plush, painted lips. I'd have said she was around my age; except she was far more woman than I was man.

'Sorry,' I said, even though I wasn't sorry at all, because I definitely wasn't staring.

A doctor came into the room and hesitated, acutely aware she'd interrupted something, but unsure what.

'William?' she looked at me.

I nodded and rose, followed her to her office. Over the years, I imagined what my mother would be like, how she would react in certain situations, what she'd wear, how she'd speak. The doctor was exactly like the mother I conjured in my visions. Warm and endearing with a hint of spice. Passionate and caring, if not a little *too* invested. Her kind smile and recognisable manner made me trust her, a stranger with a big heart, with my life.

'What brought you here today, William?' she asked, and leaned forward, as though she were my friend, my equal, wanting me to share my secrets with her.

'I'm depressed,' I revealed. As simple as that. It was out in the open. My wounds on display for her to examine. She made a noise of compassion, like a non-verbal hug.

'Or at least, I think I am. Or *was.*'

'What happened?' she asked, resting her chin in her hand.

'My grandmother died,' I said. As though my depression were situational. 'I met a girl, but it turned out she had a boyfriend. I moved here, but I don't know anybody. My boss is evil.'

The doctor nodded but I wasn't getting my points across. They were coming out muddled and when I tried to correct myself my words jumbled. I took a deep breath.

'I have no friends. I'm terribly lonely. There's a pain in my heart every time it beats. Sometimes, I just wish it would stop.'

'What kind of pain?'

'It feels like it's hollow. Like I'm empty. A meaningless case of a man just coasting along from one thing to the next trying anything just to be . . . happy.'

My quavering breaths weren't enough to fill the void inside me. She sat silent as I collected myself.

'You say you want everything to stop, sometimes. Is that your way of telling me you wish you were dead, sometimes?'

'I planned my death,' I said. I couldn't stand to look into her honied eyes, so I looked down at my hands. My fingers knotted and wouldn't come undone like I had.

Against myself, I spilled like milk, revealing I hadn't moved to London for a fresh start like everyone thought, and like I'd tried to convince myself I had. I'd disguised the move as turning a page, when it was actually me running away from my past because in truth, I'd been alive for twenty-two years and there was nobody in all that time who cared about me.

I expected her to argue, to remind me that Caitlyn cared, that my grandmother loved me unconditionally, that Alex was my friend. Instead she latched onto my hand and said nothing.

'William,' the doctor said after a time. Her voice as delicate as the first snow of winter. 'I think you've felt down for quite some time. Is that fair to say?'

I gave some short, gentle nods, wiped the tears away from my cheeks.

'I could prescribe you with anti-depressants, but I'd rather we didn't go down that road,' she gave my hand another squeeze. 'Honestly, they do more harm than good. They mask problems instead of providing solutions.'

I made a noise, all I was capable of, to show I'd heard and understood what she was telling me.

'I am going to refer you to a psychiatrist, though.'

Concealing my pain sounded more appealing, but I continued nodding, still unable to look her in the eyes. Speaking out wasn't something I was capable of, and I didn't have the strength to lose another battle. I took the tissue she offered and wiped my face, collected myself, even poised a smile, though I knew I'd be blotchy-eyed and puffy-cheeked. She handed me leaflets that I knew would lie unread in my drawer until I eventually threw them away, then talked me through the process in great detail, listing every stage.

'This is a new chapter in your life, William. It's a clean slate. Take it as that.' She gave my hand a final squeeze and smiled to herself, as though I were an accomplishment, and I thought that to her, I probably was. Just another item on her long list of to-dos that she could easily tick off and discard.

When I left the surgery, stray clouds rolled by, bringing a small shower with them. The woman from the waiting room stood by the edge of the kerb. She lifted fake diamond-studded sunglasses away from her face.

'Are you cured?' she asked.

'Excuse me?'

'The doctor. Did she fix you?'

'Turns out I can't be fixed,' I said, then walked away. She followed in my steps, caught up with, then matched my pace. I wondered if she'd been hanging around waiting for me.

'They say that about me too.'

She stopped walking and as if connected, I did too. She introduced herself as Penny, and when I told her my name, she asked if I wanted to grab a drink. While I deliberated, she pulled over her hood, and in a way she resembled *Little Red Riding Hood* and I thought that if I wasn't careful around this precarious girl, then I'd end up in the wolf's belly. But then again, maybe this would turn out to be my next renowned adventure.

'Okay,' I said.

Instead of walking, Penny strutted in strides,

I struggled to keep up. We passed King's Cross station and headed along Pancras Road.

Incapable of silence, she talked rapid-fire, shooting words from her mouth without filtering her thoughts in a mostly one-sided conversation. We turned right from Goods Way and came into Granary Square. Abruptly, Penny stopped in front of a rainbow-panelled, rickety building sitting bravely over the canal. The sign above the door told me it was The Rusty Fox. Very aptly named, I thought.

She pulled the door open. The hinges squealed, like a warning. The dimly lit bar gave the illusion of being busy with most of the seats occupied, though on second glance, there weren't many available in the first place. A whistling coffee machine pierced through the low hum of chatter as we made our way to the counter.

Penny ordered a large red wine and looked at me expectantly, so I asked for a lager. She trotted to a booth by the window, leaving me with the bill and the drinks.

At the table, she thanked me, at least, then took off her raincoat. Bare-armed, I saw that her skin was decorated with hundreds of intricate scars. The pain of her past.

'Did you miss your appointment?' I asked.

'I decided I didn't want to see the doctor, after all,' she said.

'Why not?' I asked.

'Turns out I'm not sick.' She took a large gulp of her wine. 'So what is it you're running from?'

'I'm not running from anything,' I said without conviction.

'We're all running from something.' She leaned into me. Her breath already infused with a sickly wine scent. 'You don't need to disguise yourself for me, William. I can see the ache beneath your eyes.'

With a fixed stare, she pulled away. Her eyes were dark and bottomless, her grin unabated.

'Well . . . what's your story?' I asked.

'It's still being written,' she said.

I couldn't think of a response to that, and she didn't ask me anything in return, so I took a swig of my drink.

She changed the conversation by asking about my family. Instead of telling her about Jo, I did something I'd never done before. I told her the whole truth.

'My parents died when I was a kid,' I said, surprising myself with how casual the words came out. Her eyelids narrowed; her lips drew together. She seemed to drink me in.

'How did it happen?' she asked.

I let out a long sigh and for the first time in my life let someone else hear how their deaths had unfolded.

'My mum was an alcoholic,' I said. My breath caught in my chest. It was true that the walls I'd spent years building had begun to crumble when I was with Caitlyn, but I'd never expected the remains to rain down on a total stranger.

'Everyone thinks the worst of alcoholics.' I spun my drink around in the glass and took a sip, recreating the unyielding crave for a taste that I imagined my mother must have faced. I never learned what her poison was. Whisky or wine? Vodka or Gin? 'She was always lovely. To me.'

'My dad stuck by her through thick and thin. I've been told she would kick him, spit at him, throw things at him and he never hit her, not once. Never so much as raised his voice. One night, he threatened to leave so she told him to go. He threw an empty sports bag in the back of his car to scare her and took off. She'd had more than a few glasses of wine and believed him. Furious, she stole the keys to my gran's car and chased after him. It was a Tuesday evening in September. The sun was setting. I was playing with plastic dinosaurs in Jo's—my gran's—back garden when she took the call. My mum drove into the back of my dad. She wasn't wearing a seat belt. Died instantly. Sometimes, in my worst nightmares, I imagine her sprawled across some farmer's crops. My dad lost control, spun out, hit a wall. He died in hospital that night.'

I finished the drink in my glass and looked at Penny. Her face was unreadable. I wondered what thoughts were running through her head. Why I burdened her with my past, I'd never know. She asked if I wanted another drink and I nodded; she went to the bar. Telling the story of my parent's deaths was like cutting a cancerous mole from my body. A dirty, rotten hitchhiker of a lump attached to me for most of my life suddenly gouged out.

'I'm an orphan too,' she whispered as she placed my fresh drink in front of me. I swore softly to myself, wondering if there was some unseen force that had brought us together.

'My mum died in childbirth,' she said. 'There were serious complications. I'm the reason she didn't make it.'

My face dropped. The guilt she must have carried probably outweighed any hatred I held for myself.

'It wasn't your fault,' I said.

She shook her head.

'No, it was. If she hadn't given birth to me, she'd still be alive. My dad stepped in front of a train not long after. Sometimes I wonder if looking at me was just too much to bear. People say I have her eyes.'

I'd met no-one my own age before who had already lost both parents. I couldn't muster the words to comfort her. Her pain seemed deeper rooted than mine. I'd coped because I had Jo. It seemed like Penny had nobody. As flaky as I'd initially thought she might be, I felt a spark ignite between us. I reached out across the table and lay a hand on top of hers, like how the doctor had comforted me. We sat in silence for a moment, giving thoughts to those who had left us behind. She was right; I realised. I had been running all along, but not in the way she suggested.

'What do you think of the future?' I asked. Suddenly it seemed brighter.

'I try not to,' she shrugged. Her lack of discomfort was inspiring. I got the sense that unlike me—who would burrow and hide and avoid thinking of the future—she was just taking life as it arrived. She would never understand what it was like to be me; to sit on the sidelines and not want to engage with life, and there was something refreshing about that.

'Do you have a lot of friends around you?' I asked. Loneliness is a silent killer.

'I have some close friends,' she said. 'But people tend to let you down or outgrow you. I think we tend to cling to the friends we had when we were young, but that isn't healthy or normal. People are brought into our lives at certain times because that's what you need at that time, but I think it's healthy to let friendships expire.'

'I've never thought of it that way before,' I said. The way Penny's brain worked was a mystery to me.

'Lets go for a walk,' she said, and threw her coat back on. I knew if I went with her, I'd be igniting a spark that could light up my life. Or burn my whole world to the ground. My stomach turned to snakes, writhing and knotting wildly as I took hold of her outstretched hand. I wanted a taste of the freedom she possessed.

11

The Invitation

A golden streak of sunlight shone through the window and landed on Penny. Her skin was almost translucent. Sleeping, she looked like she could bring no harm, cause no pain. A different version of herself. What, I wondered desperately, are you dreaming? What runs through your head?

Nine months of waking up in her bed and she was still a complete mystery to me.

She stirred as though she sensed me watching. The heaviness of a hangover hummed in my head. Empty wine bottles sat on the counter, along with two glasses, one stained with a crimson kiss. Penny's studio flat was small, but cosy. Our clothes were strewn around her already messy room. I spotted her lacy underwear on the lid of her upright piano, mine lay in a heap on the floor. The water in the glass by the bed had been there for days, but my throat burned. I reached over and took a drink.

'Do you have time for breakfast?' she asked, her voice still groggy, yet to adjust to a new day. I checked my phone and cursed loudly, threw the covers to the side and jumped out of bed. Penny shuffled upwards, pulled the covers over her naked body.

'No, I don't have time for breakfast,' I snapped. 'You switched off my alarm.'

I darted around the room, picking up the clothes she'd peeled from me the night before.

'I thought it'd be cute if we spend the morning together.' She whimpered and pulled her legs to her chest. 'And now you hate me.'

I froze mid-action, my trousers halfway up my legs. I jumped smoothly, pulling them all the way, and fastened the button at my waist.

'I could never hate you,' I said and sat beside her. 'I'm sorry I snapped. Things are a bit stressful at work and you know I can't afford to be late.'

'I accept your apology,' she said smoothly. I rose, then finished dressing myself, burying the rest of my frustration. Only Penny could turn off someone else's alarm and still end up the victim.

In my race to get to work, I dashed through the busy streets of London to the Underground. Like a salmon, I leaped from the platform as the tube's doors closed. I landed harshly in the carriage to a small celebratory cheer from strangers. If I'd missed, they'd probably have cheered louder, but still, I smiled to no one in particular and pulled out my phone. And for the fourth time that month, I changed my password.

Above ground, I narrowly avoided colliding with strangers and oncoming traffic by opting to take forgotten thoroughfares and cobbled site streets.

'Running late?' Grace asked playfully when I burst through the office doors. The wall clock told me I'd arrived with minutes to spare.

'Nope,' I said.

I halted, catching myself in the mirror. In the rush, my shirt had come undone and my hair sported a windswept look. There were no important meetings that day so I fixed myself with minimal effort then briskly made my way to the elevator.

'Oh, William,' Grace called. She picked up an envelope lying on her desk. 'This came in the mail for you.'

I walked over and took it from her. Weighty, it was blue as sky on a late spring evening. My name and the building address were written in white, cursive handwriting on the front. Practiced and imperfectly perfect. I didn't recognise the loops or the style, and couldn't think of an occasion. Thanking Grace, I made my way back to the elevator and tore at the seal.

'Morning.'

I looked around to see Matthew approach. I was so used to blocking him out I hadn't registered that he'd entered the building. He wore a malicious smile as we stepped into the elevator together.

'Ready for the briefing?' he asked with a smirk. 'I hear Truman's got a surprise opportunity up his sleeve for one of us today.'

'I surprise,' I repeat. My stomach knots. That could mean anything. Obviously the stress appears on my face because Matthew smiles wickedly at me.

'An opportunity,' he clarifies with a confident wink.

I wondered how he could possibly know that. Truman's always been so selective over what information he shares, especially with us, those at the bottom of the pecking chain. Unless Matthew was still sleeping with Truman's wife and it was insider knowledge. If that were the case, then he'd surely be the one getting picked for whatever opportunity it was anyway, if Kimberly had any influence in the decision. Maybe that's why Matthew was so pompous, I thought, because the game was rigged.

There were only three chairs left unoccupied in the boardroom. The first was the top of the table, the space reserved for Truman. The other two were in direct sunlight and were unofficially classified as the worst seats in the room. Matthew took the one nearest the table's centre, leaving me to perch on the edge of the table, out of Truman's line of vision. As my colleagues talked, I continued to tear at the seal of my envelope when Matthew snatched it out of my hand.

'What's this, Walters? A love letter?'

I swore at him and grabbed it back as Truman came into the room.

'Personal mail to the office?' he asked in what I thought was supposed to be an amusing tone. I flashed him an apologetic smile and tucked the subject matter into my bag.

'I have some news today,' Truman announced. Matthew was right. The room settled, ears perking upwards like dogs. 'This is the most important year of your careers. We're taking on a titanic case. The biggest the firms ever seen and I want two of you to personally assist with it.'

Silence fell across the room. Each of us seemingly waiting for the punchline that never arrived. Truman presented the case, explained how he would run things, said the people in his team would work more hours than probably humanly possible. He claimed they'd be stretched over capacity and exhausted by the end. They'd also have to sign a non-disclosure agreement, which meant the case really was huge. None of that mattered to the budding group before him, still starry-eyed and eager for long-overdue recognition. Working with Truman himself was the best way to get promoted, and that was something we all wanted. To be chosen, all we had to do was research similar historical cases and write him a report.

* * *

I made my way to the office library after the meeting, thinking I'd be ahead of the game if I started straight away. I spent the rest of the morning planning my report, arranging timelines on individual pieces of paper, and writing extensive logs for each possible outcome.

By lunch time, I was satisfied I'd collected enough information to write the report itself, so I went to the staff canteen for a quick meal in order to get back to work faster. Matthew and his cronies, who had never quite forgiven me for ruining Matthew's engagement the way I had, were in front of me in the queue, taking the same approach as me. They talked and laughed in a loud, oppressive manner in a way which seemed intentionally to exclude me. I ate lunch on my own as I always did, not disconcerted that I wasn't a part of their clique.

When I left the canteen, I spoke to Grace as I passed. She was the closest thing I had to a friend at work. In that conversation she said something which made me realise I'd been focusing on the wrong parts of the case, so I carried myself back to the library, emptied my bag into the wastepaper bin and started all over again.

By the end of the day, I convinced myself I'd written a well-constructed first draft of what I wanted to present; something I could work and shape into a potentially excellent report. We had nothing planned that night, but I thought I'd go to see Penny since we hadn't left things on good terms. On the way over, I picked up a bouquet of white roses, her favourite.

I rang her doorbell, holding the flowers up to hide my face. When the door opened, I peeked from behind the roses but it wasn't Penny looking back at me.

'Hello?' I said to the man staring at me in bewilderment. His albino white hair was a wild tangle of knots. He wore a fabric suit jacket and smelled of musky aftershave and fresh mint. When he furrowed his brow in confusion he wore a face I recognised in painful detail.

'Penny,' he called, 'your admirer is here.'

A woman, not Penny, came into the hallway and strode towards the man. As she moved, her floral dress swayed with her. To examine me out of nosiness, she rested her elbow on his shoulder and cocked her head. I recognised her callous eyes in her heart-shaped face and her plump lips.

Then Penny came skipping across the hall, only to stop dead when she caught sight of me. She may have been a deer in headlights, but in that moment, I could only see her as a vixen.

'Can I have a moment?' she said to them. Their disdained faces told me they disapproved, but they retreated without protest. Penny stepped outside and closed the door.

'You told me your parents were dead,' I said. Those people had looked at me as though I were a nuisance, interrupting their night. I'd studied their combined features on their child for so long and I realised instantly that Penny had fed me a bunch of lies. The resemblance was indisputable. It was undeniable that the people in front of me were her parents, very much alive and kicking.

She scanned the space around us as though she would find excuses or lies hidden somewhere in the cobwebs or between the cracks in the wall.

'I can explain,' she said.

'Don't bother.'

I dropped the roses at her feet and turned. She called after me but her voice croaked, broken as my heart and trust. As I walked away, I held back a river of tears, replaying everything she had told me, everything she'd ever said. *Was it all just pretty lies?*

She called me forty-two times that night. I didn't once pick up. What reason could she possibly have for killing her parents? What excuses could she have for lying? Whatever they were, I didn't want to hear them.

Lying in bed, I replayed our whole relationship over as though we had been the stars of a cheap rental movie. My head reeled with information. I searched every scene, sifting for truth and lies, but I just didn't know. If there were signs, I was oblivious to them. To try to make sense out of Penny's actions, I ran through the relationship backwards too. We'd woken that day and she'd turned my alarm off. I'd gone to work. At work I'd received mail . . . what did I do with the envelope?

I climbed out of bed and found my bag, but it was empty. Grateful for the distraction from Penny, I searched my flat for the blue envelope with the perfect writing, but I couldn't remember what I'd done with it. There had only ever been one person who could write so flawlessly . . .

I gasped. The fancy W. The I's looping like a roller coaster. The intricate border. Only one person would put so much care and effort into perfecting their penmanship. *Caitlyn Donoghue.* Suddenly I had a real thirst to know what was in that envelope. Furious at myself for not opening the damn thing when I had it, I retraced my steps, pacing around my kitchen. Then it hit me. With everything that had happened, I'd forgotten I'd written research notes. Which I'd then taken from my bag and binned.

I ran to my bag and frantically tipped it upside down. Gum, receipts, pens and loose change flew out, but no envelope. I cursed, knowing fine well I'd binned it along with the papers.

My phone was on my nightstand. I had more missed calls from Penny which I ignored and found Caitlyn's number. Why had she written to me, after all this time with no contact? How sure was I that it was even her writing? Biting my lip, I put the phone back down. There was only one way to be sure.

I'd stayed late enough times at work either finishing cases or talking to Grace that I knew the cleaners didn't arrive at nights; they came early, in the morning, which meant the envelope was still in the wastepaper bin.

I set my alarm and lay my head on the pillow, buzzing with excitement and not tired at all, but willing myself to fall asleep.

The next morning—the middle of the night, *really*—I woke in a sweat of confusion to the squeal of my alarm. I'd been dreaming so vividly of hot air balloons soaring over country manors and a beautiful girl always just out of reach and I couldn't quite decipher what was real and what was in my head. All of it, and none of it, I eventually concluded as I peeled myself from bed to get ready for the day's adventure.

The air outside was bitter cold. I joined the treacle of morning workers marching to the Underground. The tube brought me to London Bridge, and I carried myself through the maze of the station leaving by the Borough Market exit.

The building was locked, and the lights were off. I stood by the doors until the security guard arrived with the cleaner I'd met only a handful of times. When they saw me, they exchanged glances.

'Morning,' I said as cheerfully as I could muster.

'You are early,' the security guard said.

I wished I knew his name.

'Yes,' I faked a laugh as though the situation were a joke. 'I couldn't sleep.'

They hesitated, looked at each other in doubt. An ounce of annoyance flared inside me. I shifted my weight from foot to foot.

'I'm afraid I cannot let you inside,' the security guard said.

'And why is that?' I asked, running out of patience.

'Grace is the building manager. Except for us, nobody gets in the building before her,' he explained.

I had no idea that was Grace's title or even her job. She never looked stressed or overworked, and yet the place wouldn't function without her. Defeated, I bit my lip, pulling away a tiny layer of skin. By the time she arrived, the bins would definitely be empty.

'Truman asked me to come in early,' I lied, using the only card I could play. 'I'm here to work on a project he assigned. He'd have your head if he found out you didn't let me in.'

The cleaner searched the security guard's face, wondering what he would do. I held my stance stronger than I felt.

'This case is worth millions,' I added.

With a hesitant nod, the security guard took out his keys and slid one of them into the lock. I thanked him with a smile, regretting that I'd been so hostile. I rode the elevator to the offices and ran to the wastepaper bin. Buried under a mountain of discarded paper, I found the blue envelope and gave a sigh of relief.

Deciding to read the letter with strong coffee and a view of the sunrise, I made my way to the boardroom. The elevator doors opened and I stepped inside and immediately knew something was wrong. The air was stuffy, stagnant. On the table, sat a near-empty bottle of whisky and a lone rock glass. Clothes—a crimped shirt, loosely folded trousers and a pair of socks—were splayed over the backs of two chairs.

'Walters?' Truman's voice filled the room. From his vantage point, he saw me seconds before I even knew he was there. I strode past the table and found him wrapped in a blanket on the sofa. He picked up his phone to check the screen. 'What are you doing here so early?'

In hesitation, vowels and broken words stumbled out of my mouth. Truman threw the blanket from himself and rose, seemingly unaware of my discomfort. He wore nothing but his underwear, but quickly grabbed his trousers and shirt. Seeing him in any state but impeccable felt apocalyptically wrong.

'I suppose I should explain,' he said as he threw his clothes on.

'You don't owe me an explanation,' I replied.

Barefoot, he walked to the coffee machine and turned it on. Neither of us attempted to speak over the crushing and grinding of beans. He poured two espressos and ushered me towards the table.

'Sit,' he offered, as though I were a guest in his home and hadn't found him sleeping in the boardroom. I sat, and only just realising I was still holding it, shoved the envelope back into my bag. Caitlyn's letter would have to wait.

He sipped his coffee. The silence between us niggled away at me.

'I didn't think it would be a problem to come in early,' I said, feeling like a schoolboy sitting in front of the head teacher.

'It's okay, it's okay.' Truman said, with the casual flick of his wrist. 'Kimberly kicked me out last night. I came here to work, and I guess I just fell asleep.' To disguise his saddened heart, he attempted a feeble shrug, but I could see the pain etched over his face. He didn't seem to notice that my eyes wandered back to the bottle of whisky. I couldn't help but suspect it had been a full bottle when he'd arrived at the firm. My throat suddenly felt impossibly dry. I drank my espresso but that only made things worse.

'She thinks I'm having an affair.'

I swallowed audibly. An admission of guilt.

'With Grace,' he added.

I choked on air and disbelief. At that moment, I didn't want to be in that room with that man. I'd rather have been *literally* anywhere else, anywhere at all. He stared at me expectantly.

'But it's *your* house,' I croaked. 'How can she kick you out of your own house?'

The room grew hotter and Truman fell into a rumbling speech, told me they'd had a massive row.

'You see,' he said in what appeared to be a conclusion, 'Grace and I went for a drink to talk about the upcoming case. She didn't want to take her bag with her, so she dropped a few things in my rucksack. At the end of the night, she took everything but her mascara. When Kim inevitably found it, well, voices got raised, and accusations were thrown. A bit of a misunderstanding, but you know women.'

Conscious that my skin felt very tight, I nodded gently. Truman continued to ramble as sweat dripped from my forehead. My skin grew so taught that it felt like a suit I was wearing, hiding underneath. If I didn't take it off, I would burst out of it.

'. . . she's a woman obsessed with the theory that I'm having some sort of illicit affair, but she's . . .'

I tugged at my collar. Was it shrinking?

'. . . I did say that. Can you believe it? I should call and apologise. . .'

The more Truman talked, the more rigid I became. Discomfort and anger stirred inside me. What right did Kimberly have to accuse Truman of infidelity when she was the one who was unfaithful?

'. . . thing is, I know I put work first. I need to stop doing that. We're thinking of starting a family. She's always wanted kids, she's—'

'Cheating on you,' I said through held breath. The air in my lungs turned into liquid regret. Truman's head flicked towards me, his eyes narrowed. He was studying me. I wanted to take the words back, swallow them whole and undo everything. I tried to look away, to avoid eye contact but his determined stare followed my avoiding gaze. One rough night and his face had already sunken in on itself. He sported a five o'clock shadow over his firm jaw and I wondered if he'd drank until he passed out.

'Who with?'

'Matthew,' I said. My voice a dull whimper.   Time stood still. My heart turned hollow and cold. I had no idea what Truman would do next and that terrified me.

'I knew it,' he whispered, and for a second, he seemed to retreat to a dark place inside himself. Isn't that what Matthew's fiancé had said, too? I wondered if, deep down, people always knew they were being cheated on, but subconsciously buried the ugly truths.

Truman slumped into one of the chairs and poured himself, then me, a whisky. He asked where all the good people had gone; how we get through life when we treat it like a game. I sat in silence. Those questions were not mine to answer. He downed the treacle in his glass and looked me dead in the eyes.

'Go,' he said. I didn't need to be told twice. I left the room without needing be told twice. As the door closed, I heard glass slam against glass. He had undoubtedly drank the whisky he'd poured for me.

I sat at my desk for the rest of the morning with a book open in front of me, wondering what was coming. As my colleagues came into the office, they chatted to each other and buzzed around the open space. Too afraid to speak or even move, I didn't lift my head from the page I stared at, unable to process any of the words. Not knowing what Truman was going to do killed me.

When the office was full, silence fell, and I knew what that meant. The door slammed shut and I stole a glance across the room. Truman had entered and scanned for his victim. Beside him stood the Director of Human Resources. I wondered what repercussions I'd face for spilling secrets like blood.

Truman marched across the room, silent as death, and slammed a file onto Matthew's desk. Matthew blinked in surprise, too gobsmacked to show embarrassment or even resistance.

'Go home,' Truman said.

Anybody who had pretended not to observe stopped pretending. In the most subtle of movements, Matthew scanned the faces in front of him, then opened the file and his face dropped. Without protest, he rose. Our Human Resources Director trotted out of the room with Matthew in tow, who, in the stillness and quiet, could not mask his sobs.

Truman marched out, but nobody dared speak.

I waited for my dismissal, but it didn't happen. Around mid-day, Grace came quietly into the room. I held my breath as I watched her approach my desk.

'There's someone here to see you,' she said in a gentle whisper. She drew her eyes to onlookers who immediately looked away. I nodded, threw my things into my bag and rose. It was my time to go.

In need of a distraction. I asked Grace what was in the file that Truman had slammed on Matthew's desk. She told me the file was a bulk of paperwork to give it weight and make the scene more dramatic.

That made no sense, though. Why had Matthew left? Why had he cried?

'Why did Matthew take the bate then?' I asked.

'The first page was enough. Truman's dramatic, but he doesn't need a whole file to put the fear of God in you. He's more tactful than that. He had a picture of Kimberly and Matthew and had written something about going quietly or getting an awful reference.'

'Oh,' I said with a sinking stomach. At least I knew what to expect . . .

The doors opened and I blinked in surprise. I'd expected Truman, not Penny, to be standing in front of Grace's desk. I wanted to pretend I wasn't surprised, but my face betrayed me by revealing my shock.

'What are you doing here?' I asked. Her smile dropped.

'Can we talk?' she eyed Grace who was blatantly watching our interaction. 'I made you lunch.'

'No, I don't think—'

'Please,' she begged.

I let out a sigh, as if that day hadn't been crazy enough, and nodded. She walked a stride ahead of me as she left the building, waving flirtatiously to the security guard as she passed.

'This isn't fair,' I argued when we were on the street, away from my colleague's lurking ears. People buzzed by us and I wished they would have carried me away with them. 'You can't just show up at my work unannounced.'

'You can't just stop taking my calls as if I never existed, like I even don't matter.' The wind swept her hair and I wanted nothing more than for her to hug me, to tell me I'd done right by Truman. The uncertainty made me feel queasy but Penny's moral compass is evidently innately broken beyond repair.

'You can't just kill your parents,' I remarked.

To hide the tears pooling in her eyes, she looked away and folded her arms over her chest.

'Let's sit,' I said, and led her to the concrete planter by the side of the office building. She pulled out a packed lunch box and offered me the contents.

I didn't realise how hungry I was until I took a bite of the tuna-mayonnaise sandwich she'd made. I ate the whole thing without talking to her. When we finished eating, she scrunched up the cling film and threw it back in the plastic box.

'Why did you lie about your family?' I asked.

She stared straight ahead. I wanted an invitation to wherever she went in her head, but I didn't know how to ask for one.

'You were just so sad when you told me about your parents, William. I didn't want to tell you that I still had mine, that I'd chosen to cut them out of my life. You wouldn't have understood.'

She wasn't wrong.

'So instead of diving into our family drama I told you they were dead. It was easy because they were, to me, anyway. But a few months ago my mum got in touch and we made amends, but I couldn't take back the lies; it was already too late. Can you ever forgive me?'

She scratched the skin over her wrists with her claw-like fingernails. Dating her was like playing a video game for the first time ever, on a difficult level.

'Yes,' I said, grasping at her hands to stop her from hurting herself.

She hugged me and it didn't feel like the world was shaking anymore. I felt stable, like I had something to hold onto. I wondered if that's what love felt like - something solid under your feet when everything else is a mess.

When she left, I rummaged through my bag in search of chewing gum to mask my tuna breath but got distracted when I found the envelope again. I flipped it over in my hands and pulled out a thick card. It wasn't a letter I held, but an invitation. Caitlyn's beautiful handwriting filled the page, spilling the details of Alex and Luke's wedding. I smiled to myself, lifted my head and caught the tail sight of Penny disappearing around the corner and for a split second imagined it was Caitlyn who had just come to bring me lunch. Butterflies fluttered in my stomach, flapping wildly. My eyes trailed from the empty space where Penny had stood, down to Caitlyn's handwriting in my hands and I decided in that moment that if I were to the wedding, I would go alone.

12

Origami Hearts

Under the loom of the Castle Hotel, on the night before Alex and Luke's wedding, I climbed out of a taxi and took a deep breath. I grew painfully aware that I was standing alone. Perhaps it had been a mistake to show up by myself, but it was too late to turn back, so I grabbed my holdall from the driver, tipped and thanked him, then headed inside. At the desk, I checked into my room and before I could turn around, felt a firm tap on my shoulder.

'Excuse me . . . you look familiar. Have we met?'

The words sang like a lullaby. The rhythm, the beat and the tone were engrained in my memory. I turned to face Caitlyn. Her blonde curls had been chopped and replaced with a razor-sharp bob, worn to shape her face in a way which made her eyes pop. Her right hand held a glass of wine; the rim stained with a lipstick kiss. Her left clung onto a small clutch bag, the same shade of black as her tight-fitting dress. Those piercing green eyes looked right into mine.

'Caitlyn,' I said, dropping my bag and my smile. 'It's me. It's William.' My heart slowed, almost to a stop. She erupted with laughter and I realised how foolish I'd been. I sighed with relief and she pulled me in for a hug. Her skin was warm, safe. When she let me go, her sweet scent still lingered.

'Don't be silly, William. I could never forget you.' She laughed again, a quieter, flirtatious laugh. No, not flirtatious, I reminded myself. Her kindness was nothing but friendship. My thoughts appeared to spread over my face, because she asked what was wrong. I told her nothing, shrugging it off, and she dragged me to the bar, the wine in her glass sloshing as we moved.

'William,' Alex sang from across the room, his voice penetrating the space between us. He held up a highball glass as though giving a toast, then broke through the people in the room to greet me with a hug. I hadn't felt so loved since the summer after Jo had died. It would have been enough to move me to tears if I weren't sober. He asked how I was, what I wanted to drink, and told me Luke was around somewhere, then introduced me to a passing family member. Enough indicators for me to summarise that he was beyond tipsy.

'Join us, won't you?' he demanded, clutching my arm with his free hand.

'Of course,' I said, 'just as soon as I drop my bag off in my room. I left it by the reception.' I bowed away from him, Caitlyn and the other guests, then crossed the bar. Before I left, I admired the happiness in the room. The pianist keyed a familiar piece of music and a fire crackled on the far wall. Laughter, song and cheer roared from the guests in a delightful blend. Nostalgia waved through me as I spotted Luke. He looked older, gaunter, somehow. His face was an echo of the man he used to be. Caitlyn grabbed him. She also looked older, but in opposition, seemed more filled with life. My heartstrings tugged as I realised she could have had a baby in the time since I'd seen her last, and I'd never have known. I tried to imagine her swollen stomach but the image was so unnatural that I couldn't conjure anything of the sort, so I shook the thoughts away. I grabbed my bag from the reception where I'd deliberately left it so I had an excuse to leave and said goodnight to the young receptionist, having absolutely no intention of joining the pre-wedding celebrations in the bar.

I awoke the next day feeling fresher than the rest of the wedding party; I found out later. Birds sang outside, their songs pouring with sunlight through my open windows. Pulling myself to a sitting position, I yawned and stretched, then tossed the silky covers from me and watched a deer graze on the lawn outside. A beautiful day for a wedding. I tiptoed to the bathroom, the ceramic tiles beneath my bare feet freezing cold, and ran a bath, pouring a generous volume of bubble bath into the churning water.

When the tub was full I sank into the bubbles and, carefully holding my phone above the water, checked social media. Something I scarcely ever did. Penny had written cryptic messages on her news feed. I rolled my eyes and clicked on Caitlyn's profile. There were no uploads from the previous night yet. I checked Luke's page, but there was nothing there either. Alex was against the concept of social media, so I didn't bother to type his name into the search bar. Before moving on, a little blue button at the top of the page caught my eye. Blinking away confusion and disbelief, I went back to Caitlyn's page and found the same box. *Add friend.* In the time I'd been gone, they'd unfriended me. The heartache wasn't a sting I was prepared for.

There's no pain like being left behind.

With a sigh, I dropped my phone onto the towel by the bath, making sure it landed with a safe plop and buried myself in the cushion of bubbles, wondering how much fun my old friends had endured without me.

I ate breakfast alone in the empty conservatory. By the time I finished, the room was filling, so I took my leave. On the way out, I bumped into Caitlyn, who dressed simple, in an oversized t-shirt and spray-on jeans. Unlike the stern, older woman she was with who wore an expensive-looking blazer and scowling red lips. The woman did not stop to talk to me, but marched ahead, disappearing into the conservatory. Caitlyn lay a hand on the top of my arm, where my bicep would have been if I'd grown attempted to gain one.

'I missed you last night,' she said, which made me blush. I apologised; told her I fell asleep as soon as I was in my room. She dismissed the apology with a friendly head shake.

'You owe me a drink later,' she said with a smile. 'We need to catch-up.'

Later, I dressed in a brand-new three-piece suit and made my way to the ceremony where anticipation was so thick I could have drowned in it.

Knowing only a handful of people, I deliberately lingered around the edges of the bar, making myself look busy, until it was time to take a seat. Then a whole new wave of anxiety struck, and I hated myself for coming to a wedding on my own. *Where was I supposed to sit?*

'Sit with us, dear,' said a woman I recognised as Alex's mum. I was sure her name was Margaret, but not confident enough to say it aloud. I thanked her as though I hadn't been inwardly battling myself and joined the rest of the family in the front row. I wondered if Alex had premeditated the situation, or if I'd looked so outwardly lost and lonely that she felt obliged to invite me to sit with her. She pulled tissues from her small bag and told me she'd need them. Suddenly, I realised I didn't understand how queer weddings worked and I felt a small surge of excitement for being at one.

It turns out they are as long and boring as typical weddings with just a few tweaks. Instead of floating through an aisle, Alex and Luke drifted from each side of their guests and met each other at the altar equally, taking on the traditional roles of both bride and groom. The marriage officiant was a woman sporting punk-styled hair and a sleeve of tattoos on her left arm. She told jokes and kept the event light-hearted. Caitlyn stood behind Alex, bearing a cushion holding rings. My heartbeat slowed as I focused on her. The hot-pink dress she wore flowed with her movements, gentle as breath. Even though she didn't need it, her makeup was flawless, perfectly highlighting every delicate feature of her diamond face. Her emerald eyes focused on the two grooms but filled the room. A flicker of a smile spread across her. I imagined she was lost in a daydream, probably conjuring picture-perfect images of her own wedding. Would she want a grand day filled with flowers and confetti, surrounded with people from all stages of her life, I wondered, or would she want something small and simple?

Poetic vows were exchanged, love declared. Tears broke out across the room. Even my eyes threatened to spill. Alex had never stood so perfectly still. Kisses were planted in a soundtrack of applause and my friends were officially wed. Their marriage was pure – not just papers signed and rings exchanged, but the binding of two people who would walk through fire to support each other.

As a merging group, we left the room. I no longer felt alone, as though in the union of Alex and Luke, I had forged my way into some spontaneous family. It didn't seem to matter that I wasn't a cousin, or a colleague. That I'd come from outside was irrelevant. I joined Alex's mum—confirmed to be Margaret when someone called her name—for drinks under the sunshine on the patio. In conversation fuelled by alcohol, she told anybody who would listen how she had always loved Alex, no matter who he himself loved, and that Luke was the perfect man for him. For a while Luke's parents politely acknowledged her, but ultimately ended up avoiding her.

The two grooms stood on the edge of the castle's shadow; their own outlines stretched in projection across the lawn. For each separate shot, the photographer choreographed their bodies into different poses. The bouquet of roses from the morning changed hands and angles frequently. Family and colleagues and distant friends watched them to begin with, but then got lost in small talk. Around us, children amused themselves by running between their parents, who themselves were enjoying the break from sombrely watching over their every move. Alex's dad, a short and stout man, swayed when the photographer orchestrated the grooms' parents into the shots. I chuckled to myself, drained the remains of my own drink, then made my way back to the bar and ordered another. I watched the party from behind the alcove window, spied Caitlyn laughing with people I recognised from university.

When the photographer was satisfied, Alex and Luke took off in separate directions as their families dispersed. Luke joined the guests on the patio, where someone passed him a tall, clear drink. Alex checked over his shoulder as he walked the length of the lawn, alone and unnoticed. For the first time that day, there were no eyes on him, all the other guests were too busy in their own version of events.

Alex walked through the garden gate. I put my glass on the window ledge and darted after him. I knew the feeling of loneliness all too well. In my flurry, someone called out after me, but I didn't stop to find out who it was. I ran across the lawn and hopped over the gate, worried about my friend. Breathlessly, I followed the twisting path through thin woodland trees until I reached a clearing at the bottom of a small hill. Alex stood on the peak. His arms outstretched with cupped hands. In them were something small, white, and numerous. It seemed like a private moment, but when I turned to leave, he called my name.

'What are you doing?' I asked as I climbed the hill to be with him. He didn't seem annoyed I'd interrupted his private moment.

'Thinking,' he said casually, 'having a moment to myself.'

'Regretting it already?'

'No,' he chuckled, though I'd been serious. 'There's been a lot of build-up to this day,' he continued, 'and everyone's been pulling me left and right. I just needed to . . . catch my breath.'

I nodded, understanding the need to take time out to recharge. I looked at what he held: intricate pieces of paper, folded carefully into origami hearts. Between the folds, I could make out his scribbled handwriting.

'What are they?' I asked.

'*They* are everything,' he said. 'My hopes, my dreams. What I'm afraid of, and what I want to accomplish. The parts of me I'm letting go. The parts I've outgrown.'

He shifted his hands, and the paper caught wind, took flight and swirled around in the air. The origami hearts were weightless, unlike real hearts which get bogged down with pain. They followed the curve of the hill and disappeared from sight.

'For example,' he said. 'Luke's just bought a country cottage, just off the M1. My pay's not great and I feel like I'll never own anywhere myself, but that doesn't matter anymore, you know?'

'I understand,' I said.

'We should spend New Year's there,' he added distantly.

I told him I'd love to, and watched the tail end of his origami hearts float away. I was sure it meant a lot to Alex, this shedding process, but to me it was disastrously underwhelming.

'They're biodegradable,' he said, though I didn't ask.

For a moment, we stood in silence and I closed my eyes, replayed the beauty of the morning over again. Leaves crunched under foot behind us, and I turned to see Luke and Caitlyn walking along the path.

'Hey,' Luke called on his approach. Caitlyn had tucked her arm between his and they swayed giddily as they walked. Alex opened his arms and Luke floated into them, planting a kiss on his forehead.

'I knew you'd be here,' Luke said. Turning to me and Caitlyn, he added, 'This spot is the reason he wanted this venue.'

'It's lovely,' Caitlyn said. 'I hope we're not interrupting.'

Insouciantly, the grooms laughed. Suddenly I wondered if I were out of place, being amidst their alliance when I'd removed myself so long before. Perhaps, I thought bitterly, Penny was right: friendships expire.

The thoughts vanished when Caitlyn linked her arm through my own. Looking down at our connected skin, I saw her muddy feet and they instantly took me back to the day we trekked across dry muck to ride in a hot-air balloon. Against myself, I smiled, grateful Caitlyn was the kind of person who didn't mind walking through mud for an adventure.

'I'm glad you came,' she said as we walked back to the castle, ahead of Alex and Luke. Once, I'd confused her friendship for flirtation. I couldn't afford to make that mistake again.

'I'm glad I came too,' I replied. I believed she meant it. 'Can I ask you something?'

'Anything.'

'Why did you unfriend me?'

There was no way to ask without sounding like it didn't bother me.

'What?' She paused, taken off guard. The way she wrapped her arm around me, the smile she wore when she saw me, the interest she paid when I spoke. Those little things told me we *were* friends, so it shouldn't matter what social media said, but for some reason, it did.

'William, it you was you who unfriended me and Luke.' She spoke with such conviction I wondered if I'd drunkenly hit the button and forgotten about it. 'It's not a big deal. I just figured you were doing a clear out.'

The thought of clearing Caitlyn out of existence was incomprehensible to me.

'Tell me about your girlfriend,' she said, tactfully changing the subject.

I told her about Penny, editing the girl I dated for a carefully constructed cardboard cut-out version of herself.

'Why isn't she here?' Caitlyn asked. The dreaded question I'd hoped to avoid, but attending a wedding alone gave people permission to ask personal questions, highlight parts of your life you'd much rather keep in the dark.

'She couldn't make it,' I lied. 'Work commitments.' Caitlyn made a noise which told me she believed me, and that she'd understood.

'What about you? Are you seeing anyone?' I asked, failing to keep my voice neutral. She told me she was still with Nick, and that he couldn't make it either, also because of work commitments.

It wasn't until I was back at the bar and she caught my eye, that I realised that like me, she may not have been entirely truthful. The lies we tell are usually formulated to protect us, but may just damage us instead.

Dinner was served outside, under the sinking sun. There was no regimented table plan, and the grooms sat at a table by themselves, so I sat next to Caitlyn and the others I recognised from university. During the meal, I worked up the courage to ask Caitlyn about her life.

She was happy with work, but not satisfied. I couldn't tell if her dreams had changed or if she'd given up on them altogether. Her smile was wide, but the twinkle in her eyes had dimmed. I took a swig of my drink, drowning my fears and asked what happened.

'Well,' she said, taking a sip of her wine. She drunkenly hiccoughed. 'Excuse me. I've been working in a bar since graduation, but they recently offered me a position in head office. Nothing fancy, but at least it's not public facing, and I think it would be fun.'

'It sounds like a great opportunity,' I said, suspecting there was more she hadn't said. I remembered the bar, and the job and was stung with pity. That wasn't what she had wanted for herself. That was supposed to be temporary.

'Thank you,' she replied in what was almost pure relief. She took another sip of wine. 'Nick obviously doesn't want me to go.'

'Is that what's stopping you?' I asked. She studied the contents of her glass, then slammed it onto the table, annoyed. Apparently the topic had created tension, but when I apologised she cut me off.

'No, you're right' she said. I furrowed my brow. 'I can't let him hold me back anymore.' She stopped to consider the things in her head. 'I'm moving to London.'

'Just like that?' I asked. With a laugh, she nodded, then drank the rest of her wine. The fire was back in her heart, her eyes ablaze.

'You're a firecracker,' I said, and we toasted to that. 'You know, I always thought you'd call, or text when I moved.'

'We tried. You never—'

'Excuse me, guys,' Alex interrupted. Fuelled by an inordinate volume of alcohol, he had connected his phone to the sound system, skipped across the lawn, and climbed onto our table, squeezing between us. He grabbed my hand, pulled me up too. He put his arm over my shoulder and motioned me to join him in dancing the cancan.

Luke shook his head playfully as we danced. Alex signalled for him to join us. Without refusal, he clambered onto the tabletop, grabbing Caitlyn's hand on his way. Having unrestricted fun and laughing freely took me back, once again, to the weeks we had spent together in the summer. The best days of my life.

It was much later when I made my way inside the castle, intoxicated and tired. From the foyer, I could hear Caitlyn's voice carry through bricked corridors. I tiptoed to the library then halted. It was wrong to listen in, but she was upset, and shouting. There was no response, so I peeked past the door and caught her yelling into her phone.

She paced the floor in quick, furious steps.

'You're being unreasonable,' she said. The other person took their turn to speak and she continued to patrol the room.

'I *am* listening . . . you're not . . . how dare you? . . . I am so . . . never . . . I wouldn't . . . I . . . .' She threw the phone to the couch in frustration and squealed in a way I'd never seen her express herself before. She stomped around, lapped the couch, her arm floating in mid-air, hesitating over the phone. When she picked it back up, she did so calmly and with a deep breath.

'This is over, Nick.' She ended the call.

I turned on my foot as she stalked the length of the library, but the floor creaked under my shifting weight.

'What are you doing?' she asked. I turned to face her. Mascara streaks ran down her cheeks. Her hair had curled at the ends and her eyes shone with tears. Despite that, she remained beautiful.

'You broke up with Nick,' I said, unable to deny what I'd heard. With a trembling lip she nodded then took a step forward and buried herself into my chest and my arms. Her hair smelled floral, and I breathed her in.

'What am I going to do?' she asked. I didn't have an answer, but when I met her eyes I realised she wasn't really asking me. She brought her lips to mine and I sank into them.

Penny flashed across my mind, and I pulled away as rapid as my heart beat.

We'd opened a door we couldn't ever close. With just one kiss, I'd ruined everything. I was more awake, more sober, than I had been in years but in a brief lapse of judgment, I'd forgotten my girlfriend and ruined our relationship. My eyes focused back on Caitlyn. In my pulling away, she wore a face of hurt, of rejection. I'd also ruined our friendship. A single kiss and I'd blown apart the new life I'd built myself.

13

In for a Penny. . .

She chewed with her mouth open. Each loud, incessant, wet, smack made me want to scream. The noises ranged from munching to slurping and everything in between. How do you even eat toast like that? I wondered.

Had she always eaten like that? Or was this my punishment?

I thought she'd dig her acrylic nails into the fatty tissues around my heart when I told her I'd kissed Caitlyn at the wedding. Instead, Penny shrugged and said it wasn't a big deal. Then we moved on with our lives. Our relationship, and my life, had turned into a habit.

Work, argue and make up with Penny, sleep, then do it all over again.

Her phone vibrated fiercely on the table in front of us. She picked it up, saw who was calling, and sent them to voicemail.

'Who was that?' I asked, expecting her to tell me it was nobody.

'Brian, from work,' she said, a little too casually. The thing about Penny was that lies tumbled out of her mouth. She told them so often, she usually ended up believing them herself. My own phone buzzed in my trouser pocket. I slid my hand down to push the button on the side, also sending my caller to voicemail. I looked at Penny to see if she'd noticed the vibrations. If she had, her face didn't give it away. I pulled the tip of my phone out. Seeing Caitlyn's name on my screen gave flight to the butterflies in my stomach she'd created so many years before. Looking back at Penny crushed them.

'Who was that?' she asked.

She had noticed.

'Alex,' I shrugged, echoing her nonchalance and lies.

Usually, silence would make Penny anxious. She had a tendency to fill it given any opportunity. But as we sat opposite each other at my kitchen table, I realised we had run out of words to fill the distance between us.

'Do you want to do something tonight?' I asked, 'watch a movie, or —'

'I'm going out,' she snapped. 'Remember?'

There was nothing to remember - she definitely hadn't told me. I sighed, picked up our empty bowls and took them to the sink. As I washed them, I asked if she had plans for the day. She told me she didn't, but the way she scrutinised herself in the mirror afterwards was a contradiction. Her confidence was self-constructed, with hardly any resilience. One hair out of place could have her frantic for hours. I sighed.

I strolled into the firm early. Grace was on the phone, so I gave a small wave as I passed. The office was almost empty except for a few partners who sat with their morning brew, leaning precariously over their laptops, and Truman, who had his head stuck in a thick textbook. His reading glasses sat halfway down his nose. As I passed, he glanced over them. I offered a smile of peace, which he ignored, and buried himself again. At my desk, I took my laptop out and got to work.

As the morning passed, the room filled with my colleagues, but no one acknowledged my existence. They blamed me for Matthew's demise, and as a result, hadn't spoken to me since. Branded as a snake, I wasn't to be trusted. Instead of utilising the graduates to help Truman on his big case as promised, he poured his own energy into it, confiding in nobody. That was also my fault.

At lunch, I pulled my phone out of my bag and saw the unanswered call from Caitlyn that morning, which I'd forgotten about. I passed through the room with the intention of calling her back when I overheard Truman tell Grace there would be no more graduate intakes.

'I think we need to focus on the talent we already have in house,' he said.

I tried to stop myself from being spotted, but it was too late. Their eyes fell on me, heavy and weighted. Silence followed. I smiled politely and walked past, feeling their stare fixate on me as I called the elevator. Only when swallowed by its metallic mouth did I hear their murmurs continue.

Outside, the sun was shining, though there was a sharp wind in the shadows. I sat on the edge of the decorative concrete planter and called

Caitlyn back, praying she would answer.

'Can you meet soon?' she asked. The urgency in her voice worried me. I caught sight of Grace who trailed out of the building. She rummaged in her handbag and pulled out a packet of cigarettes, put one to her mouth, then lit it.

'Is everything okay?' I asked into the phone.

Grace blew smoke into the air.

'Yeah,' Caitlyn said unconvincingly. 'I need to talk to someone.'

I told her to meet me at The Rusty Fox after work and ended the call. I walked to Grace and stood beside her, knowing if I lingered long enough, she'd talk to me. When she didn't, I cracked.

'Is everything okay with Truman?' I asked.

'Of course,' she said coyly. I nodded, knowing fine well not to poke my nose where it wasn't wanted, but a nagging sensation in my stomach told me to keep prodding, like when you have a peeling scab and you know you should leave it, but you can't help but dig your fingernail underneath to prize it off a little more, until regretfully, you've picked it all away and there's nothing left but a bloody mess.

'He seems off lately,' I said.

'You mean since he found out from his *mini-me* that his wife was having an affair with one of his protégés?' she asked. 'He's absolutely splendid.' Her sarcasm and sharp tone unappreciated, I sighed and turned to leave.

'It's not you, William,' she said. She trailed the lit end of her cigarette along the bricked wall until it stubbed out and motioned me to walk to the bin with her. 'He admires you for having the balls to tell him. You've been strong considering the atmosphere in the firm's evaporated overnight. Apparently, this isn't the first time Kim's fooled around. It's been going on for years and nobody's ever told him before. Between you and me, he's going to whittle out the liars and the cheats, but he's being careful about it.'

'He *admires* me?' I asked. *He had a funny way of showing it.*

'Something's changed in him, William. He adored Kimberly. I don't think he'll ever look at anyone the same after what she's done. There used to be a light in him, but I don't see it anymore.'

There was a sadness in the way Grace spoke which made me realise she was in love with him. Probably had been for some time. I wondered if Kimberly had seen it too, if that's what had driven her to acts of desperation. Had she been fighting a losing battle for Truman's attention?

* * *

After work, I made my way to The Rusty Fox as planned. Caitlyn was already leaning against the railing by the side of the neglected pub, watching a young coot paddle along the river when I arrived. Seeing her made me appreciate that it had been a mistake to meet her there. It felt wrong to take something which belonged to Penny and me and turn it into a thing between me and Caitlyn.

I thought she'd mention our kiss, but she didn't. She hugged me like it never happened.

As we walked away from the pub, I asked her how she found London so far.

'It's a little lonely,' she said distantly, as though desolate memories blanketed her.

I agreed that it could be a cold city if you let it. She was struggling to find a graduate job and found applications daunting. Rejection followed rejection; she was riding a wheel of no experience - where she couldn't get any because she had no job and she couldn't get a job because she had no experience. She worried if she settled for something, like she had before, she'd never escape.

'It's hard in the beginning, but you need to put yourself out there,' I said.

As though I were in a position to give advice. Since moving to London, I'd lost more than I'd ever had.

'Yeah, I guess so,' she said. 'In other news, I made one friend this week. Her name's Amanda and we're meeting up this weekend. Are you free?' Her voice piqued. 'You should come. You'd love her.'

I smiled. I wanted Caitlyn to make friends, to be happy. But I figured she should establish foundations before she brought anyone else along, so I told her I was busy, even though Penny was on a trip away that weekend.

We continued walking for a while, following the natural curves of the canal. After some time, we took a seat on a bench in an open park and she asked if I'd ever got around to finishing Jo's bucket list.

'No,' I admitted, knowing my answer would disappoint her. Silence fell between us and I bitterly wondered how we had arrived in a place where we could barely hold a conversation. And more importantly, I questioned how we would get out of it.

'What about you?' I asked. She shook her head in discontent. To cheer her up, I reminded her of the time we got stranded when the last ferry left without us. She giggled for a moment, but her laugh trailed away with the breeze and died.

'You promised me on that trip you'd never change,' she said in an accusatory tone. The conversation was footing dangerous territory.

I saw the changes within myself. No longer flinching when people touched me, speaking confidently without hesitation, grabbing opportunities. I hadn't even struggled to ask Caitlyn to meet me that day - something I'd have debated and worried over before. The way she bit her lip suggested it wasn't a change for better.

Did she want me to stay poor, broken, and insecure forever?

I thought of the day I'd made that promise to her. I remembered the storm, the moonlight like a spotlight shining just for us. I should have kissed her then, told her how I felt.

'That was nothing but a moonlight wish,' I said, my voice filled with insouciance. 'It's like pillow talk. It didn't really mean anything.'

'It meant everything to me,' she said.

Me too.

Somehow, I'd said entirely the wrong thing. Regrets collect like old coins.

'In what ways have I changed?' I asked, uncertain I wanted to know, but wondering if I could convert back.

'Well, for example . . .' Her words hummed in the air as she thought. 'Would you ever say you suffer from anxiety?'

The question was out of the blue and I was certain there was a hidden agenda beneath the surface. I looked away, studied a woman flagging down a black cab across the street. Her leopard print skirt and red high heels were almost as painful to look at as our conversation was to be in.

'I wouldn't say I *suffer*,' I said carefully, bringing my attention back to Caitlyn. 'Are you suffering if you aren't suffering?' I asked, almost rhetorically. She gave me space to elaborate. 'My anxiety isn't crippling. It never stopped me from doing anything, achieving anything. So no, I don't suffer.' I said, almost convincing myself and her.

'But you do have it?' she probed.

I watched the black cab halt in traffic, thought about *having* anxiety as though it were a possession I claimed ownership of - like it could be given away if I ever chose not to want it anymore. *If only it were that simple.*

'Do I feel a high level of unease over mundane tasks other people often do with ease?' I asked. 'Do I overthink and over analyse almost all conversations?' I took a moment to let my ridiculous queries mull in the air.

'Yes,' I answered, then took another pause. 'I think it's fair to say I've lived in my head for quite some time. I have *a lot* of feelings. There's so much wrong in the world. Children are starving. Our grandparents are dying lonely. Icebergs are melting. And we try to block the pain by diving headfirst into our phone screens, but it's not enough.'

She looked at me with a mischievous smile, like she was right, but also a little wrong, about me. I might have been different, but I hadn't changed that much.

'See,' she said, 'you're more confident now, so sure of yourself and the world around you.'

'Is that a bad thing?' I asked.

'I suppose it's not.'

As much as I detested being psychoanalysed, I felt relief. Finally, *finally*, I had told somebody about the pain inside my head.

Finally, somebody had asked.

'What do you want to do?' she asked, tilting her head so she rested on my shoulder.

'I don't know what I want.'

'I have a suggestion,' she said.

I looked at her with raised eyebrows.

'Now that we're in the same city again, we could finish Jo's bucket list.' She pulled away and twisted to face me, excitement pulsing like electricity inside her.

'That would be nice,' I said, worried it was just another *moonlight wish* which would dissipate in time, but even if it was, at least I got to see her smile again.

By the time the sun set, we had ended up in Russell Square. We made our way underground and hugged goodbye at the bottom of the escalator. Instead of heading home, I went to Penny's hoping we could make amends for the way things had gone between us. From the street, I could see her open window on the third floor. Grey curtains flapped gently with the breeze and between them the soft glow of her reading lamp shone. I imagined she'd be sprawled over her bed, writing in her diary, spilling the details of her day. Once, she'd told me she wanted to publish them when I found them hidden at the bottom of her dresser drawer. I'd scoffed since she never let me read them.

Excited to deliver my apology, I fished the spare key out of my pocket and let myself inside. I passed by the bland walls, chipped paint and piss-stained walls in the communal entrance, and climbed the stairs one at a time. Once, I'd been everything to Penny, but I *had* changed; I'd turned into the kind of man who would kiss someone else at a wedding. I wasn't sure I liked the version of myself I'd become

I changed once, I could do it again.

Scorning myself for the hundredth time, hating myself more than ever before, I pushed the key into Penny's lock, twisted, and opened her front door. I stood in the hallway, the space in front me was, as always, filled with clutter. Shoes lay in disarray and clothes were strewn across the floor. In front of me stood the internal door to Penny's flat. From the other side, gentle, rhythmic moans spilled. My heart skipped a beat. Would she want me to walk in on her intimate moment? Would she be embarrassed?   I tiptoed along the hall, deciding not to interrupt her, but instead join her. Then I saw a pair of shoes I'd never seen before. They were large. Too big for Penny's doll-like feet, too big even for me. A man's shirt lay crumpled on the floor. Then I heard him. Slowly, I pushed the door open, bracing myself for what I knew I was about to witness, but nothing could have prepared me for what I saw. I tried to dismiss the images, to shake them away, but I stood frozen, taking everything in.

'William,' Penny cried. The man on top of her flew to the side, covered himself up with her duvet. The covers I'd lay under just that morning. She clambered from the bed, but it was too late, I already turned away. My legs carried me faster than my brain could process where I was going.

I didn't stop running until I was home. Even then, as I lay in bed with my heart beating erratically, my mind refused to stop wandering. Over and over again it replayed the image of Penny's arching back underneath the man who had taken my usual place.

Every time she rang, I sent the call to voicemail until eventually I threw my phone across the room. I buried myself in the safety of my blankets, wishing everything would go away.

The next morning, I woke in a puddle of sweat and confusion. Everything was dark and my body remained groggy, like it needed more time to wake. I couldn't remember closing the blinds, but they had been drawn. My phone sat on the bedside table, through I swore I left it on the floor.

Metal clanged from another room, the kitchen, it sounded like. Somebody was in my flat. Slowly, I dragged myself out of bed, threw my dressing gown on and opened the bedroom door. I tiptoed through the hall, stopping dead when I saw her.

'What are you doing here, Penny?' I asked. She stood at the cooker, rocked the pan on the hob then turned to see me. When her eyes met mine, she smiled warmly.

'Morning, sleepy-head,' she sang. 'I'm making eggs. Take a seat.' Airily, she gestured towards the already set table. Steam trickled from the cafetière sitting between the placemats.

'What are you doing here?' I asked again, this time sharp enough to cut the butter she held. 'How long have you been here?'

'I came to apologise.'

Ignoring me, she buttered two rolls, then plated them. There was something about her—her stance, her demeanour, her *essence*—that shook me to the core.

How could she be so brazen?

'No,' I protested. She lifted the eggs from the pan and placed them into the rolls as if she didn't hear me. She hummed tunelessly as she carried the plates to the table. 'Penny, you don't just get to come here like this. Not anymore.'

She almost asked what I meant, but I cut her off, told her she had no right to do this, to do what she'd done. She had no idea how much hurt she'd caused. With stony eyes and an ice-like stare she focused on me.

'This is your fault,' she said. There was poison in her words that she spat into the room.

'My fault,' I said, 'how is this my fault?'

'You kissed Caitlyn,' she said judgementally. As though that excused her raucous behaviour.

'That was *different*,' I hissed through gritted teeth. My fingers stretched out from the ball I had them clenched in. The fury in me had built up so quickly that I scared even myself. Perhaps if I was somebody different, I'd have hit her.

'Tell me, Penny. Was it you who unfriended them on my page?'

'I don't know what you're talking about.' She looked out the window, apparently finding children skipping in the streets on their way to school more interesting than the conversation.

'You blocked their numbers on my phone so I wouldn't get their texts or calls.'

For a whole year I'd wondered why they hadn't made contact; convinced myself I'd been forgotten. Slamming my fists onto the table, I leaned forwards so I was mere centimetres away.

'How many times did you cheat on me?' I asked, my words left my mouth in a sigh, not a shout. Her eyes opened wide like a rodent in fear. I'd taken her off-guard. The shouting she had expected—constructed armour for—but she hadn't expected I'd resign so rapid. She simply shook her head, so I asked again. When she didn't answer the second time, I rose, deliberately dragging my chair against the floor beneath me. My plate caught the flick of my hand as I moved, and it crashed to the floor.

'It only happened once,' she said, tears streaming from her face. I looked her in the eyes and told her she was a liar; said I could never believe her. I told her to give me my key back and to never speak to me again. I made my way to the door, pulled it open and gestured with a fixed stare that she should leave.

'Please,' she begged. 'Please, William. I'm so sorry. Please don't make me go,' she said. There was no pity for her in my heart. Her fake tears wouldn't bend me over like they had in the past. I didn't care she cheated on me. I just wanted her out of my life.

'Just go,' I hissed. And when she was outside of my flat, she turned on the spot. To argue, or plead, or say goodbye. I didn't know. Before she could speak, I told her to give me back my spare keys. She rummaged through her handbag and clutched her hand around them. With a thrust, she launched them at me, then turned and walked away. The keys hit me in the chest, then dropped to the floor with a rattle. I closed and locked the door, then stood. It took me a while to move, to do anything, but eventually I did. I bent down and picked the keys up, examined them in my hand. Our relationship flashed across my mind. I conjured the image of us meeting. Our hands intertwined. Us drinking wine together. Arguing with her. Dancing under the sinking summer sun, her hands on my shoulders. So many echoes and recollections sailed around my head. I would have drowned in the memories if I wasn't careful. A quaver escaped me, and I slammed shut the door in my mind, locking those memories out. They weren't welcome anymore. I turned, and on the floor where the keys had lain, a glint caught my eye. In their place a shiny penny had been left behind.

14

. . .in for a Pound

The following Monday, I sat at my desk and tried to push everything to the back of my mind, but that proved impossible. There were so many thoughts back there, they couldn't help but spill front and centre. Over the weekend, Penny had called me an impressive ninety-four times. Each resulted in a voicemail; a plead, a cry, a beg for forgiveness. I deleted them relentlessly but more always arrived.

'This is all your fault,' she spat through the microphone. 'You did this to me. You made me like this.'

In the end, I did all I could do to lift the weight she put on me: I blocked her.

When Grace called me later in the day to tell me I had a guest at reception, I made my way to the front desk with rising dread.

As expected, Penny stood tall and firm when I walked out of the elevator, greeting me with a lipstick smile as though nothing had happened.

'What are you doing here?' I asked, feigning chirpiness in my voice, conscious Grace was listening.

'You've been so busy lately. I thought we could go for lunch,' Penny said, mirroring the pretence of my tone. 'Truman just passed. He said you should take longer today.'

She couldn't hide the triumphant smile from her face. It hadn't occurred to me to warn people that we'd broken up, evidently a mistake on my part. She knew I wouldn't make a scene.

'Go on, Walters, take your girl for lunch,' Grace said.

I knew Penny was audacious, but I never appreciated just how conniving she was before. In her mind, there was a fickle line between morally questionable and socially acceptable. It seemed the more I tried to remove myself from her, the more the line blurred. I began to wonder what lengths it would take to be free of Penny.

We left the building together. As usual, she walked a fraction of a stride ahead of me, her ponytail swung from side-to-side, showcasing the pride of her victory. I couldn't have lunch with her, sit there playing my part in her delusional charade. I grabbed her arm and she twisted into me.

'You can't do this, Penny,' I said, shedding any reserved niceties. 'You don't get to show up unannounced. You don't get to leave voicemails. You don't get to play the part of the broken-hearted girl when you did what you did.'

'You kissed Caitlin,' she said. Deadpan.

'And I've apologised. It was one kiss, and if I could undo it—'

I stopped myself. *Would I really undo it?*

Would I really unkiss Caitlyn?

She seemed to read my thoughts. Her face broke from the character she played; her lip trembled in an unmanageable manner. And there it was, her heartache displayed for the world to see.

I did that.

I broke her.

My own heart sank.

'I'm so sorry, Penny,' I said. 'I'm sorry I did this to you.'

There was silence while she wiped away a falling tear from her eye. Unable to meet my stare, she looked towards the sky, then settled on something beyond my vision. She truly believed she was the sun in her own little universe, and that everything revolved around her. That's why she thought she could do what she wanted. In leaving her, I believe I'd made her realise that the sun was just another star in the galaxy. One of millions. Without another word, she walked away. She sat on a kerb in a side road, looking like a shattered porcelain doll. To ease the blow, I joined her.

'Remember when we met?' I asked. She made a noise to show she was listening, even if she didn't want to be. 'Why were you at the doctors that day?'

So much time had gone by and I'd never asked, never brought it up. But the truth was there and I had turned a blind eye to it: Penny needed the psychological help we both walked away from the first day we met.

'I don't know,' she said, but sensing a pending rejection from me, she continued, 'Sometimes I just need someone to tell me I'm okay. Then I met you, and you were even more lonely and broken than I was. You didn't have anybody, or anything. You were just like me.' She paused to wipe away her tears and catch her quavering breath. 'How was I supposed to know I'd fall in love with you?'

I learned in that conversation, I could never save Penny. I couldn't change her or be what she needed. It wasn't my place.

Delicately, I took her hand and planted a kiss, but she pulled away.

'You changed,' she said. I sat up a little straighter. The accusation a throb in my heart. 'You found success. You're more confident now. It's like you got happy, and it had nothing to do with me. How am I supposed to live with that?'

I didn't—*couldn't*—answer. I stood and so did she.

'You need to move on,' I said. 'We both do.'

As I walked away, I refrained from looking back. If I did, I'd have given her false hope, and there was nothing more dangerous.

Re-entering the building, I soldiered to the security guard and instructed him to remove Penny from the guest list.

As I strode past Grace, she looked at her watch in confusion, but didn't speak.

'We broke up,' I said, without a second glance.

I arranged to meet Caitlyn in the British Museum after work. Arriving before her, I took a seat in the café and lost myself in a daydream, imagining how different life would have been if I'd asked her out before we graduated. The horrendous scraping of metal against tile pulled me back into reality. She wore a summer dress and had her hair in tight curls, which bounced as she took a seat. In front of me, she placed a disposable cup.

'It's tea,' she said. I thanked her as she tucked her backpack under the table. Without prompting, she delved into the details of her day, telling me she'd had a late lunch with her new friend, Amanda.

She'd been in the city less than a month and already had friends. Soon, I knew, she wouldn't rely on me to keep her company. I was just an old acquaintance with nothing new to give.

'She just got engaged,' Caitlyn said.

'Who?' I asked.

'Amanda. Her boyfriend proposed in Rome, by the Trevi fountain.'

I bit my lip, nodded. I didn't want to feel bitter or taint the evening with heartache, but I wasn't in the mood to hear about strangers in love.

'We broke up,' I said quickly. 'Me and Penny.'

Caitlyn reached over, cupped her hand around my own. Compared to mine, it seemed so small.

Her face was apologetic as I told her everything that had happened.

'To be honest, William, it sounds like you've dodged a bullet,' she said. It didn't feel like it. It felt like a bullet had ripped through my flesh and lodged itself inside my heart.

'This might make you feel better,' she said, and picked up her backpack. She pulled out a pink, leather-bound diary I recognised instantly.

'You still have this,' I said in awe, taking the book from her. She nodded, almost guilt-ridden, as I flicked through the pages. My grandmother's handwriting filled the diary, along with glued down photographs and doodles of her adventures.

'I also have this.' She pulled out a second, thinner and newer diary. 'We should keep Jo's diary as it was, and write our own adventures in here. I already started.'

I opened the new diary and couldn't help but smile. Caitlyn had copied the unfinished items of the bucket list on the first page, but had left room for more items to be added. The next few pages detailed the adventures of our summer together. It was rejuvenating to focus on something that wasn't Penny.

'This is incredible,' I said. 'So thoughtful.'

'I left enough space for us to add our own things if we ever wanted to.' She blushed, drew her eyes from the diaries to me.

'What would be on your bucket list?' I asked.

'I don't know,' she shrugged. 'Kids, marriage, I guess. I haven't really thought about it. That's what makes Jo's so special. She put so much consideration into everything.'

'She was like that,' I said, and tried to imagine myself picking up a baby, claiming it as my own, but my mind slid into darker places. I saw a father shouting, a mother drinking. I shook the memories away like cigarette smoke. There was so much evil in the world. I couldn't comprehend how anybody could want to bring life into it.

'Where do we start?' I asked.

'Well. . . we *are* in the museum, and it just so happens Jo wanted to visit every single one in the country.' She leafed through Jo's diary to show me a broken down, bulleted list of every museum. There were a lot of things left undone. If Caitlyn was serious about finishing the list, we'd be spending a lot of time together.

The British Museum is a large and pristine building. We begun our expedition by exploring the ground floor and worked our way upstairs to the narrower exhibitions.

I was reading about Roman coins when a flicker in the glass case caught my eye. Turning, I saw a trail of yellow cloth, an article of clothing, I thought—a coat or a cardigan—disappear behind a cabinet. The lights were dim, and suddenly I felt very vulnerable. I walked, on tiptoes for some reason, to the container, throwing a glance back at Caitlyn. Seemingly unaware, she studied a passage on Seneca the Younger. There was nothing behind the case, so I crept along a passageway of ancient artefacts, unable to shake the feeling I was being watched. Arriving at a fork in the displays, I carried on through the central path, disappearing further into history's maze. Through glass, I saw a blaze of loosely flowing yellow material again and instinctively I turned, reached out, as though to grab the fabric. My hand clasped nothing but air. A clanging noise filled the space around me. The sound of a coin landing on a tiled floor. I turned and saw that under the spotlight, sat a shiny penny.

I crept forwards and picked it up.

'What have you got?'

I screamed louder than I should have. Jumped too. Even though I knew the voice belonged to Caitlyn. She found it funny and crippled over. Her heavy touch on my shoulder sent a shiver down my spine. I didn't want to worry her, so I said nothing, but clung to her side as we meandered through the rest of the exhibitions in the museum, still unable to shake the feeling we were being watched.

All the way home I craned my neck, stealing glances, certain I'd catch someone following me, unsure what I'd do if they were. When I arrived at my flat, there was a single red rose taped to the door. I peeled it off, pricking my finger on one of the sharp thorns. Thick globules of blood pooled on my finger, then dripped to the floor. I swore as I unlocked the door and made my way inside.

In the kitchen, I ran my finger under the cold water and wrapped a plaster around the damage, momentarily forgetting I'd been worried about being watched. I poured a glass of water from the filter jug in the fridge, then took a seat and messaged Caitlyn to ask if she'd got home okay.

As I waited for her response, my eyes grew painfully heavy and drew together, binding as though glued shut.

Through my eyelids, shadows flickered around. Terrified and alarmed, I tried to pull myself up, but that proved impossible. I had no energy to do anything except fall into the darkness surrounding me.

When I woke in the morning, I lay still for a very long time, feeling heavy and groggy, as though I'd been pulled from the depths of more than just a dreamless slumber. Unsure of myself, I sat up, completely forgetting about dancing shadows and my unnatural pull into sleep.

I dragged myself out of bed and made my way to the kitchen, feeling like a living mannequin. After strong coffee, I forced myself to get ready for work and before I left for the day, pulled open my curtains. On the window ledge, on the inside of the flat, sat a row of shiny pennies.

I left a message with Grace. Said I'd be late for work because I wasn't feeling well. In reality, I was waiting for a locksmith. Changing the locks was easy. Getting rid of Penny was proving to be the hard part. Did I really think she was capable of coming into my flat when I was asleep? Or worse, when I was out? I feared the answer and as a precaution, poured the filtered water down the drain.

I didn't even have her number anymore - I'd deleted and blocked her, so I couldn't call to tell her off. She'd have loved that anyway - it would have supplied the attention she craved.

Caitlyn gasped over the phone when I told her what had happened.

'Are you sure it was Penny?' she asked.

'Positive,' I said.

'You need to go to a hospital,' Caitlyn said. 'You could have anything in your system.'

'I can't,' I said. 'I need to get to work. Besides I feel fine. I'm sure nothing happened. Penny's just a tad . . . unhinged at the moment.'

She wasn't happy with my protests, but didn't argue. She told me to meet her outside Waterloo station that night, and even with everything going on, I took comfort in the thought that we were growing close again.

After a long day filled with copious cups of coffee and time-critical cases at work, I left to meet Caitlyn. As I walked the length of Southwark Street, I found myself almost constantly checking over my shoulder, certain I'd find Penny following me. That was the worst thing about her. I saw her everywhere, all the time. Always a flicker in the corner of my eye. Walking through the streets. A body in a window. A gleam in a passing bus. Waiting. Watching. In crowded places, I grew convinced her outstretched fingers would creep through the space between other people and latch onto me.

In my visions, she looked at me through hurt eyes.

Her pain a cry so loud and true it stained the skies grey. Her hand welded an impossibly sharp knife, her knuckles white as bone around the handle. Her nails red as the blood she was out for. Her empty eyes fell on my own as she plunged the knife into my skin, puncturing my arteries. Blood would spurt and as I fell to the ground, small wails of disbelief and pain would escape me. I'd try to apply pressure to my own split skin, but it wouldn't be enough. The hole left behind would burn, but I'd shiver from the cold as fiery ice shot through my veins.

The look of pleasure over the wicked features of her face would be the last thing I ever saw.

I'd imagined my death so many times the concept no longer shocked or scared me. Usually, it was always my own doing: a pill, a rope, a train. But never like how I imagined it in that state of mind.

Never by the hand of another.

I shook the thoughts away, and crossed to Stamford Street. Walking along, a quarter of the London Eye appeared, along with the OXO tower, both lighting up the darkening sky. As I neared the roundabout at the end of the road, I saw the police had blocked off the pavement, so I took a right onto the deserted Cornwall Road. There was no-one around, and yet I was convinced someone was watching me. Quickening my pace, I turned left onto Upper Ground speed-walking past the back of the National Theatre. That's when I spotted her out of the corner of my eye. I ran into the underpass then stopped in the dank, darkly lit tunnel. A man stood, urinating by a pillar. A witness, I thought, as I leaned against the brick wall to catch my breath and calm my nerves. No signs of Penny. Had I imagined her? Perhaps she hadn't seen me.

The man finished, threw a glance at me, and wandered off. I continued through the tunnels. High-heels clopped in thunderous echoes around me, and when I stole a glance backwards, I saw a gaggle of girls had come down the stairs. They turned left in the underground labyrinth.

I walked through the tunnel in the direction of Waterloo Station, wondering when and how my fear would ever go away. As I neared the end of the passage, a silhouette cut the bright lights shining between two pillars. The stance of a powerful woman leaning with a hand on her hip. Heart racing, I stopped dead, considered running back, but it was too late. I carried myself one step forward. The forest-green dress she wore was short with a sizeable bow fashioned onto her left shoulder. Her blonde hair was pinned in large, bunching curls to the right side of her head. She also took a step forward and I saw her in a less blinding light. I'd been very wrong about who was following me.

'You destroyed my marriage,' she spat.

'Kimberly,' I said, my heart thumping.

'You little twerp.' She took another step closer and struck me across the cheek. I almost lost my footing, but caught myself against the wall. My face stung.

'It's not my fault you cheated,' I said, collecting myself. 'I'm not responsible for your actions.'

'Go to Hell,' she said, and stormed off, shouting obscenities and curses. Her furious words echoed around me, shrinking me in fear and pain.

I crumpled against the wall for a second time. My heart thumped in my chest. I was grateful to have only been slapped. It was Kimberly, not Penny, I'd seen by the National Theatre. She must have seen me disappear into the underpass and gone around to cut me off, to confront me - she hated me that much.

'Did you run here?' Caitlyn asked when I met her outside Waterloo Station, slightly late and very sweaty. I nodded and motioned at her to walk with me. Standing still felt too dangerous. As we crossed the main road and trotted down Sutton Walk towards the London Eye, I told her about Penny's latest antics and my run-in with Kimberly, skimming over my growing paranoia. Caitlyn inspected my face, said I was fine, and suggested I report Penny to the police. I reminded her there was no evidence Penny had done anything wrong. It isn't a crime to call someone or stick flowers to their door, and there was no proof she'd unlawfully been inside my flat. We turned the corner and the London Eye came in glorious full sight.

'But she's stalking you,' Caitlyn said.

Was she? She wasn't a masked man or a creepy internet loner. She was Penny. The woman I'd chosen to sleep next to for the better part of a year, suddenly and drastically out of control.

If love makes you crazy, broken hearts render you insane.

'Has she ever seen a doctor?' Caitlyn asked as we joined the queue. An echo of a memory slivered into my mind. I had a sudden impulse to run away. Not only from the conversation, but from Caitlyn herself.

'What's wrong?' she asked.

I'd never told anyone how Penny and I met. Mentally, I replayed the moment. Sitting in a run-down waiting room. Penny in a yellow rain-coat and me with my nervous disposition. I recalled the way our eyes locked. Until recently, I'd never asked her why she was in the waiting room that day and even though I'd always known, I never forced her to go and see a doctor. *Was everything my fault?*

'No,' I said finally. 'She never got help.'

Caitlyn's left eyebrow rose. Indicating she knew there was something I wasn't telling her. If I didn't say something quickly, she'd poke and prod until I broke.

'I knew she needed help though,' I added. Mostly true.

I was the reason she never got it.

'You can't blame yourself,' she said. Evidently my thoughts were strewn across my face.

The memory of our meeting was in screaming technicolour playing on loop in my mind. We were *both* supposed to get help. We had distracted each other so much we'd forgotten we were broken. Penny was much better at hiding things than I was, and until then, I thought she was okay.

We reached the front of the queue. Walking past, the London Eye had always seemed nothing more than a giant Ferris wheel, but standing underneath looking up, I could take in the enormity of it. Caitlyn flashed our tickets and we moved forward.

'I can't believe you've lived here so long and never done this,' she said as we shuffled along. The conversation about Penny slipped away as quickly as it had arrived.

'It's never appealed to me before.' I moved forward. The ride had made it's way onto Jo's bucket list, and I welcomed the distraction from real life.

We edged into a moving pod with strangers. Being a weekday after work, the landmark was busy but we weren't crammed. Caitlyn made her way to the far glass wall to look at the other famous landmarks across the city. If I was the kind of person whose breath could be taken away, the views would have taken my breath away. They were spectacular. Soaring in the heart of the city and watching the buildings light up around us was both incredible and inspiring. So much happens every day and usually, I passed through each hour oblivious to the beauty around me, but from up there, I could see everything, take it all in.

'It's stunning, isn't it?'

I recognised the northern accent immediately. It wrapped around me like a python. Slowly, I turned. Sweat broke from my brow, my palms, the back of my neck. The hairs on my arms shot up, like soldiers standing to attention, ready for war. I stepped backwards, knocked my head on the curve of the pod. My rabbit heart pounded in my chest. The world seemed to be slipping around me, or maybe it was me who was slipping from the world.

Caitlyn didn't notice because she was too busy shrieking excitedly. She wrapped her arms around the person who had spoken, around Penny, pulling her in for hugs and air kisses.

'It is beautiful,' she agreed when their shrieking excitement dimmed. I looked from Penny to Caitlyn wondering what was going on.

Had they been in cahoots all along?

Out to get me?

'What are you doing here?' I asked Penny, rather flat.

'William,' Caitlyn announced, superficially embarrassed by my venomous tone. 'This is my friend, Amanda. The one I was telling you about.' Caitlyn turned to Penny. 'What are you doing here?' Though she echoed my words, her tone was friendlier.

Dumbfounded, I couldn't speak. Couldn't move. Penny stole the opportunity and spoke for me.

'I'm being a tourist,' she said, lacking gravitas.

Realisation hit hard. I'd only ever spoken about Penny, had never showed Caitlyn a picture. There was no way for Caitlyn to know the identity of the woman standing in front of us.

'Caitlyn,' I said. My voice sounded more stable than my legs felt. 'That's Penny. That's my ex.'

'No, it's Amanda,' Caitlyn said, almost as a reaction. When my words sunk in, she relentlessly faced Penny with a furrowed brow.

'No. It's Penny,' I said. 'She lied to you.'

Caitlyn looked to Penny for clarification but didn't get any. Penny simply shrugged, as though borrowing an identity was no big deal. Caitlyn's mouth dropped open. The thought of being lied to, of being manipulated, so far out the reach of her imagination.

'Why would you lie?' she asked in vain.

'Because that's what she does,' I said to Caitlyn. Turning to Penny, I asked how she got in our carriage. 'You weren't even in the queue,' I said.

'I was,' she replied.

She wore the self-defence of a liar caught red handed. There was no obvious weapon on her, but I wouldn't have put it past her to have one tucked away up a loose sleeve or hidden in the lining of her bra. I thought of her striking Caitlyn with a jealous blow, and knew I somehow needed to create distance between them.

'Penny,' I said, continuing with razor sharp words, 'please go stand at the other side of the pod. Please, leave me alone.'

'You lied to me,' Caitlyn finally said, looking to Penny for an explanation.

The round features of Penny's face drooped to the point where they sagged.

'I needed to see her. My replacement. She's so pretty,' she said. The way she looked at Caitlyn worried me: with dangerous wide eyes, so full of wonder, intrigue and distaste. A lethal combination. A hot flush of anger swept through my body. She was *always* there. Always in the way. Always creeping around a corner or showing up unannounced, leaving notes, voicemails, and inexplicable pennies. It had to stop.

'She didn't replace you,' I said with a sigh.

'How do you just switch off love?' she asked.

'It didn't switch off,' I said carefully. 'It expired.'

Penny's eyes widened, her movements small and twitchy. Her self-destruction simultaneously baffled and angered me. On one hand, I felt sorry for her. On the other, I hated her. 'We haven't cared about each other for a very long time,' I added in agitation, refraining to highlight that she was the one who had cheated in the first place.

'Expired?' she repeated. 'Like milk?' she threw her hands into the air, drawing attention to herself.

'I didn't mean it like that,' I said, keeping my voice low, conscious the people around us were looking our way.

'Did you ever love me?' she asked, scrunching her face in pain and desperation. Caitlyn held her hands up between us. If it was in attempt to diffuse the situation, she failed drastically.

'I think you guys need to relax,' she said. 'Maybe go for a coffee when we're on the ground and talk things through. It might be good to have closure.'

She placed a gentle hand on each of our arms, sending a small jolt of electricity across my skin. Penny pulled herself away as though she'd been shocked.

'Nobody asked for your opinion,' she spat.

Caitlyn, who had only ever experienced warmth from strangers, looked horrified.

Welcome to Penny's wrath.

'Why don't you care?' Penny howled. 'Why don't you care that you're breaking my heart?'

'You cheated on me,' I said. 'You think I don't care about that?'

I trembled, hyper-aware the people around us had stopped pretending they weren't listening. There was a moment of silence. I didn't know whether Penny would attack me, shout at me, or burst into tears. Traces of fury disappeared from her face. She flipped back to being innocent and broken.

'I didn't cheat on you,' she said, her tone matter of fact. Was she pretending it never happened? Or did she truly believe her own lies?

I didn't want to argue, to engage, but she had already drawn me in. She still had that effect on me.

'You're killing me, you know that?' she asked, 'you're gallivanting all over London with *her* like you never cared about me at all. About us.'

A flicker of pain flashed across her face. I saw then that she wouldn't hurt me, that she was just bruised and broken, unable to move on. Then I remembered to never underestimate the power of a broken heart. There was no telling what revenge she'd want.

'I still love you, William.'

'Our relationship should have ended long before it did,' I said as gently as I could. 'We both made mistakes, but we both checked out months ago.'

'No, please,' she pleaded. Her body twisted, it seemed to only dawn on her that she was sitting in the ruins of our relationship.

'This needs to stop,' I said, harsher than intended. 'No more flowers, no more letters, no more following me. This ends now, okay?'

'You're ending us?' she asked.

I stared at her for a second. In my head, I prayed Caitlyn would intervene again, somehow save me. How could Penny not read what I was putting in front of her?

How had I been with her for so long and never seen any warning signs?

'We're the same you and me, William. Don't you see that?' She sidestepped so she was in front Caitlyn and forced her hands into my own. I tugged free.

'It's so easy for you to move on while I'm still hurting.' She scowled at Caitlyn who was patient enough to stay silent. I was not so understanding. We reached the peak of our journey in the wheel.

'I don't know how to say this any clearer,' I gritted my teeth. 'I just want you to go away.'

There was confusion in her eyes. I felt my face grow red. The strangers around had fully tuned into our conversation like it was an evening soap. They watched our to-and-fro with faces of concern and discontent. I wanted everything to stop, but Penny lived for the drama. She needed it to breathe.

'I can't live without you,' she said.

'Well, you're going to have to,' I replied, smirking at the ridiculousness of the situation.

'I'll die, William,' she said.

'Then go die then,' I responded coolly.

It was easy to be cruel knowing she wouldn't let the words sink in. Her armour of psychosis protected her. She began to cry and to my surprise, she wiped her tears away quickly instead of showing them for sympathy to the surrounding crowd.

A tourist, a burly middle-aged woman lay her judging eyes on me. She approached Penny as though she were a wounded animal and with gentle earnest, wrapped an arm around her.

'Be careful,' I spat, 'that one bites.'

Caitlyn slapped my arm and the tourist scowled at me. They didn't need to, I knew I shouldn't have said anything.

'He's so mean,' Penny cried in a high-pitched voice, basking in her newfound pity. Just like that, I'd become the bad guy. I muttered an apology and the crowd dispersed.

'She's only going to keep going, you know?' I whispered to Caitlyn. There was no escaping her. It would never end, I'd spend the rest of my life looking over my shoulder wondering where she was, if she was watching me. And if not me, someone else?

To stop my shaking hands, I clenched the handrail, focused on the world outside the glass. Words, both said and unsaid, raced through my mind. If I could change it all, I would have. But the spoken word can never be taken back.

Caitlyn led me away from the crowds when we landed on the ground. We walked along the river in silence until we reached Shakespeare's Globe, where I finally apologised.

'You don't need to—'

'No, I do. I'm not proud of how I've handled things,' I said.

She nodded. Understanding as a saint. 'I don't think any less of you,' she said, 'it's been a long week and she's tested you. People say all sorts of things they don't mean when they're tired or angry. She knows that.'

I nodded, less sure of myself.

Caitlyn was right, but that didn't take the looming guilt away.

The argument replayed over and over in my mind later that night. I lay in bed creating impossible scenarios and new conversations, wondering how I could make things better - apologise without leading Penny on.

My doorbell rang, and my heart sank. I held my breath, as though this would indicate I wasn't home. Three sharp knocks on the door followed.

'This is the police.'

I dropped my thoughts, gathered myself and made my way to the door where I stole a glance through the peephole. Two officers stood on the other side of the door. I pulled it open and welcomed them inside.

They had come to confirm there was no taking back what I'd said. There was no undo and there would never be a do-over. It was already too late for that.

Penny Heart had killed herself.

15

Gone

Could I have done more?
Is it my fault she's dead?
If I'm not responsible for her actions, am I culpable for her choices?
Was I a catalyst in her death?
What more could I have done?

16

Aftermath

Proving himself once again to be the nicest human on the planet, Alex came to London to spend time with me. He was there for me when Jo died. And there he was again. Sometimes I wondered what I'd done to earn his friendship. He sat opposite me in my kitchen. The silence between us burned my ears. The smell of scorched coffee filled my nostrils, made me want to throw up. He checked his phone, rose from the table without a word, and made his way to the front door. I stared at my phone, willing it to ring. It never did, not like it used to. He came back into the room followed by Caitlyn. She greeted me with a gentle hug, and I pulled her in close, knowing it couldn't last and not wanting it to either, for everything I touched surely died. When she pulled away her presence lingered. The tiny hairs over my body clung onto her.

'How are you?' she asked.

I shrugged, unable to bring myself to look into her gorgeous eyes. There was no need for honesty. No reason to lie. Since the funeral, my final argument with Penny ran through my head on constant loop. Over and over and over again. I analysed each word as they echoed around, twisted them inside out and turned each of them over. Guilt consumed me like a fire, sizzling away, blistering my skin and charring my core, but there was something else there too, buried in the embers. An emotion so unwanted I could barely even bring myself to acknowledge it.

Relief.

Did that make me a monster?

I hadn't wrapped the noose around her neck but was I accountable for her demise?

It was her lies that caught up with her in the end, not my words.

Her lies, always so well-crafted and polished. She presented them so well, and people were always delighted to hear them. As a consequence, they adored the drafted version of herself she presented to the world, and that's what drove her to insanity. All she ever wanted was to be loved, but her desire for admiration ultimately destroyed her. Because of her lies, she had gone home and wrapped a rope around her neck as though it were a tie.

And all because of me. I had been warned, threatened, held to ransom. I told her to do it.

I told her to die.

Tears formed in my eyes. I shrugged again, wiped them away. Reality had set, hard as stone. Death is final. Death is forever. And Penny died thinking I didn't care about her.

But I was free from her and that's what I wanted, wasn't it?

In freedom, I learnt the cost of what you say is the greatest price to pay for your actions. I wanted to tell everybody who wished me well that I wasn't a victim; not the boyfriend left behind, but I couldn't find the words. Instead, I found myself remaining quiet, incapable of speaking out.

The silence between us was broken when the buzzer rang almost an hour after Caitlyn arrived. Alex answered the door again. When he came back, Truman sulked timidly behind him. He poked his head around the door frame as though checking the kitchen was safe to enter. He quietly asked Alex to make him a coffee and traipsed towards me. Greyed stubs of hair poked from his chin at wild angles. Heavy bags lay under his eyes. He placed a careful hand on my back.

'How are you coping?' he asked, his voice much deeper than usual.

Question of the week.

'Surprisingly okay,' I lied. He was the only person in the room who didn't know how desperate Penny had been in her final weeks. I hadn't briefed my friends, but I hoped they'd keep their mouths shut. She didn't deserve to be rendered as crazy or insane.

'How's the office?' I asked. Truman had forced me to take compassionate leave. He shuffled, leaned against the windowsill and took his coffee from Alex with a muttered thanks.

'Quiet,' he said. No mention of new cases or promotions. My chances of those gone for the foreseeable future. 'This is tragic,' he said, more to himself than the table. His words didn't hold their usual weight. 'Were there any signs?'

I'll die, William.

Then go die then.

His hazel eyes searched the room for answers. There was no official reason. No note. No final goodbye or explanation. When his eyes settled on me, I thought, that's right, Truman: *I am the reason she died.*

'No,' I said. 'None.' Then to change the topic, I quickly thanked him again for giving me the time off, which was purely a formality since I wanted to be at work. It would have been better than sulking at home, regretting the past.

'Not at all.' Truman shook his head, tried to smile. His lips seemed smaller, traces of what once was there. 'I can't imagine it, Walters. I really can't. Committing suicide. Such a waste.'

'A waste?' Alex asked, unable to resist such a cue.

'Yes,' Truman said, looking at his fidgeting hands as though they could answer for him.

'I've thought about it a lot. I can't stop thinking about it, actually. She had so much . . . *oomph*. Remember William, she came to the office that morning . . . she seemed so happy . . . was it all just a lie?' As an afterthought, he turned to Caitlyn and added, 'you know, I've always seen William as a son. It was selfish to leave him like that.'

I had no idea he held me in such high regard. Before I could say anything, Alex spoke.

'Taking one's life isn't a selfish act at all,' he said, quite disgruntled. 'She battled internally with her mental health and came to the decision that she'd rather not be here than fight another day. To decide that must have been impossible and draining and exhausting. It's not fair to call her selfish. It's not selfish to be so desperate you truly believe there's only one way out.'

Holding my breath, I shot Caitlyn a distressed look, but she didn't see, for she was dabbing her eyes with a tissue. I expected Truman, the lawyer, to argue against Alex, the bulldog for the underdog. Neither would back down for a case they believed in. Truman leaned forwards, propped his chin in his hand with his elbow firmly planted on the table.

'You're right,' he said. 'The world's such a horrendous place, and we're awful to each other. We fight over politics, we break hearts and we lie, and cheat, and steal.' He looked around at his audience. 'How do you stop from drowning in the pain?'

Grace had told me the divorce had affected him, but I was only just seeing it with my own eyes.

'You don't forget to live,' Alex replied, resounding what Jo had once said to us. 'You stop and appreciate the small things in the present.'

Truman nodded.

'I used to say if you were anxious take a pill and get over it. I used to think the worst thing to do could be to give in to depression, to stew in your own pity. But now . . . everything's different.' Truman fell silent, a shadow fell over his thoughts. 'How do we fix a broken world?'

He shoved the tip of his pinkie between his lips, clamped down and bit what remained of his nail, something I'd never seen him do before.

'I think we educate,' Alex said. His eyes found me, as though he were searching for permission to go on. I nodded my head a fraction, like it mattered, and he continued. 'Small steps to begin with. For example, you said she *committed* suicide, but suicide hasn't been a crime in this country for almost five decades.'

'People are so afraid of mental health,' Caitlyn chimed, 'because they don't know enough about it. A person suffering from a psychosis is more likely to harm themselves than someone else.'

Speaking it through made things seem so simple. Penny had sought help from a doctor, but hadn't seen it through, and the system never chased her. There was a crack in the system and she never got help because she could pretend she was fine. People who can function, who can hide their illnesses, slip through all sorts of cracks all the time.

I slipped through the same cracks in the same system.

The realisation hit me like a train. I couldn't be mad at the doctors for not diagnosing me when I hadn't been wholly honest in the first place. The stool beneath me seemed to wobble, as though it was going to eject me. Before it could, I excused myself from the table. The cumulative weight of opinions sat heavy in my head, giving me a rush of vertigo. The walls slanted and twisted. Gasps left the table as I stumbled.

'I just need to lie down for a second,' I said, ignoring their worried pleas. I went to my bedroom and collapsed on the bed.

I couldn't bring myself to sit when there was a tap on my door a moment later. I grumbled something: a combination of 'come in,' and 'go away.' The knocker pushed the door open. For a second, I imagined Penny coming in, perching beside me, and running her hand through my hair the way I liked. My eyes followed Caitlyn as she walked across the room. When she sat beside me the old mattress springs creaked beneath us. Slowly and gently, she caressed the skin over my arm with her nails. I watched her gaze trail over the two tall piles of boxes by my wardrobe. Stuffed animals and diaries poked out.

'It's some of Penny's things,' I explained, my eyes falling on her cat calendar sitting open on my desk. It was, and would forever, be stuck on May.

'Truman seems to be really affected by this,' said Caitlyn.

'I think the divorce is hitting him hard,' I replied.

'Poor soul,' she said. 'It's not your fault, you know. None of this is.'

'I'm the one who told him his wife was having an affair . . . I'm the one who told her to die.' My voice cracked but I'd already run out of tears.

'You said a stupid thing because you're a stupid boy. That's not what made Penny decide to end things. You're not God, William - you're not responsible for anybody else's life. Or death.'

I smiled through my pain. There was a truth in her words and a comforting authority in her voice. She stopped caressing me and twisted away. Her touch lingered like a ghost.

'You couldn't save her, William,' she said. 'It wasn't your job to.'

I thought about my parents. Imagined, as I had a million times before, their final moments on Earth; the crash of metal, the stink of burning like gun powder in the air, the rain of shimmering glass around them. I thought of Jo, who had worn such a face of pain when she collapsed at my graduation, who had clutched at her heart as it broke it her chest. I thought of Luke, remembered the prescriptions I'd found in his medicine cabinet. The secret battle he fought. The pain over Truman's face when he learned his wife was having an affair. The glimmering scars that shone on Penny's arms.

Death is a promise which never breaks.

'What if it's me?' I asked.

What if I was addicted to pain and chaos?

Caitlyn jolted her head back to look at me with sorrow-filled eyes. She brought her hand back to my arm, and for a second, everything seemed okay.

'Everything I touch dies,' I said, fearing no amount of time would mend the pain that Penny left behind. Caitlyn let my words hang in the air. Because she didn't know what to say, or perhaps because there was nothing to say, I couldn't tell.

'*I* haven't,' she replied simply. 'It breaks my heart to see you like this.'

She bent her neck so that she was staring down. As though the weight of her broken heart anchored her. After a lifetime, she kissed the tips of her index and middle fingers then placed them firm on my lips. When I kissed them back, she returned them to hers and kissed them again.

'What was that?' I asked.

She shrugged. 'A paper kiss,' she said with the hint of a blush spreading over her cheeks.

I furrowed my brow and felt a smile break over my face. I'd never heard of it before, was certain she'd made it up, but it was sweet, and gentle and most importantly: it was ours. Light and airy, her love carried from her to me in the form of a paper kiss.

I pulled myself into a sitting position and she rested her head on my shoulder. I was no longer naive about the world. Caitlyn was flirting with me, and I knew it. Penny and I had been drawn together because the world had broken us. Maybe Caitlyn was in my life for a reason too.

'Do you ever think about us?' she asked.

All the goddamn time.

'What do you mean?' I asked, squeezing my fingers deep into my pillow.

'Like, as a couple.'

'What are you asking?' I writhed uncomfortably.

'We'd be a great couple,' she said.

I couldn't bring myself to look at her as thoughts of Penny raced through my mind. If Caitlyn broke in the same way Penny had, I'd never survive.

'Caitlyn—'

'—don't. It's stupid. Forget I said anything.' She got up and marched across the room. I threw my head into the pillow as she left.

I walked back into the kitchen and apologised to Truman and Alex for running out, but my rudeness was waved off immediately. Caitlyn stood with her back to me, boiling the kettle and arranging mugs.

'What have you been discussing?' I asked.

Truman turned bright eyed, holding his phone in the air. On the screen, I could see he'd looked up sponsorship for local events.

'I want things to change,' he said. 'I've thought it through, and at the firm, we're going to start a mental health campaign - in Penny's name, of course. I'm going to arrange something, a sky-dive or a marathon of sorts. We can do it annually, so we never forget. And once a week, or once a month, we'll partake in a wellness day to support each other. Otherwise, life passes by and we miss the good things. And what will it all have been for?'

The idea of doing something for a cause left me a little less hopeless, and the feeling seemed mutual around the room. Truman announced he'd have to take off, and as a parting note, turned to me with a heaviness spread across his face, and said: 'You grow from this, Walters.'

In the passing weeks, Truman stuck to his word. He was no longer a man who formed opinions of people based solely on what they brought to the table, a trait I had personally benefited from on several occasions. The new Truman listened to people, really hearing what they had to say, taking time to learn about the decisions they made and why. On Wednesdays, we finished work early, regardless of cases in hand and traipsed to a yoga class or a mindfulness lecture. After Grace profusely protested to throw herself out of an airplane, Truman instead arranged for associates at the firm to run in the London Marathon supporting mental health charities.

My practice for the big run grew into a routine, where I would meet Caitlyn each morning before work and together we'd run laps of Southwark park, followed by coffee and a goodbye hug. Neither of us brave enough to bring up the conversation Caitlyn had started in my bedroom.

Each Thursday afternoon, my colleagues and I jogged lightly around the city, finishing the evening off with dinner and wine in a small Italian restaurant not far from the firm.

There was a slight chill in the air on the morning of the marathon and the winds threatened to bring a light drizzle down from the north. I threw up after breakfast. I'd trained and practiced, but I wasn't ready to race. My stomach churned and contracted in protest as raw bile burned my throat. No amount of preparation could have readied me for the day ahead. Still, I persevered. The Tube was crowded beyond belief, and finding Caitlyn outside Maze Hill station, where neither of us had ever been before, was a miracle at best. She had come wearing her sports attire, despite not actually running in the race. Somehow, she'd managed to dodge that bullet. In her hands she carried a polaroid camera, and the maroon diary containing our personalised version of Jo's bucket list. She snapped my picture, and we found Truman who was elevated by the atmosphere around us. She took another picture and wished me luck with a hug, then disappeared into the swarming crowd.

In the chaos of it all, I shuffled to my starting place between other runners, losing sight of anyone I recognised. As they often did, thoughts of Penny treacled across my mind but as I waited for the race to begin she fully preoccupied me. If it weren't for her, I wouldn't have been there. Truthfully, I missed her. Her drama. Her lies. Her smile. I missed it all. Gunshot blasted, and I ran. In taking off, I forgot about the dread and worry. I forgot about the pain of being alive. There was nothing to run from anymore. My mind cleared as the miles passed. Reading my name from my vest, spectators cheered me on. I threw smiles and waves as I crossed Tower Bridge, not thinking about Caitlyn until I reached Wapping.

Running back towards West London, I realised I had to bite the bullet and ask her out already. What was I waiting for anyway? She enjoyed my company and I needed to live my life. She flirted with, and supported me, even confessed she thought about us. *She loved me . . .*

My feet hit the ground, one after the other, carrying me towards her. I passed the finish line to a roar of celebration and ran straight into her arms. I didn't, couldn't, speak, but just held her, grabbed her face and planted a kiss on her lips. It lasted forever. It was over too quick.

'Caitlyn Donoghue,' I said, rather breathlessly, and before I could stop myself added, 'Be my girlfriend.'

She looked at me as a smile broke over her face. I wiped the hair from over her left eye, tucking it behind her ear and she bit her lip and nodded.

'Right,' I said, my face breaking into a smile. 'Well . . .' She leaned in and kissed my parted lips, interrupting my hesitation. When she pulled away, I laughed. 'What do we do now?' I asked, though I didn't need an answer, because for once, I was happy in the moment, right where I was.

Caitlyn thrust the camera into my hands, opened the diary to the newest entry and scored out the latest addition, *to run a marathon,* with a single red line. Tracing her her pen lightly across the page she stopped seemingly at random at another item on the list.

'We go to Italy,' she said with a smirk.

17

Mudslide

Caitlyn shielded her eyes from the sun as it beamed through the large airport windows. We'd arrived with enough time to have pre-flight drinks in the departure lounge, which was a cosmopolitan city of itself, with glamorous shops, coffee houses, an array of hot-desk workspaces and an eclectic mix of bars. We settled for a quiet upmarket place nestled close to the departure gates for an easy getaway when boarding began.

Luke asked Caitlyn about her job, unaware the topic was a sore spot for her. She said she was enjoying work despite it not being as fancy as our graduate jobs. I hoped Luke wouldn't push. Being related to her, he tended to get away with prying deeper than Alex and me.

'How's Truman coping?' Alex asked, removing the pressure away from Caitlyn. He took a sip of his pint.

'He's good, still obsessed with mental health. I had a meeting with him yesterday,' I said. Caitlyn's neck cracked as she shot a look at me.

'You didn't tell me you had a meeting,' she said. The accusatory tone in her voice sent panic across my heart.

'Sorry,' I said. 'I wanted to tell you, but we've been so busy between now and then.'

'Tell me what?' Caitlyn asked. I probably should have told her before, but it was too late now. I hadn't been able to find the way to announce the news naturally. It all seemed so random, quick, and a little too good to be true.

'He's selling me his house,' I said. Alex and Luke exchanged glances. Caitlyn wore a face of betrayal. Something I'd said or done had triggered her, and though I didn't know exactly what it was (and I doubt she did either) there was nothing worse than letting her down. With tones of confusion my friends pushed me to continue.

'He's giving it to me at an *unbelievably* super-discounted, *can't-turn-down*, rate,' I explained in caution, hoping to ease the blow.

'What?' Caitlyn hissed, 'how did that happen?'

'We talked about the firm, how he started it, how far he's come, and I told him I needed to grow up. One thing led to another and he offered to sell,' I said. 'Privately.' *Cheaply.*

'And you didn't think to tell your girlfriend,' Caitlyn said. Her eyes wandered to the ceiling, saying more than her words or tone. I apologised, but it wasn't enough. When I tried to explain myself, Luke interrupted, said this offer was an amazing opportunity that I couldn't let pass me by. Bitterly, Caitlyn agreed.

'Cheers,' Alex proposed, holding his glass in the air. 'To William and his new home. The world really does just open up for you, doesn't it?'

It didn't feel like it.

Caitlyn let out a high-pitched noise as our glasses clinked over the table. Alex grimaced. Luke avoided eye-contact. I could tell they found the situation awkward. I wished it had never been brought it up.

'Not the world,' Caitlyn said. 'Truman.'

'What's that supposed to mean?' I asked viciously. If Alex and Luke had something to say, they hid it well. *Did they think so too?*

'Every opportunity you've had has been because of Truman,' she said bluntly. She downed the contents of her glass. Beyond tipsy, and growing resentful. An explosive combination.

'I admit I have been lucky,' I forced a laugh and drained my own glass as tension grew thicker around the table. *Luck was not a trait I possessed.* I scanned Alex and Luke's expressions, but couldn't read their blank faces.

'I got to where I am—'

'—with a blend of hard work and a little bit of luck,' Alex butted in. His tone and fixating stare told me not to open my mouth again. I thought my friends would be happy for me, share in my success but they were angry and bitter, even jealousy had leaked into their tones. *How quickly they forgot what they had.* Did they not understand I'd trade those *lucky opportunities* in a heartbeat if it could mean waking up with family on Christmas day? I stopped myself from asking them. It was, after all, a purchase made with a combination of monies I'd inherited from the untimely deaths of my parents and grandmother as well as all my savings.

Luke welcomed the end of the conversation when our gate was called. He grabbed Alex by the hand and led him away.

'This decision affects me too, William. You'd think as your girlfriend I'd at least get to hear about it first.' She stormed ahead.

I opened my mouth to defend myself, but she was quick to join the departure queue and I didn't want to fight in front of anyone else. To busy herself, she played peek-a-boo with the child in front of us. The fence she'd built seemed to instantly dissipate. I'd never seen her so broody before.

'I'm sorry,' I said again. 'I should have told you.'

Technically I had, but she blushed, apologised too and hugged me. We'd survived our first lover's tiff.

'Plus, I really want to get out of my flat,' I said. 'Penny's been haunting me there. A change of scenery will do us good.'

She smiled at my deliberate use of the word us. In comparison to life with Penny, that disagreement was nothing but a blip on the radar. Penny would have dragged it on for days, if not weeks. Despite the practice, I still struggled to navigate unreasonable arguments so to lighten the mood, I made a joke about Caitlyn playing with the child. She reddened, showing a vulnerability I didn't know existed in her. To hide it, she pulled me in for a kiss.

We boarded the plane together, hand-in-hand, the way things were meant to be. For me, her mood was nothing to worry about. It's easier to snap at a lover than anyone else. I took it as a sign that we'd transitioned beyond the comfort of friendship and settled into a place of openness and love.

Previously, I'd imagined when our flight landed in Naples, we'd struggle to navigate the foreign streets and unusual public transportation. I foreshadowed angry rows with taxi drivers about money and arriving so late the hotel would be closed. In reality, things happened a lot smoother than I'd anticipated. Luke managed to form a bond with the driver who acted as a personal tour guide as he drove us across the city. He pointed in all directions shouting excitedly in a mixture of Italian and broken English. Luke, who could speak basic Italian, loosely translated facts about the best restaurants in the area, places to avoid, things we should see and where we should go.

We checked into the hotel with ease and dropped our bags off in our rooms, then took to the cobbled streets to explore the city. Agreeing we'd only have a couple of drinks that night, we settled in a bar tucked away in the corner of a central plaza where we watched late-night street performers. Music reverberated against old bricks as locals and tourists alike cheered them on. We settled the bill and headed back to the hotel.

The next morning, I awoke with sun pouring into the room through the open balcony doors. Caitlyn was outside leaning against the railings and talking on her phone. From context, I worked out it was her mum she was speaking to. The early morning breeze caught the delicate nightdress she wore, blowing the material in wisp-like waves. She turned to face me when she heard me yawn. As I stretched, she said goodbye to her caller and hung up the phone. She threw it onto the bed, then prowled towards me like a tigress.

'Coffee?' she asked, but before I could answer Alex's voice echoed around, bouncing in from the walls outside. Curious, we walked to the balcony and saw that he and Luke were waving to us from the street below. They wore matching denim shorts and similar vests in different bright shades. Once, Luke had been bulkier than Alex, but looking down at them, it was hard to tell them apart.

'Ready for a hike instead?' Caitlyn joked.

I was neither mentally nor physically prepared for what the day would bring.

We showered and dressed, then met Alex and Luke outside. Luke told us they'd bought water, snacks and food for a picnic-style lunch.

The Path of the Gods - *Sentiero degli Dei*, in Italian – got its name as it was believed to be the path the Gods took from Heaven, or Olympus, or somewhere—I missed that part of the story—to meet sirens in the Ocean. But even in mythology I couldn't accept that. No higher being would choose to trek hours along dangerous cliffs, no matter how beautiful the scenery.

We passed through small residential towns in the beginning, taking the leisurely walk in our stride, but grew secluded from locals as we progressed along the path, and eventually we found ourselves in deep hidden layers of the mountain. Frequently, Luke and Caitlyn stopped for selfies and scenic pictures, christening each occasion as a photo opportunity. Those were especially common in places where the sea was exposed, sparkling beneath us. I had preference for the moments where trees loomed overhead and glimpses of sunlight were rare, because it reminded me there's darkness in everything beautiful. In those areas their photos turned out underexposed and no good. We walked out of a shaded stretch, and came into a large rocky space where the mountain curved naturally to form what looked like a dragon's face with its tongue sticking out.

'Good place for lunch,' Caitlyn said. She steadied herself carefully on the rock formation and took a seat. Under the Mediterranean sun, she had a glow about her, and as she balanced on a rock, I leaned over and kissed her smooth cheek, basking in the perfection of the moment. Caitlyn blushed and ventured further out, almost transfixed in the beauty, as though the heavens were calling her home.

'I'm glad I took out travel insurance,' Alex said after I wobbled. He took his backpack off and climbed to join Caitlyn. I followed suit, trying not to focus on the seductive drop beneath us. *Wonderful holiday destination for someone with suicidal tendencies.*

To capture the moment, Luke set his camera's timer and balanced his phone haphazardly on a pile of nearby rocks. He told us to smile as he gathered us together for a picture.

'Does anybody hear that?' Caitlyn asked in alarm. We stopped talking, stopped moving. Faintly, somewhere above us, an animal cried.

'It's a kitten,' Luke stepped forwards and pointed. 'Look, up there.'

I squinted my eyes, shielding them from the sun. Strokes of ginger shone amongst the vivacious canopy greens. The animal wailed, it seemed, directly at us, as though it were trying to catch our attention.

'She's stuck,' cried Caitlyn.

Alex hovered frantically, looking for help from each of us, then hoisted himself onto the lowest branch of the tree, but it snapped under his weight. He flew backwards but managed to stabilise himself. Luke rushed to his side, but Alex swore he was fine. Expectant eyes locked on me.

'Me?' I asked.

'I'd break a bone if I tried.' Luke said.

'I can't climb,' Caitlyn said, her eyes wide with fear. Her arms flailing desperately. 'Please, William. She's so scared.'

As if agreeing, the cat meowed loud and sharp, cutting the debate.

'Right,' I exhaled and gripped onto the next branch, lifting myself up. The bark under my fingertips was flaky and dry, like a thick powder, and pieces crumbled onto my face. As I shifted my weight, the branch wobbled and bent threateningly, but didn't snap. Wrapping my legs around the trunk, I pulled myself upward again. The higher I climbed, the easier it became. Branches were thicker and closer together and—

'Lookout,' I shouted as a rotten branch came away with my weight. I managed to swing myself around the tree and save myself from falling. It was probably a bad omen to damage the woodland on a path which belonged to the Gods, but surely leaving a kitten to starve or burn was worse, so I continued to pull myself upward, taking my chances. As I climbed, the branches thinned and when I was close enough to reach out and grab the kitten, the tree wobbled with a gust of wind. It's all in your head, I told myself. *Just like the rest of your problems.* The kitten batted at me with its tiny paw when I reached across.

'Come here,' I said in my softest voice. 'I got you.' Like a human claw machine, I swooped the tabby with one hand and held it close to my chest. Razor sharp talons pierced my skin, but I didn't mind. Tiny purrs escaped from the kitten, which I took as a thank you.

As if climbing the tree in the first place hadn't been difficult enough, climbing down with a handicap in the form of a squirming kitten trying to burrow into my t-shirt was a whole new challenge. Close to the ground, I dangled it in the air, tiny legs flailing in protest, then plopped it gently into Luke's outstretched hands. I swung my weight and let go of the branch I clung onto, landing with a terrible pain in my feet. Alex fountained water into Caitlyn's cupped hands. She looked at me with eyebrows twisted upwards as the kitten lapped up the water she held.

'This wasn't on the list, but it definitely should have been,' she said.

I smiled, checking my body for signs of damage. My palms had grazed, and blood dotted the inside of my thighs where my skin had torn, but I'd live to see another day. Somewhere along my solo adventure, the skies had turned an angry gun-metal grey, so I suggested we call it a day and head back down the mountain. The decision was unanimous. The kitten, christened Ivy by Caitlyn, darted affectionately between our feet as we walked, slowly arching its back and affectionately wrapping her tail around our ankles.

'Was it supposed to rain?' Luke asked as heavy droplets of water fell from the sky. Alex said it wasn't, and then checked his phone, only to find he had no signal.

'I guess one of us annoyed the Gods,' he said.

Low thunder growled around us. From our height, it sounded as though we were in the stomach of a drum. The grumbling grew loud, livid and within seconds a downpour of rain cascaded over us. Like a switch had been flicked, we were engulfed in darkness until electrical streaks of lightning ripped across the clouds, turning the world around us purple and yellow. Ivy darted into the bushes and to no avail, Caitlyn threw her hands over her head. The rain was warmer than the English downpour I was used to, but I was drenched like never before. In a hurry to evade danger we scuttled down the path but the ground beneath our feet turned from solid muck into a rapid mudslide. A sharp scream of horror left Alex as he slipped into the devastation. His silhouette disappeared from my line of vision. I watched someone—I couldn't tell if it was Luke or Caitlyn—dart after him. I clung onto a tree, frozen in horror, the weight of fear anchoring me. Lightning flashed again and the sky pulsed like it was made of lasers. A hand wrapped around my wrist. Caitlyn's. She was crying, shivering. Then she was gone. I reached out, grabbed the air. She wasn't there. Another strike of lightning and I could make out her figure sliding through muck. She swished in and out of my vision. I shouted her name, but the rainfall carried her away. Fighting trembling legs, I went after her, careful not to fall victim to the landslide.

'Alex,' I shouted, grasping onto a figure by a thick tree.

'It's Luke,' he called back. 'Alex is hurt.'

Thunder grumbled again. Lightning struck and I could see Alex crouching on the ground. It was obvious he was injured. We're not going to make it out of this, I thought. I couldn't tell them Caitlyn was gone, couldn't voice it. I told Luke to hold onto Alex, to call for help and left them, knowing there was no way I could ever leave this mountain without Caitlyn by my side. I struggled to fight the resistance of thick murky water rushing past me. Each time I lifted my feet I sunk deeper into the ground, the gritty earth trying to swallow me whole. I called Caitlyn's name with a quaking voice. There was no response. She had evaporated into the mountain under the ballad of rain. *Into the mountain*, I wondered darkly, *or over it?* I trudged to the place where the earth met the edge of the world. Tried to shout, but unable to open my mouth. My lips trembled. Ready to give up, I caved in on myself. Then, in a bellowing roar, I screamed her name. Silence. I leveraged myself against a tree and leaned over, peering into the abyss. What would it feel like to fall? Would death bring peace, after all this time? Would it be everything I imagined it to be?

I put a foot over the edge, hovered in the air for a second and closed my eyes, ready for the end. Ivy appeared, clawing at my leg, as though a sign. Pulling myself back, I told the kitten to go away, to go find Alex and Luke. She stared at me innocently. If she meowed, I didn't hear.

Lightning struck again, and for a moment the world stilled, like I was in a picture. Then I heard her. Her scream, a harrowing noise carried through the trees, filling my ears in the way that water would have filled my lungs if I were drowning. *How close to the end I was.*

Ivy darted and a pulling in my stomach like a magnetic force told me to follow. Caitlyn wasn't far. Relief flooded my heart when I saw her. She lay in a heap on the ground on the other side of a small rope bridge. I called to her. She moved slowly, shouted my name. I footed the ground deliberately, treading carefully onto the bridge, knowing it could snap at any moment. Ivy watched as I swayed with the wind. Clasping firmly onto the rope handle, my thoughts turned to Penny. Is this what it felt like, I wondered, when she held the rope in her hands? Did her heart beat like mine? Or did she solemnly surrender her life with no fight? I thought about the way she must have dropped through the air. *Neck breaking on impact.*

Battling wind and rain, the rope craned under my weight and then gave way. Half of the bridge smacked the rocky mountain while the other half plunged into darkness and I leapt through the air. I landed with a thud, and clawed desperately at the solid muck beneath me, my legs dangling dangerously over the edge.

This, I thought, this is how I could go. I almost saw myself as though outside my body - like my spirit had left the physical restraint and I watched from above. In split seconds, I thought about dropping, contemplated giving up the fight. It would have been so easy to just cease existing.

For the first time in my life, dying seemed like a choice.

Before, I'd taken pills out of sheer desperation, as though there were no way out, no other options, but hanging over the ledge of the mountain top, I had a choice. I could pull myself up, or I could go.

'William,' Caitlyn groaned.

My leg kicked the side of the mountain, a rock broke free and fell.

'William?' Caitlyn called with enough panic in her voice that told me she had registered how perilous my situation was.

Caitlyn Donoghue. The woman who had changed my ending.

I hoisted myself up, climbed over the edge and crawled over to her.

'Are you okay?' I asked foolishly, not knowing what else to say, how to express my gratitude that she was alive.

'I'm fine,' she said, though her voice was raspy, weary.

'My ankle's stuck on this rope,' she said weakly.

I picked up the closest rock I could reach without moving and smashed it against the ground with the rope caught in between. Consumed with anger and guilt, I screamed and lashed at the horrific visions and the dark images in my head. I screamed, and hit. Screamed, and smashed. The rope eventually splintered and Caitlyn was freed. She wrapped her arms around me, and I held her tight.

'I told you that not *everything* you touch dies,' she said.

We both shook violently, but time halted in the precious way it can when you're holding onto a good thing. *We were safe.*

For a long time, we lay silent in each other's arms as the rain washed over us.

'Are you guys over there?' Luke called.

How much time had passed? The rain had stopped, and the late afternoon sun had broken through the clouds. Alex and Luke stood on a nearby peak with Ivy at their feet.

'Yeah,' I answered. 'Caitlyn's twisted her ankle and the bridge is gone. We need help.'

'Alex already called mountain rescue. They're on their way,' Luke said.

Mountain rangers and paramedics arrived and we were carried to the bottom of the mountain on stretchers. The paramedics checked us over, and deemed there was nothing severely wrong, but told us to take it easy over the next few days. The rangers, taking no pity, scorned us for not checking the weather, and for damaging the environment, cursing us in their foreign tongue. They drove off, leaving us to find our own way home. The bus stop wasn't far, and Caitlyn was able to walk but leaned heavily on me. Ivy stuck around while we waited, purring peacefully in Alex's lap.

When the bus arrived, we hobbled on, deflated and defeated. Caitlyn sank into my shoulder silently crying. I gave her hand a squeeze and kissed the crown of her head. I looked back towards the mountain through the window, giving a small nod to Ivy, who sat on the road, seeing us off. Internally, I thanked her for keeping us alive.

18

The Answer

At the end of summer, on a Saturday morning, Truman called to let me know the documents for the house were ready. He'd been so busy at work we'd barely had a chance to talk, but he wanted to exchange and give me the keys in person. I met him outside Raynor's Lane Underground station that afternoon. It was only mid-August, but the weather had already turned and there was a slight chill in the air. His Porsche idled as he waited in the pickup bay. Excited as I was, I couldn't help but wonder if I was making a mistake - the thing about those is that you don't usually know you've made them until it's too late. I swallowed my fears and made my way towards him. He greeted me with a flick of his fingers in a simple waving gesture. I climbed into the car and studied him. The sleeves of his light blue shirt were rolled up, his cream shorts shorter than anything I'd ever seen him in before. For the first time ever, his smile reached his ears.

'Ready?' he asked. I nodded and cranked the volume dial. Classical music burst from the speakers as he took off. I shoved my sunglasses onto my face to block out the sun we drove towards.

Driving faster than the law allowed, Truman raced out of the city and followed the familiar woodland roads which stretched on for some time. We arrived at the extensive gate and he grabbed a small, white, device from the cup holder between us. He clicked a button and the gates swung open obediently, welcoming me into my new life.

The house stood proud as ever at the end of the trailing driveway, basking under the mid-afternoon sun. I climbed out of the car and took in the supercilious building, not quite yet believing I was the owner.

With the lights off inside, it was impossible to see through the glass walls; instead, they tossed my reflection back at me in the most condescending of ways, reminding me just how small I really was. Truman dangled the keys in front of me like a carrot.

'She's all yours,' he said.

I waited for him to pull them back, for a wicked smile to spread in place of his generosity, but he never did. He dropped them onto my outstretched hand.

When I unlocked and pushed open the front door, people from all areas of my life stood around the entrance in a semi-circle, shouted 'surprise,' and it truly was. Caitlyn skipped over and threw her arms around me, kissed my cheek. She wore a yellow sundress, highlighting her glowing complexion. Grace followed, ruffled my hair. Luke and Alex stood by the fridge, toasted me with champagne glasses, and the celebrations began.

'You can tick *party-like-Gatsby* from the bucket list,' Caitlyn said an hour or two later. We stood in the kitchen alone, watching people drunkenly socialise in the garden. Truman had erected a marquee and had rented outdoor heaters. There was a full buffet and a self-serve bar. Office parties were always held there, and I knew I'd have to learn how to serve everybody else whilst still having a good time, as well as maintaining a relaxed appearance when I hosted in future. A tightrope I wasn't keen to tread, one Truman seemed able to walk over effortlessly every time. I wondered if he'd learned the skills, or if it was a trait the super-rich were inherently born with.

'Are *Gatsby* parties even on the list?' I asked, dismissing my fears.

'They might as well be, it's another one down,' she smiled, bit her lip and ran her finger around the rim of her glass. There was a gleam in her twinkling eye, but underneath I sensed there was something she was keeping from me.

'How long has this been planned?' I asked.

'Only since we got back from Italy. Very impromptu.'

My nerves twitched as I scanned the scale of what Truman had been able to pull together in such a short space of time. Fearing Caitlyn would wonder what I was thinking, I tried to meet her eye, but she looked away.

'What are you hiding?' I asked, taking a sip of my drink. I leaned against the counter, studied her gorgeous face. Her whole figure shook as she laughed.

'Who says I'm hiding something?' she avoided my stare, glanced down at the floor. Her hair, poker straight that day, fell over her eye.

'I know you, Caitlyn Donoghue,' I said with a small hiccough. I pulled her into my arms. 'You know, you don't have to live here with me if you don't want to. You can still live in Finsbury Park if you like,' I said playfully. Her lease was expiring and we'd discussed living together. Until we found somewhere close enough to both our work, we'd agreed to stay in the house and do the long commute.

'You're showing off, William,' she said. I ran my finger down her spine, pushing hard. The way she liked.

'Have a drink with me. You've got some catching up to do.' I twisted away from her, held the remains of my drink up. 'What do you want?' I asked.

'Vodka coke,' she said with a slight blush. 'I'll get them.'

I knew Caitlyn Donoghue better than anyone else in the world, even better than I knew myself. Her excessive blinking and deliberate attempts to avoid my eye told me was lying. As she turned away, I grabbed her arm gently.

'Why are you lying?' I asked, taking her glass from her hand. I took a sip.

When she met my eye, my heart sank. In a split second I convinced myself she was going to tell me she didn't want to be with me anymore. She stole a glance around the room, checking we were still alone, and patted her stomach.

'I'm pregnant.'

Excitement pulsed through me. Seeing my reaction, a smile burst across her face and we grabbed each other in a hug. I wasn't ready, hadn't expected her to say that, but when she had I knew everything had fallen into place.

'How long have you known?' I asked. My eyes trailed down her body in the way women hate, but I couldn't help myself. There were no tell-tale signs.

'Roughly thirteen weeks, give or take—'

'You were pregnant in Italy,' I said, alarmed. My thoughts raced to Caitlyn falling on the Path of the Gods, the alcohol we'd consumed.

'The baby's fine,' she said, instinctively patting her stomach again. 'I've had the first scan. Sorry, I should have told you before, but I didn't want to until I knew everything was okay.'

'What's got you two cooped up inside?' Truman asked. He sauntered into the kitchen with a beer in his hand. He pulled his sunglasses from his face and tucked them between the buttons on his shirt. Caitlyn said 'nothing', at the same exact same time I told him she was pregnant. Catching her expression, he smiled gracefully, congratulated us, then air-zipped his mouth shut, pleasing Caitlyn who scowled at me.

'Thank you,' she said sharply. Truman excused himself to use the bathroom, leaving me alone with my sullen girlfriend.

'What?' I asked, genuinely unaware if I'd done something wrong.

'I just thought we should keep it to ourselves for a bit,' she hissed.

'Keep what to yourselves?' Luke asked, parading into the kitchen. He made a beeline for the fridge but didn't take his eyes off Caitlyn.

'Cat's out of the bag now,' she shrugged. 'We're pregnant.'

Luke gushed, hugged us both in turn and when Alex came into the kitchen, he told him our news.

'I thought you wanted a wedding before a baby,' Luke said.

'It's not planned,' Caitlyn admitted. She looked at me and smiled. 'If I'm being honest, I don't really care. I'm so happy.' She grabbed my hand and swung her arm.

'We both are,' I said with a smile and a small squeeze of her hand. That moment was sheer perfection.

At that point, there was no need to hide it from the rest of the party. Caitlyn made the announcement and almost immediately relaxed. Freeing her secret seemed to take a weight from her chest.

With elated spirits, we stood in the garden, in the centre of attention, answering questions we'd never even discussed intimately, about our futures, our hopes and our dreams. Truman, I noticed, grew rather reclusive, tidying empty bottles and clearing discarded paper plates. Later, when our guests had gone and we were left alone in our exhilaration, I asked Caitlyn if she had noticed. She was drying washed glasses with a dishcloth but paused to think it over.

'He did leave early,' she said, as though it had only dawned on her. She noted other points where he had been standoffish as she continued to twist the dishcloth around the glass in her hand.

'He changed right after we told him . . . Oh,' she gasped and put the glass on the counter but held onto the dishcloth, waving it in the air as she continued, 'It makes sense though, doesn't it? This was his home, he probably saw himself raising kids here, and instead he ended up with a divorce. Even his protégées let him down,' she said. Then quickly added, 'no offence.'

The towel drooped as second-hand pain seared across her face. I felt a wave of pity and sadness for my friend and mentor. Perhaps that was why he was so eager to sell so quickly; he couldn't stand to be surrounded by the tormenting memories anymore.

'I suppose you're right,' I said, worrying Truman had just put a brave face on for the world, burying his emotions deep. I knew all too well how dangerous that was, but it wasn't my place to approach him about it, and was certain he wouldn't be pleased if I tried. 'What do we do?'

'There's nothing we can do except be there for him.'

I opened my arms, an offer Caitlyn welcomed by bringing herself in. I kissed the crown of her head, told her I loved her, and smiled in defeat. I couldn't help but wonder what the future would bring.

Caitlyn added a happy marriage and healthy kids to the bucket list. Specifically, in that order, so I proposed on a snow-filled evening in December. Even though we'd talked it through, I still couldn't believe my luck when she said yes. I was certain she'd tell me we were too young, that we weren't ready, but the tantalising dream she'd envisioned for herself was too enticing to pass up.

With the baby due in March, we set the wedding date for the beginning of February. We planned a humble affair, a back garden ceremony, as elegant as our small budget would allow for in the given time.

All of the fifty invited guests showed up. Alex, my best man, stood beside me as I watched them socialise from our bedroom window.

'How do you feel?' he asked.

'Like I'm not old enough, yet,' I paused. 'To have all of this: a house, a career, a job, a wife, a baby. Plus, I still don't think Rose likes me very much.' I spied Caitlyn's mum flirtatiously fix Truman's bow-tie by the marquee. As though she could feel my gaze on her, she flicked her head in my direction. I moved away from the window, wishing Jo could have seen me. Life was moving at a million miles an hour, and I wanted nothing more than to snatch that moment in time and just hold on to it, appreciate how precious it was.

'If that's what you're worrying about, then you haven't had enough to drink.' Alex pulled a hip-flask from inside his jacket pocket. 'Because what Rose thinks of you is not important.' He unscrewed the cap and took a swig. Passed me the silver container. I took a mouthful and swallowed. The liquid burned my throat. I stuck my tongue out, involuntarily scrunching up my face.

'Whisky,' he said, answering my unspoken question.

Caitlyn had a strict seating plan to keep certain guests as far away from each other as possible. In the end, the arrangement turned into an almost perfect map of where we had been, each of the tables representing parts of our journey in life, both alone and together. I slipped past the empty tables nearest the house and strolled past the rows of our friends, colleagues and her family further down the garden, taking the time to speak to each person individually; laughing at their jokes or thanking them for their attendance. The photographer we'd hired snapped away on her camera as I moved.

Every breath. Every mistake. Every heartbeat. They all led me to that day; to our alter: a stage made just for me and Caitlyn. I took my place and ran my fingers through my waxed hair, checking each strand was still fixed in place, not used to it being so tame. The minister beside me chuckled. My stomach churned as I checked my watch. It was time.

I stood with my back to our guests, pictured Caitlyn climbing out of the wedding car, carefully manoeuvring in her dress so it didn't spill to the ground. Butterflies fluttered in my stomach as I saw her in my minds eye, walking through our house. Would she have a sip of champagne to settle her nerves? Just a little. Or would she be so against the thought of harming the baby she wouldn't even be tempted?

The drummer we'd carefully chosen began to drum. Murmurs erupted, then died, only to be replaced with gentle sniffs and the rustling of tissues and clicking of buttons to capture the moment. I couldn't see, but I imagined how perfect she looked as she glided down the aisle in time to the music. We were going to make perfect parents, I thought, and was then surprised to find my own eyes stung with unshed tears.

The drumming stopped, and the minister subtly nodded to me. Permission to turn. Caitlyn stood; her arm linked through Luke's. Impossibly wide smiles covering their faces. Her hair flowed in loose curls around her face and her green eyes shone just for me. Then I noticed something she tried to hide. A glimpse of pain shot across her face. Her smile, full and bright, dimmed, for only a second. Luke let her go and she joined me on the alter.

'What's wrong?' I whispered, leaning into her. An onlooker may have thought I told her she looked beautiful. She waved the notion away and the minister began to talk. In exchanging our vows, words flowed from me like water, pooled with her own. When the question was asked, there was only one answer. Life had never seemed so simple, and it would never be so easy again. Words, when spoken aloud, can often be used as bullets. But that day, in that instance, they were a promise. One we sealed with a kiss. We turned to face our audience.

Rose's scream penetrated the surrounding gasps. The wail, sharp enough to pierce my ears and heart, drowned me. Luke shot over to us, smacking the decorative floral archway we stood under as he moved, sending it crashing to the ground. Caitlyn and I, for a second, stood frozen on the spot, unaware of the horror. Caitlyn looked at me, then slumped her head downwards, taking in the horrific sight. Trancelike, she raised her hands. *Her blood-stained hands,* and stared at them for a long time, like she couldn't figure out where the blood was coming from. *There was so much blood.* When she fainted, she landed in my arms. I don't remember putting them out, didn't think I was aware enough of what was going on to respond, but it must have been instinctive. Luke was already on the phone, demanding an ambulance. Dissatisfied with the answer, he scooped Caitlyn in his arms and told me to come. She flapped rigid as he ran through the aisle. I followed in his footsteps, still not quite sure what had happened.

'Get in,' Luke said. His Range Rover was parked at the side of our house. I climbed into the back seat and helped navigate Caitlyn inside too. She lay her head in my lap and groaned in pain. The noises, like a wounded animal, cut through everything else. I stroked her hair as Luke got in the driver's side. He started the engine and raced down the driveway, knocking over our garden fence and tearing up our bushes on the way.

Our guests watched in horror. Rose and Truman were already clambering in another car, ready to follow us. Others looked lost, frozen and helpless.

'William,' Caitlyn said. Her hoarse voice barely more audible than a whisper. I shushed her, hoping she'd conserve energy. She sobbed inwardly with tiny jolts and shudders in my lap. 'I lost my baby.'

19

Born Sleeping

We were in the hospital no longer than ten seconds when an army of nurses ran to our aid. In a whim they had Caitlyn in a wheelchair and whisked her away without so much as acknowledging either myself or Luke. I stood, too stunned to speak. I thought I knew what heartbreak felt like, thought I'd met tragedy before, but standing in that dank hospital entrance was when I learned just how cruel the world could truly be.

In the maternity waiting room, Luke sat me down as my tears fell. We remained silent as the world carried on around us. The room both filled and emptied as minutes turned to hours; each expectant mother and giddy partner at different stages of their journey.

For the first time since I'd met her, Rose greeted me with a hug, dropping her harsh exterior to play the role of devoted mother-in-law. Truman sat with the tip of his thumb constantly in his mouth, biting away at a loose piece of deadened skin. Alex had brought spare clothes for me and Caitlyn. In the rush he'd been in, he grabbed the first comfortable things he could find in our bedroom, oversized loungewear. Having changed in the bland hospital toilet, I fiddled with the draw string of my old university hoody. The insignia, faded and washed after years of ware, took me back to a time where all I'd wanted was to get to know Caitlyn.

The reception doors burst open and a burly nurse tumbled into the waiting room. She moved towards the wall, as though hoping to sink into the shadows, not to make another spectacle of herself. Heading towards me, she moved with the concentration and determination of someone who had a job to do that they did not want to do at all.

'Mr Walters?' she asked. I nodded, wondering how she knew who I was and deciding she had simply looked for the most tragic man in the room. I sent a million silent prayers into the air.

She led me to a room beyond the reception she called a birthing suite, even though it was only a small, rectangular room with very few items inside. On a bed by the window my wife lay perfectly still, undisturbed by our entrance. She held a knitted yellow blanket close to her chest, breathing in whatever scents she could from the material. Her eyes had glazed over. I walked to her, perched beside her. After a moment, I took her hand and gave her skin a gentle kiss. She retreated back to the blanket, pulling it up so the bottom half of her face was hidden and all I could see were her round, empty eyes.

'I'll give you time,' the nurse said. She closed the door gently behind her, but the room was so still that it seemed like she had slammed it shut. I looked around, taking in my surroundings. There was a desk with a dated Windows desktop sitting atop, a rocking chair in the corner, and an empty crib by the end of the bed. Desolate items. I don't think Caitlyn even registered my presence and we sat in reticence for the longest time.

Rose came in after a lifetime of silence. She brought with her a smell of musty old books.

'May I have a moment alone with my daughter?' she asked.

I left them to it.

The nurses let me see him, my son, born sleeping. His eyes were shut, like he really was just asleep. If eyes were the windows to the soul, then where had his gone if his eyes had never opened in the first place?

My tears fell onto his soft skin. It hurts to live on after somebody has died. I knew that kind of impossible pain, but losing our son was on a whole other level. Caitlyn had never experienced real loss in any capacity before. My heart broke for her, and for me; because the castle we had carefully constructed in time crumbled around us as though it had been made from sand. And there was nothing we could do to stop it.

We eventually left the hospital. Caitlyn opted not to get changed and walked into the street in her hospital gown and a blanket hanging from her shoulders. Truman offered to drive us home, but Caitlyn refused without opening her mouth. We climbed into the back of a taxi and drove away from our concerned and heartbroken family and friends in complete silence.

Caitlyn had gone into the hospital with a baby and had left without one. That kind of torture tears a human apart. At home, she cried, wailed, on the couch. Her raw pain erupting in bouts of agonising anguish. Sobs so infeasible and inhumane escaping in irregular intervals. Her body ached for the baby she had lost. Milk seeped from her. A vicious jest from a cruel world. She cleaned herself up, seemingly numb from ache, then carried herself to our bedroom. I followed behind, forgetting I'd previously placed rose petals in the shape of a heart on our bed. Seeing them brought a new wave of agony for Caitlyn, who erupted into a burst of rage and threw the petals aside as quickly as she possibly could. When the bed was clear, she climbed atop the messy sheets, grabbed a pillow and thrust it into her face to muffle her cries. There was nothing I could do but watch.

She didn't eat, couldn't sleep. Alive, but not living at all. Sometimes, she would pat her tummy, as though to check if it were true; a way of confirming that she was trapped in a godawful nightmare. And then she would cry all over again.

Her lips, constantly dry and cracked, never told me they loved me again. They had lost our secret language. Her silence was a constant shrieking. Stabbing, piercing me.

I couldn't bring myself to enter the room we had decided would be the nursery. It wasn't a room at all - it was a mould, infesting our lives. A constant reminder of what could have been. I closed and locked the door then went to the kitchen, poured a glass of whisky and leaned against the counter.

Three weeks passed, and nothing had changed. At dinner one evening, Caitlyn forked pieces of macaroni from one side of her plate to the other. Even in her devastation, she looked beautiful, but there were no words for me to tell her that.

'Truman called,' I announced. Waiting for her to respond, I sipped my whisky, enjoying the burn in my throat. 'He was wondering if I could go back tomorrow,' I added when she didn't say anything. She dropped her fork, letting it clatter to her plate and looked at me without looking at me at all.

'That's great,' she said. 'Just great.'

'I can take longer off. If you'd like. I can stay.'

She gave a mighty headshake, looked at me as though I'd spat at her.

'No,' she said. 'Go.' She pushed her plate to the side and left the kitchen. Once again, I was alone with my thoughts and my drink, which I swiftly threw back. I rinsed my glass under the running water, covered my hand over my mouth to stop noise escaping and let out a suppressed sob. I allowed myself one or two a day, before washing my face with cold water. The chill was refreshing.

Hazily, I carried myself to the bedroom. Already, the lights were off, and Caitlyn pretended to sleep. The distance between us was a living, breathing creature, growing from our pain and misery. It took its sharp claws, and slowly tore into our marriage. I wondered, as I lay my head on the pillow, how we could ever be happy, when we were sleeping beside a monster. As I drifted in and out of sleep, I found myself hoping, as I had almost every other night, that the monster would smother me before I woke.

I did wake. Caitlyn had already left the bed when I peeled my eyes open. Her side of the sheets already primp, as though she hadn't slept there at all. I found her sitting in the lounge, her feet tucked under her bottom, a blanket draped over her shoulders. Rain pattered lightly against the windows. She didn't speak or acknowledge my existence in any way at all. I got ready for work in a zombie state and left her alone in the house for the first time since I'd married her.

When I arrived at the office, it became a soundless vacuum. I walked through stolen sideway glances and took my seat at my desk. My colleagues continued to stare at me as I pretended to gather paperwork. My nerves shattered as a rush of emotions stirred inside me. I wanted to shout across the room, beg them to talk to me instead of about me, but when I scraped my chair back and brought myself to my feet, I ended up leaving the room entirely. Grace watched in silent horror as I closed the door and leaned back against it, catching my breath.

'Not you, too,' I said.

'Tough start?' she asked.

'Try impossible.'

She asked me to join her for "fresh" air, flashing me a packet of cigarettes.

We rode the elevator, passed security and left the building. With suave, she pulled a cigarette from the packet and poked it into her mouth. Lit it. Took a long drag and blew out a steady stream of smoke. I studied her posture, her style. Laid back, yet glamorous. She belonged on a catwalk, not behind a reception desk.

'How's Caitlyn coping?' she asked.

'She isn't,' I replied. 'This has really darkened her world—' my voice cracked, and I paused. 'I don't know what else to do.'

'What have you tried?'

I frowned to which the receptionist smirked. She'd caught me off-guard.

'I've been there for her—'

'A shoulder to cry on? A cup of tea? Made her dinner?' Grace checked the items against her fingers as she rattled through her list. I gave a grave nod.

'You need to do more. She didn't just lose a baby, Walters. She lost part of herself. Right now, she's in this pit and you're on the outside looking in. She needs you to be in there with her.'

Guilt riled around my stomach. What could I do? Grace read the thoughts displayed on my face, because she told me to go buy flowers after work. Give them to Caitlyn.

'Aren't you guys working through a bucket list together?' she asked.

In one syllable I confirmed that we were.

'Then go do something from it. A romantic gesture, some unique activity, something just for you two.' She waved her hands around as she spoke, smoke pluming from the tip of her cigarette. 'It doesn't need to be grand; it just needs to be *something*.'

Grace had planted a seed in my head. After work I stopped by the supermarket to buy a bouquet of flowers. As I browsed through the flower section by the door, I was hit with an idea. I left the bouquet on the shelf and ventured further into the shop.

I drove home, quite satisfied with my purchase. Arriving later than I'd wanted to, I bounded up the stairs and found Caitlyn lying in bed, staring into space.

'Come on,' I said. 'You need to get out of bed and put clothes on, quick.' If I stayed in the room, she'd have argued, so I turned around and ran down the stairs. Back in the kitchen, I could feel the strain from the exercise in my chest. A sign I needed to get back into an active routine.

'What's this?' Caitlyn said as she walked into the kitchen. She'd thrown on skinny jeans and a baggy t-shirt and eyed the carrier bags suspiciously. Soil and pots were scattered across the kitchen table. The bags were filled with seeds, planting baskets, small spades, and gloves.

'Gardening materials,' I said. 'You always wanted to grow your own garden.' I didn't add that it was on the bucket list. It felt too soon. 'I figured we could make a start tonight, in time for Spring.'

She looked at me with a face that told me there was a million things she would rather do. Under the kitchen lights, I couldn't help but notice her eyes were lined with dark, heavy bags. I knew when she got into it, she'd feel better. The bucket list had always been our answer, even when we didn't necessarily know what the question was.

'And you don't get to say no,' I said in the most optimistic tone I could muster. I pulled out the gloves and tossed them to her. She caught them, studied them for a heartbeat.

'I don't want to,' she said.

'You don't get to say no,' I repeated. 'Now come on, it's going to be dark soon, and I want to make a start.'

She exhaled but put the yellow gloves on. I took the bags from the counter tops and carried them outside. She followed but didn't help. I held any negative thoughts inside as I went back for the rest of the equipment.

'So I bought peony seeds, because they're your favourite.'

Her face remained neutral. In further attempt to please her, I told her I'd planned to buy her flowers, but instead came away with the idea for the garden. Caitlyn remained unobtrusive. I refrained from directing her to areas I thought we could start and let her do her own thing. On the way home, I'd played out the evening in my head. How we'd plant seeds together, perhaps have a drink, maybe even share a laugh. But Caitlyn sighed again and heaved her way through planting. She seemed to be getting into it when she picked up one of the smaller pots. As she walked across the garden with it, her grip loosened and it dropped, landing on her foot. She swore loudly, plonked herself on the ground and massaged the damage. I ran over, perched beside her, and rested my hand on her back. She yanked away, hissing at me like a scared animal.

'I'm sorry,' I said. 'I was just trying to help.'

'Well you're not,' she said. 'You're not helping. This doesn't help. You think growing a garden together is going to fix me?' Anger flared in her voice. She brought herself to her feet in full fury. 'I'm not *damaged*. I didn't even want to plant a stupid garden, anyway. And now my toe is broken.' She stomped her feet, showing that her toe was not in fact broken. Tactfully, I didn't point that out. She marched back inside the house while I stood rooted, holding back tears. *I was just trying to help.*

I didn't tell Grace about the mishap, and instead of throwing myself into cases at work, browsed online for unusual things to do around the city, certain I'd just chosen the wrong activity. If anybody in the office noticed I wasn't being productive, they didn't seem to care.

There was nothing on our bucket list which would inspire or reach Caitlyn in her catatonic state. I needed to branch out or risk losing her. Failing again wasn't an option, so when I found the perfect activity, I told Truman I wouldn't be in the next day because we had an appointment with the mental health nurse. As expected, he didn't ask any questions.

Back at home, I could barely contain my excitement, certain my plan would work. It would remind Caitlyn that we were fun, that life had its ups and downs, that we'd get through them together. When I told her I had an activity planned for the next day, she merely shrugged and excused herself from the table having eaten none of the soup from her bowl. When she was gone, I tipped it down the sink, then poured myself a drink, hoping and praying she would get better.

'Where are we going?' she asked the next morning. Her face showed her peaked interest. Strictly, I'd told her to wear a sports bra and exercise clothes, but gave no other hints. I shrugged with a smirk, like old times. We drove in silence; I focused on the road in front, and she leaned her head against the window.

'Why won't you just tell me where we are?' she snapped when I pulled into an almost empty car park by what appeared to be an abandoned warehouse. Her tone was a slap across my cheek; she'd never been so impatient before.

'I thought we could go to trampoline world,' I murmured.

'No. I don't want to go trampolining, William,' she said. 'Are you insane?'

No, I'm hurting too, I thought.

'I just want to do something different, Caitlyn.'

Her ponytail swung freely as she shook her head. The look on her face told me she was seething. Before she could protest, I twisted towards her, picked up her hand.

'Please, Caitlyn. Please, do this for me.'

She let out a long sigh and said, 'Okay'. Under her demeanour, I could see the gears in her head turning rapidly. Once, I'd known what she was thinking just by looking at her at her face, but I could no longer read what was going on in her head.

Resentment radiated from her as we registered at the centre. The teenagers behind the counter threw odd glances at each other as they took our details. I tried my best to ignore them, pasting an excited smile on my face. We were taken to a colourful room filled with sponge coated walls and several long, padded benches to watch a safety video. I sat on the edge of the closest bench. Caitlyn walked across the room and sat on another. I got up and moved towards her.

'Can't you see I don't *want* to sit next to you?' she hissed, folded her arms over her chest.

'What do you want?' I asked, giving up.

'You know, that's the first time you've asked me that,' she said in defeat. Folding her arms, she twisted her body away from me, I suspected, to hide her tears. 'I want the world to go away.'

The door burst open and a swarm of kids flooded into the room, running riot. An oversight on my part. Caitlyn's head tilted upward as she focused on the ceiling tiles, refusing herself to catch glimpses of the children around us. My heart thumped in my chest. I had clearly made a mistake.

The safety video was repetitive and dull. Conscious we were the oldest people in the room without kids, I tried to avoid eye-contact with curious parents around us. Our wrists were stamped with a black ink pattern and we made our way into the bounce palace. Caitlyn walked ahead of me, past the children's access gate, and the overbearing mothers and climbed onto the first trampoline. Within ten bounces she was laughing.

No longer trapped in our pain, we jumped our way to the foam pit. Against the rules, I picked her up and threw her in. She sank with a smile on her face, climbed out and chased me. Bliss. We jumped in together, our laughs bellowing louder than the kids.

When we were hungry, we had overpriced hotdogs at the café. I didn't make a big deal of it, but it was the first time Caitlyn had eaten substantial food since . . . since it happened. To me, that was monumental. Before we left for the day, we partook in a dodgeball tournament, losing when the kids teamed up against us. Then we left the trampoline palace hand-in-hand, and the day was over.

We climbed into the car and sat for a second. I turned the engine on and Caitlyn burst into a fit of tears. I tried to touch her but she pulled away. She needed a moment. When she collected herself she looked straight ahead.

'That *was* fun,' she admitted, a tiny smile formed in the corners of her mouth. It's like she believes she isn't allowed to have fun anymore. That breaks my heart, brings a tear to my eye, but I dared not let it fall. Like the morning, we drove in silence, but the pain that existed before no longer lingered between us. It was a shared pain, like for the first time, we were in on this together.

When I pulled into the drive, she told me she was going to bed. From her tone, I understood she meant alone. Before she left, she hugged me, gave me a kiss on the cheek and thanked me for trying. There was a trace of a smile on her face. We weren't fighting separate battles anymore; it was like we were finally on the same side.

'You should go to work today,' she said the next morning. We were lying together, but instead of turning away, she faced me. 'I'll be okay. I'm better. I'm going to take the time to work on myself.'

I believed her, so I climbed out of bed knowing things were going to be different, and got dressed. Before I left, she let me hug her. She *was* better. I went to work, excited to tell Grace everything had worked, that Caitlyn was back to her old self. I told Truman, too. They were excited for me but reminded me that recovery was a long and winding road. I knew it would be; I knew grief better than anyone.

On the way home, I stopped by a stationary shop, wanting to buy Caitlyn a present. I picked out a notebook so she could let her feelings flow. She could spill her emotions onto the page instead of bottling them up. At least if she wasn't talking to me, she would be venting to something.

Caitlyn never felt the need to lock the door when she was home alone. The area was safe enough, and I imagined in her lacklustre mood she didn't have the energy to get up and lock it when I was gone. So I was surprised to find that the door had been locked when I got home. My heart constricted as I made my way inside, wondering what was waiting for me. Early summer sunshine cast a beam through the window, illuminated the glass coffee table in the living room. On top, sat our bucket list diary and on top of that, a torn out page folded in half. It would have sprung open were it not for Caitlyn's golden wedding ring pinning it down. My heart sank. I knew exactly what this meant.

She was gone.

20

Rock Bottom

Alex appeared on the other side of my front door with Luke. Despite being summer, there was a slight bite in the evening air. The whisky in my glass danced around as Alex pulled me in for air kisses. The thick wool of his turtle-neck sweater scratched the skin over my cheeks. Luke greeted me with a hug. In the months since I'd last seen him, Luke had gained a healthy volume of weight and was looking like his old self again. Alex, who never seemed to age, had simply grown out his hair. They'd brought beer and games with them. *As though my problems could be solved so easily.*

'Have you seen her?' I aimed my question at Luke. He shook his head firmly.

'We're here for *you*,' Alex said. Don't ask about her is what he didn't say in words. I was no stranger to loss, but Caitlyn leaving had taken the life from my soul.

I wasn't particularly pleasing to be around at that stage, but they stayed anyway, despite my flaws. We played *Life*, and I tried not to ask about her again except when Alex went to the bathroom, I couldn't help myself. I leaned in close to Luke, careful to keep my voice barely more audible than a whisper.

'How is she?'

'William,' he said firmly.

'I know, I know,' I said. 'But how is she?'

In his hesitance, he opened his mouth to answer, to tell me something, but Alex walked back into the room and the conversation died.

'Let's play something different,' I announced louder than intended. 'A drinking game.'

I suggested *ring of fire*, selling it as a visitation to the good old days. In reality I just wanted to get Luke drunk enough to open up to me, preferably without Alex intervening. Long gone were the days where either of them could outdrink me.

I awoke the next morning with an exceptional pounding in my head and an electronic imitation of cheerful music looping around the room. With dry eyes, I focused my vision, trying to find the offending source. Alex splayed himself across Caitlyn's armchair. Bubble-gum pink and soft as heaven, she'd once described it. His limbs dangled in precarious angles, and his neck was bent in what looked like an extremely uncomfortable position. His hands held his phone close to his face, his eyes flickering across the screen.

'What are you doing?' I asked.

'You're awake.' He pushed the side button on his phone, sending it to sleep then hoisted himself so that he sat normally. He pocketed his phone and stared at me. The way the sun kissed his olive skin reminded me of Caitlyn, the way she used to read in that very chair, not in a dissimilar sprawl to how Alex had been lying. For some reason, that annoyed me. The chair had been her favourite piece of furniture and yet she'd left it behind. *A habit of hers.*

'There's tea by the dresser if you want it, though it might be cold now,' Alex said.

He studied me as I leaned over for the mug. An unwelcome glimpse of the previous night flashed across my mind. I'd drunkenly revealed that I'd been told to take another leave of absence from work. My third one that year. Shocked, he'd turned to Luke and asked what that meant. Before Luke could weigh in, I said, 'It means I'm walking on thin ice'.

'You've had a painful year,' Alex had said in response, as though I wasn't excruciatingly aware.

I sipped my tea which was stone cold and thanked him as I placed the mug back on the dresser.

'How are you feeling?' he asked.

'Probably worse than I look.'

He rose and walked to me, cupped his hand over the covers, resting it on my shin. I imagined he thought it would be comforting, but it wasn't. There was a thing he was doing—*a hovering*—flirting around with his actions in a way that made me suspicious.

'Where's Luke?' I asked.

'He left,' he said, speaking in a way which suggested I wasn't to ask any more questions. No longer an open book, he'd turned into one of those people who only dish out information on a need-to-know basis.

'What's wrong with him?' I asked bluntly.

'What?'

'Something's wrong with him. I know he takes medication. I know he's tired—'

'—you don't know anything,' Alex burst. Clearly, I'd hit a nerve.

'I know *something*,' I argued.

'No you don't. And why?' He threw his hands in the air. 'Because you never ask, William. You've never once asked about Luke, or me for that matter.'

'I . . . I'm asking now.'

'And if you must know, his medication is for HIV.'

I didn't know what to say to that. All I knew about HIV was that it was a death sentence or *was* a death sentence at some point. I realised I didn't know anything.

'Why didn't you tell me?' I asked cautiously.

'You see,' Alex burst. 'This is what I'm talking about. Not everything is about you, William. We came here to be with you, and the first thing out of your mouth was "how is she?"' He jumped to his feet. The tension between us had come from nowhere but simmered profusely. I didn't want our friendship to boil over, but it was too late to turn down the heat. 'You didn't even ask about us.'

'Well I'm *sorry* if what I've been through has made me a little depressed—'

'More than a little,' he said after a long sigh. 'Do you remember how nasty you got last night?'

'That's not fair,' I said, suddenly feeling very attacked.

Alex didn't respond with words. He held a hand to his hip and cocked an eyebrow. Evidently, he had said enough to prove his point.

'If I'm so awful, then why are you still here?'

'Because I'm your friend.' There was something in the way he refused to meet my eyes that alarmed me. I leaned into him. Underneath the caring exterior he was trying so desperately to put on, there was an ulterior motive. I wanted to voice my impression but couldn't find the words. He twisted his wedding ring around.

'Why are you here?' I asked again, my voice an echo of what it once was.

'News flash, William: People care about you. *I* care about you,' he said.

'She doesn't.' Saying it was an automatic response, a knee jerk reaction.

He shook his head, exhaled sharply through his nostrils.

'She does,' he said. 'She misses you.' He paced, then stopped.

I sat upright, quick as lightning.

'You've spoken to her.'

His small eyes widened in fear, then searched the room as though he'd find a suitable response on the bedside table, between the plaits in the curtains, in the folds on the sheets. I repeated myself, this time announcing each syllable slowly. In defeat, he sighed, stopped fidgeting and perched himself back on the bed. Regret drew over his face. Anger beat in me like thunder. He had given away the secret he'd harboured, the one eating him up.

'Luke has—'

'—you're lying,' I said. 'I knew you were hiding something.'

He cocked his eyebrow again. Ignoring his offended pretence, I mulled the situation over.

'She's staying with you,' I threw my hypothesis into the room, testing the plausibility. He shook his head too quickly. I clenched my fists, brought them to my face.

'Why won't you just tell me?' I asked, frustration pouring from me. 'If she's not staying with you then where is she?'

'She doesn't want to see you right now.' His voice croaked, as though it was tearing him apart. His words were a knife that he stuck in my back. *Then twisted.*

I'd once plunged into a dive pool, felt the sting of ice-cold water on my skin like the prick of a thousand needles all at once. Dragging the truth out of Alex was not dissimilar to that experience.

'Give her time, Will. She'll come around.'

'Where is she?' I brought my face so it was inches away from his and spoke through gritted teeth. 'Tell me.'

'I can't—'

'You can,' I yelled. 'You're choosing not to.'

He backed away from me too quickly, stumbled and fell. He lay on the floor for a second, looking at me through betrayed eyes. If he was waiting for an apology he'd be waiting forever. I didn't have one to give.

'You're supposed to be my friend,' I said pathetically. Tears of defeat came to me. I blinked them away. He told me everything when he told me nothing.

'She's staying at your country house,' I deduced.

'William—'

'—don't.'

He stood, stared at me expectantly with upturned eyebrows and a quavering lip. He opened his mouth to speak.

'Don't,' I said again. It came out as a broken whisper.

'How did you think I'd feel, Alex?' I asked. 'You've been squirrelling her away from me this whole time. You've lied, pretended you care, but you obviously don't.'

'I do.'

My pain. My loss. My torment. They blurred into a confusing concoction in my body resulting in a bubbling angry mess. I began to speak, told Alex he was a liar and a bad friend. The more I said, the louder I became until eventually he snapped, and shouted back at me.

'She's *my* friend too,' he bellowed. 'She's family.'

I snorted, swore at him. I didn't want to argue, to fight. But I was so furious I couldn't keep anything in.

'How do you think *I* feel, William?' He snapped, taking me by surprise.

'How do I think *you'd* feel?' I mocked, 'are you seriously making this about you right now?'

'No because it's *always* got to be about you. Doesn't it? You make it really difficult to be your friend. You know that, right? You never ask me how I am; you never take an interest in *my* life. I've been struggling with anxiety for years and *you* make it worse.'

'You don't *have* anxiety,' I said. It was a low blow—to dismiss someone's mental health like that, but he *didn't*—life was so easy for him. He had loving parents, a perfect husband, a good job with prospects and a world of support around him. He didn't understand what it was like to have nothing, to be beaten up by the world day after day, month after month, year after year. He didn't understand that anxiety was crippling; that when it came, it came from nothing and nowhere, crept up on you like a shadow lurking in the dark. Anxiety isn't feeling a little timid at a party—it's being physically sick at the thought of even *going* to the party in the first place.

'I'm done,' he held his hands in the air, 'I'm done with this friendship. It's toxic. *You* are toxic.' He pointed at me with a long, bony finger, spun around and left through my open bedroom door. Too shocked to move, I stared into the empty space he'd left behind, willing him to reappear. The stairs creaked as he descended. My stomach dipped, as though I was on a rollercoaster and I was at the point where I hurtled towards Earth from hundreds of feet in the air. *How could it end like that?* I chased after him, stopping myself on the top stair.

'Alex,' I called. 'You're really going to leave me?'

There's no pain like being left behind. He didn't answer, but he did look back. His hand wrapped around the front door handle, his eyes looked into my own. I balled my hands into fists and ran down the stairs, taking them two at a time.

'Alex, don't go. I'm sorry.'

I meant it, the way my voice cracked showed my sincerity. I stood and he stood, frozen, wondering what was coming next. I wanted to fix things, and in his hesitance, I thought he'd maybe tell me everything was all right; that it would all go back to how it was before, but instead, he shook his head and pulled the door open.

'I give up,' he said, so quiet it was more to himself than me.

'No, Alex, no,' I shook in desperation. 'Please don't give up on me.'

He walked out of the door letting it slam shut behind him. My mouth was dry. My knees weak. I dropped to the floor and swore repeatedly as I slammed my fists into the tiles beneath me. None of that should have happened. In some sort of self-destructive episode, I'd pushed away the last, and only, friend I had.

Weeks passed before the doorbell chimed again. In that time, the summer air had turned colder. Leaves curled and fell lazily to the ground, turning to an auburn-red mush. Often, I'd stare out of the window, watching nature change before my eyes, wondering if there was anybody out there who ever thought of me. It was a Wednesday morning when the chimes rang through my house. The loud, incessant rings were unbearable. From the lounge, I stole a glance through the window, but there was nobody at the door. In tiptoe, I made my way to the kitchen, as though heading somewhere I shouldn't, and took a peek at the side of the roller blind covering the large window.

Peter Truman stood outside my back door. I deduced he'd have known I'd have ignored the front, but that he could spy me from the other side of the house. Using a cane to lean on, he examined what was left of the flowerbeds with the sadness of a keen gardener. Like the rest of the house, only dust and memories remained. He looked directly at me as though he knew he was being watched. I jumped back from the window but it was too late. I'd been spotted. Cursing myself, I answered the door wearing my best fake smile.

'Truman,' I said. 'What a surprise.'

'It wouldn't be if you'd pick up your damn phone, Walters.' He shook his head and pushed hard on the door with his cane. The force took me by surprise and the door flung open. He barged past me with a force that suggested there was no requirement for the cane in his hand, made a beeline inside and stood in the middle of the room. His eyes wandered around, taking everything in. They landed on the palace of dishes in the sink before moving to the overflowing bin. Distain was written over the aged features of his face. I couldn't tell if this is what he'd anticipated or not.

'I wasn't expecting guests,' I shrugged.

Between a pinched thumb and forefinger, he lifted a stiffened, beer-soaked tea-towel from the kitchen stool and discarded it to the side. His face scrunched even more when he caught site of the stain on the stool beneath. His tiny head shake spoke volumes.

'Evidently,' he said. He caned his way across the room and settled for leaning against the fridge instead.

'You hurt your leg?' I asked.

'Skiing,' he said sharply. He wasn't there to talk about that. Again, I saw him look around the room. The last time he'd been there, the surfaces had shined pristine, and from an exterior view, so had my life.

'What's going on, Walters?' He crossed his arms over his chest.

I shrugged. He knew what I'd been through. What did he want, a breakdown of events?

'That's not good enough,' he spat. Any patience he had brought with him had disappeared.

I resisted the urge to shrug again.

'What happened to the kid I took under my wing?'

'He died.'

'Walters.'

Hearing my name spoken so sharply was like being slapped. He let out a long sigh and I lay my armour down.

'What do you want, Truman?' I asked, my voice nothing more than a whine.

His face softened as he took a moment to gather his thoughts. In the time since I'd last seen him his hair had greyed over.

'I came here to check on you. I came because I wanted to make sure you were okay.'

'Well I'm *not* okay,' I confessed. 'Are you happy now?'

I rubbed my temples, a rising pressure underneath threaten to explode.

'No, I'm *not* happy. If you would just *try*—'

'I did try,' I argued. I threw my hands into the air. *He didn't understand how impossible life was.*

'No, you didn't. You need to move on. You need to get over this.' His face flooded with disappointment. I wanted to tell him I didn't need his tough love, but he continued.

'Pick yourself up and get on with your life, and for God's sake, have a shave,' he threw his hand up, gesturing towards the irregular stubble growing around my mouth and over my chin. Once again, I wondered how much he needed the cane.

'Do you think I could have built an empire if I crumbled so easily?'

'You don't understand,' I began, desperate for him to hear me.

He sliced the air with his hand. 'I taught you better than this. You're a waste of talent.'

The words stung. My defensiveness turned to rage.

'You. Are. Not. My. Father.'

We stood in silent rancour for a time, both refusing to back down. We had gone too far. Eventually, Truman broke. He let out another agonising sigh, focused his attention to the window.

'No,' he said, 'I'm not.' He turned to me. 'Do you think he'd be proud? Look at you.' His mouth twisted at the corner as though I was vermin. 'Everybody told me I was wasting my time coming here today - said you're a lost cause. Obviously, they were right. I'm afraid I've got no choice but to let you go.'

He shook his head.

'I'd already quit,' I argued. Technically, I hadn't. I'd just stopped going to work. The thought of calling in sick had crippled me. He fished inside his suit jacket and pulled out an envelope from his breast pocket. I recognised the size and shape instantly: a formal letter from HR, stamped with the firm's official seal. *A letter of dismissal.*

He hadn't been to check on me at all, he'd arrived to fire me. That didn't matter. I had enough savings to see me through. With slight hesitance and a lot of regret, he placed the envelope on the counter. I narrowed my eyes, hoping he wouldn't see that I was upset.

'You could have sent that in the post, you know,' I said. 'It would have saved you the trip.'

He met my eyes with intent. If he noticed the break in my voice, he was kind enough to not mention it.

'You used to play your cards so well,' he said with a small shrug. 'I honestly hope you get through this, Walters. I hope you get the help you need.'

Defeat lingered between us like a bad smell, stopping us from getting too close to each other.

'One thing I never got,' I said. 'Why me? Why'd you pick me?'

His mouth twisted like he couldn't believe I'd finally asked him. He let out a heave of a sigh.

'I thought you had potential you might otherwise never have met,' he said. 'I once thought the world had burned you so much that you'd never give up. Turns out I was wrong. And it was wrong of me to come here today. I could never help you.' He turned on the spot and smacked his cane so hard into the floor that it left a crack in the tile. The bang showed that he had seen more than enough.

'I'm just done.' My words were a sigh, so quiet Truman didn't seem to hear them. Or pretended he hadn't. He walked out of my house, letting the door close with a slam behind him. Just as it had before. When Caitlyn left. When Alex left. It was a cycle I was trapped in.

I fell to my knees. I couldn't understand how I'd gotten there: to a place where everybody was at me constantly. At my neck with a noose, out to get me.

Is that how Penny felt?

I hadn't asked for them to visit - I only wanted to be left alone. I wanted them all to leave but they kept coming for me as though they were a part of a club who were determined to keep me down. I imagined them laughing as they pushed me from the pedestal they'd put me on in the first place. I'd never asked for their tainted opinions.

I wished the world to go away.

After Truman left that day there were no more visitors and I found myself plagued by the silence I thought I needed. Loneliness rose like an unwelcome tide. I found it comes when you're alone and you have no option but to be. It stopped me from getting the help I needed. *Not that I deserved help.* I spent the next few weeks dissecting where things had gone wrong, living very much inside my head. Every turn I took. Every move I made. All of them, it turned out, had been bad. Everything that had happened was entirely my fault.

* * *

I stayed in bed for days, sometimes weeks at a time, paralysed by something deep inside me - pain or fear, perhaps. Only leaving for food or drink, living on a diet of whisky, rarely water, the occasional beer, some crisps, and a lot of biscuits. On a good day, I'd get a takeaway. I wasn't entirely alone in the house though. I lived with ghosts. Memories of what once was. So many moments replayed in my mind. Over and over and over again. A personalised movie made just to torment me. Worse than that were the dreams and nightmares of what could have been - the ones where Caitlyn and I were still together and there was a child laughing in the background.

Depression followed, arriving in the form of an invisible rash spread over my body, consuming me. The battle in my head raged on like a storm. Self-hatred and guilt took so much space in my mind there was barely room for any other emotion. Sometimes, I'd find myself sitting in the shower for hours at a time. The water rushing over me, comforting me. A temporary healing of my permanent pain.

There was nothing particularly peculiar about the early December afternoon that I spent in the shower watching the first snow of the year tumble past the window. I found peace in observing the flakes which had battered against the glass melt on the pane. My heart battled a different kind of storm. Every day, I'd replay my last encounters with Truman and Alex, the things they said to me. I often thought about Penny and Caitlyn and the way they hated me. Water drizzled over my body, but it was their words which truly soaked me. They crawled under my skin and seeped into my bones. My fist, a wrecking ball, hit the wall as I reached a conclusion. *Once and for all, it was time to end the war.*

I got out of the shower but left the water running. There was nothing else to do. Everything I worked hard to build had fallen apart. There was no one to miss me. No one to notice, to care, if I disappeared. I took my razor blades from their box in the medicine cabinet. The thin metal gleamed in my hand. I sat in the shower again and brought my knees to my chest in despair.

There was so much hatred, so much pain and so much guilt. They flowed through my blood. The only way to get rid of them would be to physically set them free.

Gently, I traced a line with the blade along my forearm. Then I dug the metal deeper into my skin and dragged it against my flesh. It wasn't painful. *It was nothing.* I kept going, sliding the blade deeper and deeper and longer and longer. At first, lines of protuberant red dots appeared. They became a line of tulips sprouting from my arm. The dots joined together until the blood ran across the sides of my skin. At first it trickled and then ran, staining my hands, my legs, my waist. The water in the basin turned pink, pooling around the drain. There was so much of it. Even when I began to panic, I couldn't stop cutting. It was a need, more than a hunger or thirst. I cut and I cut.

Then the pain came. Sudden, sharp, shooting and searing. I tried to breathe through the ache, but air had a consistency of cement, and I couldn't take any in. All I could do was continue to cut, tearing myself apart.

21

Not the End

As my blood pooled around me, the pain grew more and more unbearable. I didn't want to die, but I didn't want to live either. I just needed to escape myself, if only for a moment, because I'd been in a perpetual state of emptiness for so long. I'd spent a lifetime burning bridges I couldn't repair. I didn't even have a single friend anymore. No one to miss me if I were gone.

The noise of my phone in another room made me realise what I was doing, as if I was being pulled from a dream where I watched myself from a distance, not really in my own head. *What had I done?*

Wincing, I turned the shower off, grabbed a towel and wrapped it around my self-inflicted wounds. Applied pressure. My blood soaked the white cotton. Dripping wet and in my make-shift bandage, I rushed to the bedroom following the sound of my phone, unable to recall the last time I'd used it or even the last time it had made a noise.

I hovered on the spot, certain the sharp tones were coming from the wardrobe. First, I pulled out my suit jacket. The pockets were empty so I dropped it to the floor just as the melody stopped. Cursing loudly, I pulled out my winter coat. Empty pockets again. In a frantic search, I pulled out garment after garment. The make-shift towel bandage, stained red, unravelled and fell. My arm stung a blinding pain. I found the phone in the side pocket of my backpack. Alien in my hand, I pushed the button on the side and the screen lit with the dead battery symbol.

I found a charger under the bed and plugged it into the phone. In the time it took to come alive, I fixed the towel back around my arm, this time using a safety-pin I found in my drawer to secure it in place.

While I waited, I sat on the bed, caressed my arm and watched the snow fall. What had started as a light frosting, turned into a horrendous blizzard. One that Britain, inevitably, would not be prepared for.

My phone pinged to life seizing my attention. The lock screen image was still of me and Caitlyn. Seeing her smiling gave me pause until a notification popped over her face and the phone let out a sharp ping. A reminder: that's what had distracted me. I pushed the rectangular box with my thumb. It was Jo's birthday. *Would have been, anyway.*

I considered calling an ambulance, to have my wounds dressed properly, but I didn't want to waste their time—I didn't deem myself worthy of help, and I knew my deep cuts would heal in time. If I was the type of person to believe in fate, I would have said there was a reason Jo's birthday reminder had interrupted me from slitting my wrists any further; that it was all part of some grand plan. But I didn't believe some higher power had steered my life, because who would have planned for me to have been in such a rut in the first place?

Yet, as cynical and sceptical as I was, it was nice to think that Jo might be out there somewhere, watching over me. I collapsed backwards, spreading myself over the bed, mulling events over in my mind. Life hadn't turned out quite like I'd hoped it would, but I only had myself to blame. I watched the storm rage on outside. Snowflakes battered down. Their cascading shadows danced on the adjacent walls around me. The images gave birth to an idea.

Fuelled with a motivation I hadn't felt in months, I unclasped and peeled my blood-soaked towel from my arm and placed it in the washing hamper, then pulled the first aid box from under the bathroom sink and rummaged through the contents until I pulled out a cotton bandage. If I could avoid going to A&E I would. I wrapped the material around my arm as best I could with one hand, which proved to be more difficult than before, with the towel. The bandage didn't stay off-white for very long. Satisfied, I picked up the clothes strewn across the bedroom floor and dumped them into the washing hamper, then made my way to the bathroom.

From the shower, I picked up the unused razor blades and put them back on the shelf. I winced, remembering the slick way the sharp metal had sliced through my skin. Catching my reflection in the mirror, I vowed to never harm myself again. Whilst there, I decided to shave, which ended up taking years from my face. After, I dressed myself in jeans and a t-shirt for the first time in months. Once, clothes had hugged me, but as I walked, the material flapped around my skeletal frame.

The storm showed no sign of calming. It was late in the afternoon, but I had a fraction of an idea in my mind and a burning desire to start straight away. I couldn't risk the excitement fading. From kitchen cupboards and behind hallway doors, I collected all of the alcohol in the house and sat them in a long line by the kitchen sink. In total, there were twenty-three bottles, staring at me seductively. Such a dependent, I had become. There was no excitement in my life anymore, no pain either. There was only an addiction to booze and a driving need to numb the pain. No future. No escape. Only booze. I didn't want it anymore. Simple as that. As though a switch had been flicked. I uncorked the wine, refrained from inhaling. *The first step in stopping is starting*. I tipped the bottle upside down over the drain and the rustic liquid chugged away.

When I opened the first of the beers, I had a strong impulse to take a sip - almost convinced myself it would help me get through. But I stayed strong. Just one taste would lead to another. I tipped bottle after bottle upside down. Then came the whisky. Pouring the amber liquid away both physically and mentally hurt.

At first, I quickly moved from room to room, tidying and organising the hangover of a house as I went, worrying if I stopped, even for a second, I may never start again. In protest to my sudden bursts of energy, my bones creaked and cracked, but still, I pushed on.

Somewhere along the line, my home had morphed from a private paradise to an island of seclusion. I opened most of the windows, just a fraction, to get rid of the musky smell I'd previously ignored. Cold air blew inside in sharp gusts. I scrubbed, dusted, and hoovered each room in turn, making slow progress. I collected rubbish, gathering seven black bags of unwanted, broken or unused items, and sorted books in alphabetical order. It had been dark outside for several hours and a thick trace of sweat lined my body by the time I'd finished cleaning the house – all but one room, anyway. Slowly, as though trespassing, I carried myself into the room which had once been allocated as a nursery. Nostalgia and regret washed over me. It was supposed to have been so many things but neglected wasn't one of them. The walls were yellow. Jo's favourite colour. Standing in the thick of it, I realised that choosing yellow had been a mistake. It reminded me of the bungalow; of the peeling wallpaper, the screaming happiness the bright colour enforced and memories tainted by raw emotion. Some ghosts needed to be let go. There were boxes lying around. I didn't have the strength to open them knowing that like a coffin, they held the clothes my baby never got to wear. Everything had been newly bought. They should be donated, I thought, so I carried the boxes to the garage and placed them carefully in the boot of my car. The car battery would probably be dead, but that was a problem for another day. Walking back across the garage, I saw a metal rack filled with tins of paint I'd forgotten about and I thought about that horrible, awful yellow room upstairs.

I was awake all night. I could tell because the sky transitioned in a long drawn out ache from a rich velvety moonscape to a sugar-frosted expanse. I stood, paint spattered and exhausted, taking in the freshly-painted beetroot walls. Dark, but sometimes that is better – if it weren't for darkness, we'd never appreciate the light. Heavy-eyed, I carried myself to bed, and for the first time in forever, fell asleep without the aid of a drink, quite satisfied that I had achieved something.

I slept lightly, tossing and turning. My body craved alcohol. Usually, I'd drink to hush the noise of regret, so without it the mistakes I'd made in my life chorused around me. There had been so many mistakes. My mind craved peace and forced me awake. After changing my bandages, I picked up my phone, opened my messages and almost text apologies, but they wouldn't have been appreciated. Words on a screen would be cold and flat. The gesture wasn't grand enough. Instead, I looked up therapists and councillors. I read about the frustrations and despair people faced when they joined year-long waiting lists. I learned that to jump the queue, I could treat the system as though it were a game, exaggerate my pain to my GP and get the help I needed over someone else. I didn't want to do that, be that guy, so I opted for private counselling and emailed to book an appointment. Internet forums suggested I write down my issues before I go, and I thought there wouldn't be a piece of paper big enough.

More awake than I'd been in years, I kindled a fire in the lounge, found a notepad, and in bulleted form wrote down what I'd experienced. Then I twiddled my thumbs and wondered how I could occupy my wandering mind. *Writing what I'd experienced.* Somewhere in my house, I remembered I had all of Penny's diaries. Hadn't she wanted her story told? Didn't she deserve that?

I found them in a box in the attic. There were twenty-eight in total. I arranged them in chronological order, opened my laptop and began blogging Penny's version of events, calling the website "Penny for your thoughts".

By the time I typed up the last of Penny's diary entries, the website had been visited over a million times, and I could tick another item from the bucket list: *to write for an audience*.

It had taken me two weeks. After which, I was purposeless once again. Depression breeds depression, I thought, and so to stop my mind from battling itself, I gathered the paints from the garage and brought them to the beetroot room. With an idea in mind, I cut out stencils taken from the internet and added designs to the wall, letting my creativity flow. As I crafted, I longed for a drink. Whisky. Wine. Gin. Tequila. Beer. Any would do – I didn't care. I just wanted my fingers wrapped around a cold glass, to feel the condensation drip from the glass onto my skin. Have the cool liquid sit on my tongue and for an explosion of flavour to follow. In substitution, I painted, filling my days with productivity, grateful I'd already thrown all of the alcohol away. The end product was a feature wall covered with the events of the bucket list - the adventures I'd been on. No Picasso, but not all bad, I thought, admiring my work.

My first therapy appointment was scheduled on a Tuesday afternoon. I packed my notebook into my backpack, threw on my anorak, gathered my nerves and travelled into the centre of London. After checking in at the reception, I took a seat in the empty waiting room and filled in the forms I'd been given. One of the doors opened, and a lady I recognised walked through. Tall and lean with flaming red hair, dressed entirely in black with heeled boots which clinked the floor beneath, and an inviting smile wide as ever. I'd gone from seeing her almost every day to never speaking to her. Grace. I lifted the clipboard over my face, watched her thank, and wish the receptionist a happy birthday. She climbed the stairs and left the practice without noticing me at all. I wished, too late, that I'd made the effort to say hello, to have spoken to her, but fear and anxiety took over. I made a mental note to mention that to my therapist.

'William Walters?'

My therapist was an astute, tall, and slender man. He looked at me through half-moon glasses which lay on the end of his pointed nose. Deep wrinkles were embedded over his willowy face and he had a smile that showed yellowed teeth. When he walked, his feet barely touched the ground, as though he weren't really a part of the world at all, but simply spectating from above.

The furniture and décor in his office was strictly from an undetermined era prior to my birth. The walls were lined with books, and framed educational certificates were displayed boldly. In the corner of the room sat a fish tank with no fish inside, and on his desk sat a globe with a sizeable hole where Poland should have been. He sank into an armchair, releasing a squeak as he moved. I took the seat opposite him, on a much more comfortable looking maroon sofa and shook off my anorak, carefully wasting as much time as possible by folding it into a neat bundle.

'What's brought you here today?' he asked. He crossed his left leg over his right and propped his elbow on his knee, then leaned into the space between us.

'I tried to kill myself,' I said.

'Recently?'

'A while ago, actually . . . but I feel like it set me into a spiral. I wrote a list—' I opened my backpack and with a trembling hand, pulled out my notebook.

'It would be much more helpful if you could tell me about your life,' he said.

'Right.' I put the notes to one side and lulled for a moment.

'My life . . . well, my grandmother died and then my girlfriend killed herself,' I said quickly, then realised that wasn't the whole picture. 'Then my wife left me . . . after she lost our baby,' I added nervously, incapable of reading his thoughts.

'What a terrible set of circumstances,' the therapist said.

I nodded, wondering how sincere he was, wishing I could have been anywhere but in that room. Lost for words, I fidgeted with my fingers, knotting them together.

'Why don't you tell me what happened that made you come here today? What's pushed you over the edge?'

His indifferent body language as I told my life story made me realise therapy just wasn't for me. As uncomfortable as the hour was, it flew by and when my time was up, I thanked the therapist and left his office forever. Under pressure, I booked my next appointment with the receptionist which I promptly cancelled when I got home, claiming I had accidentally double-booked myself.

I'd tried therapy and it wasn't for me, and I'd tried killing myself, but learned that wasn't the answer. There was a sinking feeling in my gut that I was running out of time. I'd stumbled and fallen in the past and yet I continued to tread through life, but I knew the odds of me surviving another bought of deep sadness were against me, so I researched other ways to get help.

'And that's what let me here . . . to you.'

22

Moonlight Wishes

I pause, study the other faces in the room. Twelve of them, practically strangers, all staring at me. Each have their own stories, struggles and conquests, and yet they sat silent and listened to me. We're the type of people to invite problems into our life then complain we have problems. Some of them are dabbing their eyes. Some sit with their mouths wide open, shocked I'd drivelled on for so long, or perhaps even appalled by my truths. After all, in the year I've been coming to the church's weekly meetings, I'd never opened my mouth once. These days, I usually find it difficult to talk about myself, or open up to people at all; they only ever let me down. They leave, or cheat, or die. But once I'd opened my mouth to speak, the words cascaded from me.

Martha asks if I have any pictures of the painting I'd finished. George asks about Jo's lasagne. John asks the best question though: what am I'm going to do now?

I don't get the chance to answer.

'That was truly inspiring,' Pete says, his voice projects across the room the way only a natural leader is able to. When he stands, his shaggy hair flounces by his shoulders. 'But I'm afraid that's all we've got time for this week.' The finality in his tone makes it clear there are to be no more questions. He claps his hands together and the others follow his applause. I'd run over my time slot, but at least my story is out there.

I linger afterwards, to help clean up. I watch Pete thank us one-by-one, making sure to have physical contact with each person as he does so. He has a stout way about him making this form of connection seem genuine, allowing each of us to feel truly heard and cared for. With him, we are still human, and our humanity is very much in tact. After finding God during a particularly insightful trip, he swore off drugs and now chairs weekly meetings and serves soup to the homeless. He tells us he's looking forward to seeing everyone next week, and I believe he is. He lives for this.

I'm folding away the cheap, uncomfortable chairs when Martha approaches, and reaches for my hands. Her eyes are too big for her face and not for the first time, I suspect we are not living in the same reality.

'The painting,' she says, pulling her lips to a tight line. They are surrounded by cracks in her skin. 'What was it of?' She *needs* to know. Gossip is her new drug of choice. I lean forward, bringing my lips a fraction away from her ear.

'My life,' I whisper.

The mixed smell of coffee and cigarettes pour from her drooped mouth as she twists to face me. She doesn't understand. I give her hands a squeeze and drop them, continue to fold away the plastic chairs. Martha's at the front door when she turns around and calls my name. I look up at her.

'You can still have happily ever after,' she says. Perhaps the deepest words to ever leave her mouth, but they aren't true. Happy endings are as fanciful as *moonlight wishes*.

When I finish with the chairs, I make my way to the refreshment table. Pete is already there, doing his best to look busy, but he's achieving nothing.

'Want to take the rest of the donuts away with you?' he asks.

I scrunch my face in response. They're cheap and tasteless. I gather sugar-sachet scraps, used tea-bags and wooden stirrers and dump them into the open bin.

'I knew there was more to you than meets the eye,' he says, 'all this time and we haven't had so much as a *boo* out of you, and now . . . why now?'

'It's time,' I say quietly. For a second there is silence. I've grown comfortable with silence.

'You're not coming back, are you?' he asks. *He knows.*

He's the type of person to always know exactly what someone else is feeling, thinking. I'm pretty sure he's truly empathetic. That's what makes him so good at this job. I fixate on a greasy pink jam stain on the doughnut box, avoiding his eye. I shake my head.

With the table cleared, he walks with me to the centre of the meeting room. He's quiet as I put my jacket on and watches as I fasten the buttons with care.

'The world can make a monster of you if you let it,' he says. 'Don't let it.'

I throw a sympathetic smile and take one final look around the meeting room for what I know will be the last time. It seems smaller without the people, the chairs and the wallowing. The walls are decorated with great religious carvings and paintings, each telling a story of their own. I think that's what we become in the end: stories.

At home, I sit at my desk in the library, which is what has become of the beetroot room. Like me, it has morphed and started over in life; it's become something new. Being surrounded by books comforts me. They make everything better . . . or at least, less painful.

I switch on my desk lamp, and write my final goodbye, giving a detailed explanation for my actions in the letter. When I'm done, I fold and envelope it then write the address on the front. The bucket list was complete, my life fulfilled. They're designed in solitude, but I've learnt that life is not a journey to be walked alone.

I thought I'd found therapy in the small things; in the *moonlight wishes and the paper kisses,* but they haven't healed me, they only ever bandaged the pain. Turns out depression isn't something you defeat: it's a lifelong battle which comes back when you least expect it: an eternal struggle. Realising that makes living with it a little less unbearable.

I drive to the cemetery, picking up a bouquet of white roses and a pot of planted forget-me-nots on the way. The letter is in my pocket, but I have one last thing I need to do before I send it off.

I park in front of a row of terraced houses. Rain drizzles and when I step out of the car my foot lands in a small puddle. I take the flowers, lock the car and freeze. Across the road, one of the chestnut doors pull open and a little girl leaps from the doorway to the driveway. She twirls on the spot. The princess dress she wears flows with her. Fairy-tales exist to distract from the pain of real life. Hurriedly, two people I assume are her parents follow. The mother, a hardy woman in slick business attire, dances with her daughter while the father laughs heartily as he locks the door. On his way to the car, he joins in the dance. They are serious and hard-working, but never forget to stop and appreciate their family. They climb into the car and through the windows, become silhouettes. Pulling out of the driveway, the dad stops driving and I watch as he leans over to kiss his partner before the car drives off, disappearing forever. I've never paused what I'm doing to dance with a child. Not once. I've never stopped to kiss a lover. I was always too busy thinking and moving to appreciate the smaller things in the bigger picture; ultimately the things which make life worth living. My kisses were always made of paper. I used to think happiness wasn't possible. When I achieved it, I thought it couldn't last. *Had I predetermined the end and created my own fate?* Because I lived like that—believing the magic would fade and living in fear of the end —I created a wedge between me and my friends, me and my wife, me and myself. Everything seemed so clear in that moment. The world had been bleeding in watercolour, and I'd done nothing but watch.

Along the street, the gates of the cemetery stand tall and proud. When I walk through them, I feel like I'm entering another world, one with talking foxes and moving statues, one where fairies sit on branches and watch humans all day long. Crisp, reddish-brown leaves fall from the overarching trees, swirling as they drop. I walk along the curving path thinking about the road which brought me here, about Jo and Caitlyn; Alex and Luke; my parents and Penny. They're all gone now. But they didn't have to be. In this mystical place, where life and death are separated by the thinnest of veils, the rain stops and the sun breaks from the clouds. I stand in front of the same marble headstone I always find myself in front of when I come here. The engraved name is as bold as the person laid to rest. *Penelope Heart.*

'Hey, Penny,' I say, placing the white roses so they balance against the headstone. 'I'm sorry it's been a while . . . I finished my bucket list. I understand now . . . why you did what you did. I hope in the darkness, I was able to make things a little lighter.'

But sometimes life just isn't worth the effort you put in.

With the pot of forget-me-nots still in my hand, I meander along the cemetery. Never before have I ventured to the north graves, and habitually, I head east. Usually, when I come to the site boundary, a wall of birches, I turn around and go back, but today I hear water churning in the distance and it calls me like a siren. I take a small step over a useless picketed fence and venture into the woods. Damp leaves and moss waft in the air around me as I walk to the melody of cooing doves and hooting owls. Being a small wood, the water isn't hard to find. As I near, twigs break and leaves rustle in the distance – alarmed creatures taken by surprise at my presence. The noises combined are a beautiful piece of music, almost a lullaby. I arrive at the top of a waterfall which I didn't know existed. The water churns under pine green shadows. Nearby, there's a small wooden-and-brick bridge with an elegant arch. As I approach, I see a small, wood-carved bench and a young heron who perches on the back. When I look at the bird, it cocks its long narrow head, watching me carefully through black beady eyes. Under its careful observation, I take a seat and the bird ruffles its greyed wings with a powerful force. The feeling that comes over me is distantly familiar.

'Penny?' I ask stupidly. The bird wails like an alarm, flapping raucously. 'Jo?'

Calmly, it shuffles towards me, nestles by my side in a hunched ball. I don't actually believe it's Jo, but the ghost of a brush touches my neck and I'm comforted by the thought of her being here, watching over me. I place the pot of flowers on the ground.

'I've learned a lot,' I tell the youthful heron, speaking as though it is Jo I'm talking to. 'Probably all too late. It turns out nobody knows what they're doing. It isn't just me. The thing is Jo, you wouldn't be proud of me.'

Almost in protest, the heron stands, stretches.

'You wouldn't be,' I argue. 'Truth is, I've clung onto this life much longer than I ever intended to.' And with a breath, I add, 'it's over now.'

On cue, the bird flaps its wings boisterously then throws itself from the bench. With effortless flaps it takes to the sky and disappears into the thicket of surrounding trees.

'Goodbye, Jo.' I whisper.

'Did I really just have that conversation with a bird?' I ask aloud before carrying myself to the bridge. There's a scarf of ivy around the panels. Light bursts from the canopies above, glowing on the brickwork like a halo. I finger the cracks between the bricks and small pieces of mortar crumble away, a spider flees. I wonder how many other lives are under the surface, fighting to survive. I climb onto the ledge. It isn't hard to do. I don't want to fight anymore. I want to be at peace. I look down. From here, it's a long way to go. The river curves along as smooth and seductive as a sleeping snake, promising to carry me to faraway places. Light reflects, beams from the water's surface. I've been through so much. I can't stand anymore. I close my eyes and let myself go and for once, thoughts pass as hushed soliloquies instead of screaming songs and nothing matters anymore. When my life flashes before my eyes, I'll replay me and you, I think as I'm falling. But then I open my eyes sharp. Pieces of stone disintegrate under my feet. I watch them drop to the water below and realise I haven't left the bridge at all.

I'm still here.

It's time for me to head north in the cemetery. I can't put it off anymore. I step down from the ledge, wobbling as I place my feet on solid ground. Rain trickles through the roof of the trees. It's refreshing on my skin. In haste, I grab the forget-me-nots and walk back through the woods, retracing my earlier steps. *I don't want to die.*

I come to the clearing and head north. The grave I've put off seeing for so long is by an old oak tree which I recognise from the distance. There's already a figure there and when I catch sight of her, I stop dead. At first, I think it's Caitlyn, but on second thought, I see it isn't her at all. The stance is similar, but much taller, more slender. It's my mother-in-law, Rose. As though she can feel my eyes on her, she twists and catches me staring.

'I always wondered when I'd see you here,' she says when I approach. She's wearing a brown leather jacket and has a head scarf wrapped over her thinned hair. Taking her in, I see her skin is paler than it used to be; she is white as salt. Her sunken cheeks and blotchy, baggy eyes show me she is no longer a stern woman to be feared, but a powerless old lady, trapped in mourning. Already there's fresh purple freesias and spurting daffodils by the marble headstone. I place the forget-me-nots down, catching my son's name as I do. *Asa Walters.* My mouth feels very dry as I remember Caitlyn naming our angelic son.

'It's always been impossible,' I croak. Anything to do with that period of my life is a painful haze.

'It's impossible for me to stay away,' she says, disapproving as ever. '*She* couldn't bring herself to come here either.'

I gather the *she* Rose refers to is her daughter, and now Caitlyn's been brought up I want to ask about her, but before I'm given the chance, Rose clears her throat.

'She misses you. But honestly, William, she's better off without you.' The words have the effect Rose wishes them too. I force myself not to fall to the ground; to surrender to her strike. I feel my stomach sink and my knees give a threatening wobble. 'But I miss her. I miss her terribly.'

'Where is she?' I can't help but ask.

'Thailand.'

Rose copes with grief in a different way than I've ever experienced in a human before. When we lost Asa, I thought Rose was immune to the devastation that had washed over the rest of us, but now I see she had been a rock for Caitlyn, and even for me. With both of us gone, the woman is a shadow of who she used to be. *There's no pain like being left behind.*

'She'd come back for you,' Rose says.

'I don't think—'

'You have to *try*,' she cries. I remember an earlier argument with Truman where he'd said something similar. I stood for a second, contemplating everything. Was the ball truly in my court this time? Was it my move to make?

'How?' I asked. 'She won't take my calls, and she's not online anymore.'

'No,' Rose agreed. 'She's off the grid. But you could go there and—'

'—and stalk her? Drag her home? She's moved on.' Saying this makes my mind conjure nasty images. I picture her with somebody else. I can't stand the thought of seeing Caitlyn happy with another man. The idea of his child in her arm makes me feel nauseous.

'She wants you to, William. She always wanted you to, and when you never did it killed her inside.'

'She could have reached out to me—'

'No, she couldn't, not after the way she left. She was always waiting for you. She still is.'

'Why?' I ask, unable to decide whether this is what Caitlyn wants or if it's a desperate attempt for Rose to get her only daughter back in the country.

My mother-in-law steps forward and hugs me. She is so frail I can feel her bones, and I imagine if I squeeze she would snap like a twig. Her perfume still packs a punch and when I inhale I'm taken back to a time before any of this ever happened.

'I'll think about it,' I say, though I suspect a simple reunion with Caitlyn is nothing more than another *moonlight wish*, both on my part, and on Rose's.

She gives a polite nod and walks away. I have pity for her. She lost everything too, when Caitlyn left. I stay with Asa for a while, but the day darkens, and the soft rain begins to pelt down, so I make my leave, promising the empty space around the grave I'll be back.

* * *

I'm soaked by the time I leave the cemetery. My foot lands in a deep puddle by a blocked drain on the side of the road, and water seeps through my shoe and into my sock. I curse loudly. My hair is in strands, like little rat tails. They swish as my neck twists to check if the road I've already begun to cross is clear. There's a horn, a long offensive blast of a thing, and a flash of light and a spray of murky water. I can't avoid the collision. It's fight or flight and I've nowhere to run. I close my eyes in preparation for the strike and when I'm hit by metal there's only pain and darkness until there's nothing left.

23

Paper Kisses

Caitlyn

The damp moss is a carpet of earth under my feet. I flex my toes and pieces of rock crumble away. *Déjà vu* washes over me, as though in another place and another life I could be doing the same thing, only *different*. Behind me, birds sing to each other. The wind blows tender, carrying gentle rays of sun to my already tan skin. The world is tranquil, perfect. Looking ahead, never back, I take a step into the air and let myself fall with grace.

I pierce the surface of the icy lagoon with pointed toes and shoot through the water like a dart. When my momentum slows, I float, frozen in space. The sun glistens above me. Darkness is below. I wonder what it would be like to just cease existing. If I propel myself downwards, I could find out. What would it be like to never come back? Peaceful, I imagine. My body fights for life, and naturally I swim upward, penetrate the surface and take a big, deep breath, followed by rapid, succinct breaths, greedily guzzling as much air as I can.

I watch a water spider skate away from me. When I first came here, I'd have been terrified. But there's nothing to be afraid of. The world can't hurt me anymore. When my fingers begin to prune, I swim to the banks and climb out of the water. My towel and flip-flops are on the thick tree root which poses as a bench, right where I left them, and when I'm dry, I wrap the towel around my body and mount my scooter. It starts with a familiar *vroom* which is music to my ears.

The drive back to my rented cabin doesn't take long. I know the route by heart and it's almost impossible to get lost since the hot-pink walls can be spotted through the lush green canopies. My hair has air dried by the time I get there, and all I need to do is run a brush through the fresh knots which I plan to do later. I haven't been so hung up on my appearance since moving here. Nobody cares what I look like in the middle of a Thai jungle, least of all myself. I pull up and find my friend and colleague, Tik, waiting for me. She sits smoking on my steps.

'Teacher Caitlyn,' she says as I approach. 'A letter come for you.'

I teach English as a foreign language to the kids of the community. I've never told anyone where I live; nobody back home knows my address. It's in a small province, tucked away from the rest of the world. I am the only Caucasian person for miles around and even after all the time I've been here, some of the locals still stop and stare when I pass, to gawk at my pale skin and golden hair. I take the envelope and study the calligraphy. I recognise the writing immediately. *William Walters.*

The only way for anyone to have found me would have been to contact the agency who placed me. They shouldn't have given away my information, but life here isn't like it is in England. Expectations are different. People are different. That's what I like about it.

'Thank you,' I say, hoping Tik won't stay. I don't want to read the letter in front of her, but I need to know what's written in the contents. William races through my mind. He was never designed to live alone, and I can't help but wonder who is loving him now. Out of politeness I ask if she'd like tea, but she says she must go. She stubs her cigarette out and carries the end away with her, leaving me alone with my letter. I go inside my cabin and sit at the small circular dining table. The kitchen light buzzes above and under its soft glow I peel open the envelope and begin to read. The familiarity of William's scribbles spark a warmth in me. I carefully read what he has to say.

My Dearest Caitlyn,

I'll never convince you this was the right decision, but for me, it was the only one left. I was never the person I wanted to be; was incapable of being the man you needed. I have many regrets, Caitlyn, but loving you is not one.

Your eyes were stars in my stormiest nights; they penetrated the darkness consuming me, and sometimes I hear your rich laugh and I just smile to myself. I remember the way you used to dance in the kitchen in your underwear. Often, I hear you snoring in the middle of the night, feel your nails trace the gaps between the freckles on my back, smell your perfume in the bathroom, like you were just there. Those little phantoms bring a smile to my face. I carry those little memories everywhere I go. As impossible as it might be, you can't blame yourself for this. There is nothing you could have done to change the ending. My fate was set in stone and it was only a matter of time before this happened.

To be honest, Caitlyn, I was supposed to die the day we met. You are the reason I lived, and I'm so thankful for every second I got to love you. You, Caitlyn Donoghue, are my best friend, but this isn't about you. I've been in pain forever. It's better off this way, because old wounds never heal.

I tried, Caitlyn. I tried so hard, but I can't go on. There's nothing left for me, and I just can't stand it anymore. You built a life for yourself, and I truly hope you were able to stumble upon the peace and happiness you left to find. I hope you found a love so great it stops time. I wish I could undo things, and start again; make it so you never hurt, but I can't go back time. I can't change the past. I can't do anything anymore. It's time for me to go.

Yours peacefully, and forever,

William Walters.

I turn the letter over in my hands scanning for a date. When I find it on the back I stare at the numbers for so long they become a blur. The letter was written four months ago. Why has it taken so long to reach me? There's seven stamps on the front of the envelope, two from Britain and five from Thailand. It's addressed to the agency, who must have sent it to my school, who have in turn, sent it to Tik to pass to me. I feel sick; it's already too late. Why did I have to remove myself from the world to the point where this has been allowed to happen?

My hands are shaking and it's an effort to stand.

There's no pain like being left behind.

I rush to the bedroom and pull out my suitcase from under my bed. There's an old iPhone in the inside pocket which I kept for emergencies, but have never had to use before. I turn it on, but it doesn't have any signal and I don't have WiFi in the cabin. I curse myself again for being so far removed from society.

As quickly as I can, I throw on socks and trainers, then rush out of the cabin without locking it behind me. Thailand isn't like England. You can trust people not to break into your property or destroy your things just for the sake of it, so it's perfectly okay to leave the place unlocked. Tik's cabin is just a ten-minute walk from my own. I run it in five. Similar to my cabin, it is painted a striking colour—her's is violet —so sticks out against the lush forest greens. I bang on the door and call out Tik's name, unable to keep the panic from my voice. She isn't home. I can tell because her bike is gone, and the lights are off. She'd have answered if she was, but that doesn't stop me from running around, peering in all of the windows. I try the door and it's locked. The next thing I can think of is trying the Tesco Lotus. Being a Sunday, it'll be closed, but the public WiFi should work from the car park. I run back to my cabin and take a deep breath, trying to calm my nerves. I remind myself that whatever happened to William, has already happened, and everyone has already processed it. There's nothing I can do to change that. I lost him a long time ago, but the thought of him not being on the planet is a different kind of loss, and that comes in a wave like a tsunami. It's enough to take me down. I throw on jean-shorts and a jumper, and before I take off, check the iPhone battery will last. There's a quarter left which should be enough for me to make contact and get an update. When I mount my scooter, I think about who I should message.

The sky is coated with endless blues, streaked occasionally with puffs of white. I drive under them as I speed around the province's mountains, slowing when I'm crossing the local dam, to follow the strict speed limit. There's a cheap rented scooter parked by the wall. The tourist wears a plastic poncho that locals would never wear and is checking their phone. I drive past, my mission too critical to stop, but when I glance in my mirror, I see them turning around in circles. I gather they are aligning themselves with the GPS on their phone. It's illegal to stop on the dam since it's considered a sacred space, and the charges don't come lightly in the province. I once had to spend a weekend in the town's single jail cell, and publicly and profusely apologise. I almost lost my job, but paid a fine and made up for my mistake with community service in the form of free English tutoring which I didn't mind, because it turns out teaching is my calling. I know the way the country works and I can accept the punishment for a crime which may not seem like a big deal to most people, but I wouldn't want someone else to suffer a similar fate, especially if it taints their experience of the beautiful country. I turn my scooter around and race to the tourist, thinking a slight delay wouldn't hurt.

'Hey, you can't stop here,' I shout from my scooter. Deliberately, I don't dismount. 'You need to get off the dam,' I say and motion in exaggerated waves with my arms. The stranger stares at me behind their darkened visor. I curse myself for stopping, deciding they don't speak English and I've wasted my time. I motion again with my arms in what I'm sure is universal code for "you can't be here". The person takes a couple steps towards me and I throw an alarmed glance over my shoulder, worrying we'll be seen. I open my mouth to speak again, but when they take off their helmet no words come out.

It's William who stares at me. He looks like he's seeing a ghost, which is probably what I look like too, because I'm pretty sure I am. I'm not sure how I feel, and I wish I had somebody to tell me what to say, and how to react. I want to hug him. I want to run away. My stomach twists and I contemplate revving my scooter and driving off into the sun, but I'm too stunned to even move.

'Caitlyn,' he says, disbelief coats his tone. He takes a single step forwards, gentle so as not to startle me. *I might run away again.* It doesn't seem real. Like I've taken a step outside reality and all of my dreams and nightmares are crashing and colliding on this very dam in a different world. We stand there, for the longest of times, in silence. There are freckles over his nose and cheeks. The skin over his ears has peeled. Evidence he's been in the sun for at least a couple of days if not weeks. *Here? In Thailand?* I'm surged with annoyance that it's taken him this long to find me. I'm grateful he's alive and in front of me. Catching myself before I display irrational emotion, I force my teeth to clamp down on the inside of my cheek. His hair is longer than I've ever seen. The loose curls of his fringe fall just short of his eyebrows. I want nothing more than to run my hands through them. He doesn't speak, and neither do I.

I said what I had to say in the letter I left him. He doesn't deserve to have his heart broken twice. But his face; I lose myself in his beautiful, innocent face. The world has aged him, but there's a poetry in his pain. What's he thinking behind those deeply tragic brown eyes that I've always loved so much? Why has he come here, after all this time?

'I thought you were dead,' I say, and saying it aloud makes all of my emotions come pouring out of me. 'I thought you were dead.' This time I say it louder and I climb off my scooter and march towards him. 'I thought you *fucking* died.'

I'm at him now, we're face-to-face and I'm a fraction away from him and in his eyes I see myself. I see a furious woman standing under a melting sky and I see a naïve student, blushing when he says her name and I see myself in a wedding dress waiting to say "I do". My tears come in floods.

'I thought you died,' I say again because I can't seem to find any other words. My knees buckle and I fall to them. In instinct, he reaches out.

'Don't touch me,' I say, but I don't mean it. What I really want is for him to wrap himself around me. On the ground I notice his leg. It's gone. His right leg has been replaced by metal. I stop crying, let out a long, quavering breath.

'I'm lucky to be alive,' he says when he catches me looking. Realising what a child I've been, I pick myself up from the ground and meet his eyes, wiping the tears away from my own. There's a million things I want to say. Even more that I don't.

'But . . . but this . . . ' I pull out the letter I received, now crumpled and folded and wet from tears. Spotting it, he blushes, reaches out for it but I pull away.

'I didn't mean for that to get to you. I mean, I did, but not like this,' he lets out a long breath.

'You're not allowed to stop on the dam,' I say. 'It's against the law.' I make my way back to my scooter. 'Come on, I know a place. You can explain over a beer.'

I drive back across the dam and turn left on to a small clearing only accessible to bikes and scooters. Making sure he's following; I continue to drive the hairpin curves of the dirt road. In my mirrors, I see his helmet shift from side to side. He's taking in the immense jungle-scape beauty. Even after all this time, it can still overwhelm me, but I will him to focus on the track ahead. One wrong move and he'll . . .

I shake the thoughts away. No need to go there. The road twists and we come out into a clearing at the bottom of the dam. There's a small tiki-hut called Paradise that I visit frequently. The owner smiles and calls out to me as I approach.

'Teacher Caitlyn, you have a friend,' he says cheerfully.

'Yes,' I respond. My right hand instinctively grabs my left, and I notice the absence of my wedding ring. *A friend.*

I order two bottled beers as William kicks the stand on his scooter down. I can't tell if he's genuinely incapable of doing it quickly, or if he's busying himself so he doesn't have to awkwardly stand behind me. I take the bottles from the merchant and walk to a flat rock poking onto the water. I wish Thailand wasn't so beautiful so that this moment wouldn't seem so romantic. Slow as hell, William comes. He looks for a place to sit even though the rock is big enough for two of us and again I wonder if he's postponing the inevitable. I can't stand the tension anymore and pass him his bottle, point to a place for him to sit. Obedient as ever, he sits and fidgets with the bottle's label. I take a swig of my own.

'Explain this,' I say, waving the letter in the air.

'I honestly forgot I'd written that,' he nods. 'I guess one of the nurses found it in my clothes and thought they'd be doing me a favour.' He shrugs as though the misunderstanding is no big deal.

'How would a nurse even know where to send it?' I ask. It's not that I don't believe William, but the situation. Then it hits me.

William's lips furrows.

I sigh. 'This has Rose written all over it. . . she sent it to the agency.'

William meets my eye and I know I'm right. I can't imagine him and my mum conspiring together, but her attempts to get me home have been futile so far. She must have been desperate. I catch William's eye. There's no longer a sadness in the depth of his soul.

'Were you really going to kill yourself?' I ask.

'I was ready to die.' He takes a small swig of beer and looks at me. Anxiety and anger rise in me like a fever.

'You're a bastard,' I say. I can't help but let tears fall. 'I'm glad you didn't.'

He looks to the water, seems to study the surface and with an indifferent sigh, let's me know what happened at the cemetery, then tells me about the accident and how his leg had to be amputated.

'How did *you* find me?' I ask, and though I'm perplexed and curious, it comes out sharp and impatient.

'Rose told me you you were in Thailand,' he admits. He can't look me in the eye anymore. I can't tell what he's thinking. He's leaner than he used to be.

'When I got here,' he says, 'the agency told me where you'd be.'

He must catch the betrayal on my face because he says, 'You can't blame them. You are still technically my wife.'

The reminder is a knife in my heart and I wonder what it feels like for him, to be looking at his ghost of a wife in a foreign country. Happy. Established. It must be killing him. If it is though, it doesn't show on his weathered face.

'I understand why you left,' he says.

How could he when I don't understand it at all?

'Then why are you here?' I ask unkindly. My words are not coming out in the way I want them to at all, but how can I ask him to hug me? How can I cry on his shoulder when I'm the reason we're in this place?

'I completed the bucket list,' he says. His mouth breaks into a smile showing his dimples and suddenly I'm taken back to a place when we were nothing but kids starting out at life.

"Healed a lifetime of scars doing it, too,' he adds.

'So you thought you'd end it all?' I focus on his lips, imagine myself sinking into them. Soft and plush. I remember the way he tastes, the way he'd linger on me.

'It's not like that,' he says, ripping me from my fantasy. I'm treating him like a punching bag, he's treating me like a diamond.

'Rose misses you.'

I nod again, hiding my guilt by biting my tongue. Mum always hated William. It would have pained her to approach him. I try to think of them going for coffee together to discuss me, but the images come distorted and messy.

'I miss her, too,' I say quietly and take another swig of my drink. He's peeled the label off entirely and we sit in a horrendous silence. I can't bare it anymore. 'Tell me about the bucket list,' I say.

He basked in the blue lagoon in Iceland, and built a school in Malawi with his bare hands. He has the pictures to prove it and shows me as he's telling me. I laugh playfully at his jokes and gasp when he tells me of the troubles he's faced. He's climbed all the mountains and swam all the oceans. He's hiked Machu Picchu and prayed at Bone Church. I realise as he's talking that I'm happy for him. Never in my wildest dreams did I ever think it would be so easy to sit next to him again, talk about life without drowning in the past. Once again, I find myself focusing on his lips as he talks. Why did I always give paper kisses in place of the real thing? Life's too short for that shit.

In the distance I see Paradise's merchant bringing us two more beers. William rejects, says he has a one beer limit.

I thank the merchant and pass over a twenty baht note, telling him to keep the change. He thanks me as he always does and gives a small head bow to both William and me. William thanks me too, balances his new bottle in a groove in the rock then continues with his story.

'. . . You know the rest. I left the cemetery and got hit by a car. Was in hospital for weeks, lost a leg. Nearly died.' His voice is soft. Barriers are broken. He puts his bottle to the side and fiddles with the label in a predictable but comforting way. 'Rose and Alex visited a lot in those days, Truman too – he offered me my old job back and everything.' He took a pause, not so much for himself, but for me to process what he'd said. Life had continued without me. I guess it was selfish and naive to think it would halt in my absence.

'Strangely enough, I wasn't depressed about losing my leg. You'd think I would have been, but it kind of gave me a new lease of life. I wanted to find you. More just to tell you that I understand why you left, and to let you know that I forgive you.' He nods and tears burst from my eyes. I didn't think I needed his forgiveness but hearing the words heals me in ways I never imagined.

'I'm so sorry—'

'Stop,' he says. His voice carries an authority I've never heard in it before. 'I've built my life up from scratch. Not many people get to do that.'

I sip my beer and let any space between us sink away. I move closer to him and do what I've wanted to do since I saw him on the dam. I fall into him. There are muscles under his t-shirt which hadn't existed before. We sit for some time. The sky above is an infinity of azure but the shade dims ever so slightly. Soon it will be dark and we shouldn't be at the bottom of the dam when that happens.

I don't know what to say so I move out of his grasp and take another swig of my beer. I've almost finished my second bottle.

'Do you think you'll ever stop running?' he asks.

I pretend to think about it even though I know the answer. In waiting for me, he completely tears the label off his beer.

'No,' I say with finality, if only to formalise the thoughts and put him out of his misery. He looks away, can't meet my eye, but gives a small understanding nod. Surely he knows that coming here was a long shot. And yet, I can't bear the thought of him leaving, going off to have coffee with Mum and Luke and Alex. We take a minute to appreciate each other's company, after all this time apart. His scent is fresher than air, and when I breathe in his musk, I could fall into him all over again. But I don't. I stay strong.

'So where do we go from here?' he asks. He's letting me decide our fate – like he hasn't learnt anything, but when I catch his eye, I see he's looking around the trees in the area and I understand he's asking in a literal sense. If you didn't know where the opening for the dirt road is, you'd never catch it.

'Up there,' I point. He grunts and stands, picks up our empty bottles, binning them as we walk towards our scooters. I can't stand to leave it like this though and I can't tolerate the thought of watching him drift off into the future without me.

'What are you going to do now?' I ask, unable to help myself. He wears a face of defeat.

'Well, I found you and I've gathered you're not coming home.'

I catch his wandering eye take in the surreal scenes around him. I wonder if he is thinking the same as me: that I *am* home.

'So I go back to Rose and tell her you're safe, you're happy,' he concludes.

My stomach twists cruelly. He'd given up, as easily as that. *As easily as I had in the past.*

'I'll have to file for divorce, too,' he says carefully.

'No,' I say. I'm not ready for that. My heart turns into a jackhammer in my chest. I remember how my heart constricted, just an hour before, when I thought he'd died. I would have given up everything to go back to England, to see him if I could. He stands, looks confused.

'You don't want me. You don't want divorce. You don't want to come home. What *do* you want?'

Air escapes my nostrils even though they feel like they're closing in on themselves. What do *I* want? What *do* I want? *What* do I want?

Time.

I want time.

I want William to stay.

I want to be happy.

I want to *live*.

But how do I say that under all this pressure?

I let down my guard, lay down all my defences.

'Well you are here,' I say. 'How about one more adventure?'

He looks at me with illumination, a full smile breaks over his face and he even manages to let out a laugh.

'Okay,' he says. 'One more adventure.'

I nod and laugh too. I start my scooter and drive up the hill, taking the path less travelled with William following at my tail. We drive along the road and in the distance the sun begins to sink beyond the horizon, and I am ready for whatever comes next.

Acknowledgements

I always thought writing a book was an activity one completed by oneself, but writing William's story proved me wrong. So many people helped to shape the words and ideas that formed this novel.

First and foremost, thank you to my parents, who raised me to be the kind of person who is able to find happiness in stories and formulate ideas into realities. Thank you for teaching me to have the kind of patience needed to write and edit a novel.

Thank you to the teachers and mentors I've had over the years who helped me to better articulate my thoughts into prose and for allowing me to flex my creative muscles. For giving me the ability to craft the lies we tell ourselves into works of fiction. Jane Bell, Tasha Kavanagh, Bill Ryan each played a role in my life which has made me a better storyteller.

Thank you to James whose critiques shaped early versions of William's story.

Thank you to the numerous friends I've met along this journey; especially Amina, Matt, Sophie, Dean, and Junior, who tirelessly read countless editions of this novel, helping to make each draft more exciting than the last.

Thank you to Shona for your wisdom, guidance and support, not just with William's journey, but my own as well.

Thank you to Stephen for the late night calls when I had questions about character development. Your inspiration and input has helped bring certain characters to life.

Special thank yous go to Claire, Hattie, and Jake, who read and reread paragraphs and chapters over and over again without complaint. You each read every single word on numerous occasions, and I hope I've been able to make you proud.

Thank you Alisson for giving life to the cover design. You managed to understand what I envisioned perfectly, and it's so much better than I ever imagined it would be.

Thank you to Anna-Marie who is a constant support and always my biggest cheerleader.

* * *

And thank you, reader, for coming on this journey with me. Remember: in the chaos of life, don't forget to live.

Printed in Great Britain
by Amazon